THE SPIRIT'S CURSE
LUTESONG BOOK THREE

R.K. ASHWICK

The Spirit's Curse

Copyright © 2025 R.K. Ashwick

RK Ashwick Books

rkashwick.com

All rights reserved. No part of this book may be reproduced or used in any manner without the prior written permission of the copyright owner, except for the use of brief quotations in a book review. To request permissions, contact ash@rkashwick.com.

ISBN (Paperback): 979-8-9911992-1-6

ISBN (E-Book): 979-8-9911992-2-3

LCCN: 2025908108

First edition May 2025.

Edited by Kim Halstead

Cover art by Patrick Knowles

Map by Lucia Vázquez de Prada

Illustrations by Felix Vincent

Chapter icons by R.K. Ashwick

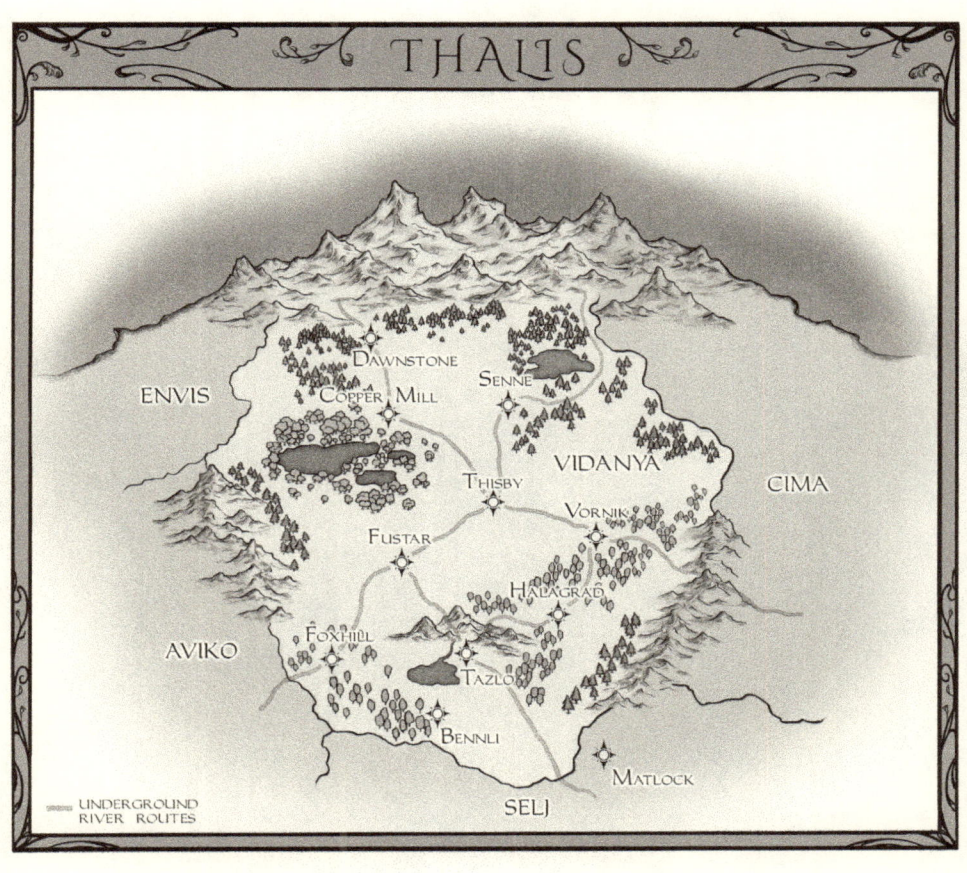

CONTENTS

Chapter 1	1
Chapter 2	13
Chapter 3	19
Chapter 4	25
Chapter 5	35
Chapter 6	45
Chapter 7	55
Chapter 8	61
Chapter 9	73
Chapter 10	85
Chapter 11	97
Chapter 12	103
Chapter 13	115
Chapter 14	127
Chapter 15	135
Chapter 16	147
Chapter 17	157
Chapter 18	165
Chapter 19	173
Chapter 20	179
Chapter 21	189
Chapter 22	197
Chapter 23	207
Chapter 24	219
Chapter 25	225
Chapter 26	231
Chapter 27	237
Chapter 28	245
Chapter 29	249
Chapter 30	255
Chapter 31	267
Chapter 32	273

Want More?	281
Acknowledgments	283
About the Author	285

CHAPTER ONE

EMRY

Emry Karic harbored several regrets in life, but none so immediate—nor so sweaty—as scheduling a music festival at the height of summer.

Not that he hadn't tried to avert the disaster that was his damp cravat. *He* had gently suggested autumn for the festival. Autumn was lovely; autumn had cool breezes. But autumn also already had the Sada festival. Then spring had the social season, winter had frostbite... So, summer it was.

And the Auric Guild had decided to schedule his backstage reception under the full fury of the summer sun.

He tried to subtly wipe his brow, desperately wishing he could escape into the cool shadows of the actual backstage looming behind him. The behemoth of temporary wood and curtains neatly divided the grand Vornik plaza in half, separating him from the festival stage, and beyond that, the festival-goers. Even now, Emry could hear the Forsgren Quartet playing their hearts out to the audience, and he longed to stand in the shadows and simply listen.

But for now, his place was behind the stage, out in the more exclusive—and horribly sunny—half of the plaza. Mingling around high tables with his manager Damir, making small talk, and holding champagne simply for the cool glass against his fingertips.

Because, as he had learned over his past two years with the Auric Guild, this was where the real work took place.

"You mentioned there might be a spirit living in your vineyard," he said to a Councilmember. Which one, he hardly remembered; he'd spoken with a dozen of them in the past hour. "Have you tried talking to it—?"

"Oh, yes, yes." The Councilmember waved her fan, the painted paper flashing in the evening light. To Emry's relief, the sun was finally setting on the first day of the festival—but the heat still lingered. "I tried all those welcoming statements the spirit department recommended in their quaint little pamphlet."

Emry held up a finger. "If I may, it was a brochure, and it actually took them a lot of effort—"

"But, tell me." She ignored his words and leaned in with a conspiratorial smile, her fan half hiding her face. "My daughters told me all about your last tour. Do your eyes truly glow when your use your magic?"

Emry stifled a sigh, while next to him, Damir barely concealed an eye roll. Half their work at this reception involved simply keeping their audience on task.

"Yes, a little. But about that vineyard spirit. It's terribly important to make the spirits in populated areas feel welcome, in case they choose to interact with—"

"Is it entirely your magic onstage? The glowing flowers and all?"

"Not at all." His smile strained. "Aspen and I work together. Not precisely how we did in Matlock, of course—but you'll be able to witness it shortly, if you watch our set. Aspen's far better at it than I am, as you'll see—"

"And can you speak to the flowers?"

He tilted his head. "I—no?"

"What *gossip* they would have! Could you imagine?" The Councilmember spotted someone across the tables and snapped her fan shut. "Oh, there's Miss Lorenz! Pardon me." She nodded to Damir, then shook Emry's hand with two silk-gloved fingers. "I *so* look forward to seeing you on stage, Mr. Karic."

"Thank you so much," he managed weakly. "And thank you for supporting the spirits—"

But she had already floated off to fawn over another Guild member, one of several milling about the reception. Emry wasn't alone in his work, at least. While Damir stuck to his side, famed musician Karlson chatted somewhere to his left, and Guild leader Ella Sorman held court to his right. His troupe mates, Sage and Riley, wisely stuck close to the refreshment table and the iced drinks. But all of them had one goal in mind: ensure every politician, merchant, and socialite at this reception welcomed the spirits in their midst.

Because for the very first time, the cheering audience beyond the stage didn't just have humans in it.

"Yes, Spiritsong, that's right!" Sage said, her voice overly bright as she mopped up a man who had spilled wine on himself. As she set down her own wineglass, Riley picked it up and downed it. "We're the first troupe with a forest spirit in it, you know. We'll be on in about ten minutes."

The time call roused Emry from his heat-induced haze. Ten minutes was hardly enough to finish up here, considering he needed to shed his formal coat and gloves before heading onstage. Then there was makeup to check, tuning to be done...

"Ten minutes?" he whispered to Damir. "Is that all? I haven't spoken with everyone here yet—"

"You don't have to," his manager advised. Though strands of his blonde hair stuck to his temple, he showed no sign of discomfort nor impatience in the heat, even in his customary black coat. Emry imagined that after two dozen years of managing Ella Sorman and the other musicians under her wing, he must have become accustomed to such ill-advised summer events.

"Most of the Councilmembers here are very much in favor of spirits," he continued evenly. "The people you'll want to target are—"

A pair of newcomers approached, the man scowling, the woman smiling. Damir briefly snapped shut, gave a grim smile in return, then turned to face away from the strangers, his shoulder brushing against Emry's.

"Here's one," he murmured, his Envisian accent spiking in disdain. "Mr. Lewis Chamberlain and his wife, Penelope. Mr. Chamberlain manages cargo routes between Vornik and several cities in Cima. You met him at the soiree last week."

"Which soiree?" Emry muttered back, then dutifully brightened just in time to greet the couple. "Good evening—"

"Mr. Karic!" Penelope eagerly took his gloved hands in hers, her touch far warmer and more sincere than that of his last Council admirer. In truth, her round, friendly face reminded him of one of his aunts back in Senne. "I can't tell you how much we love this festival idea. Don't we, dearest?"

Mr. Chamberlain gave a brusque imitation of a nod, his top hat barely moving. Penelope soldiered on.

"A music festival for *spirits*," she squealed, the long feather in her hair bouncing along with her enthusiasm. "I wish I had a spirit in my garden. Have you seen how many of them are out there in the plaza?"

Emry dared a glance around. He hadn't yet seen how many spirits Cal's festival invitations had drawn in—but there was one specific spirit who was supposed to be at this reception with him.

And he hadn't seen hide nor hair—nor antler nor leaf—of Aspen for hours.

"I haven't yet had the pleasure, no." He tried to match Penelope's warmth. "Tell me, do they seem to be enjoying the festival? All the Guild troupes have tailored their set lists with them in mind."

"Oh, yes! Why, I do believe I saw a bear dancing by the stage. Can you believe it?"

Emry could believe it—he'd seen stranger, in his time amongst spirits.

As she continued to gush, he kept one eye on Mr. Chamberlain. There was no need to worry about dear Penelope; she was clearly delighted about the mingling of spirits with human society.

But next to her, Mr. Chamberlain's ample mustache twitched.

"Is Ms. Sorman quite sure this is all safe?" his words finally escaped from under all the bristly hairs. "Are these spirits truly civilized?"

Emry hated that word—one could argue that *humans* varied widely on whether they were civilized or not—but he swallowed his annoyance. Ever since the events of Matlock two years ago, he had fielded the full range of opinions on the emergence of spirits into society. Everything from the Councilmember's misconceptions, to Penelope's enthusiasm, to Mr. Chamberlain's lip-curling contempt.

Fortunately, such negative opinions were in the minority—but a small amount of contempt could easily grow into something worse, if the Guild left it unchecked.

Hence the pageantry of the city's first music festival for humans and spirits.

"I assure you, the festival is taking every possible step to ensure that everyone here has a safe three days," Emry said. "I assume you noticed Ms. Bres"—he corrected himself with a smile—"Mrs. Karic and her team of researchers at the entrance?"

Penelope fluttered her fan. "We most certainly did. She is an absolute darling, isn't she?"

Inwardly, Emry scoffed. She was far more than a darling. She was his *wife*. A refined genius with the best laugh in the world. A rose who stooped to his dandelion. A goddess if there ever was one—

He had to keep the conversation going before he started waxing poetic about his wife's innumerable charms.

"Then you must have seen all the resources she and Aspen have made available to ensure the spirits are happy and well cared for," he continued. "Soil from all five provinces, lake and spring water, cuttings from over a hundred different plants and saplings. Everything they need to refresh the grove they're carrying with them, all on the tables at the front. If any of the spirits are even remotely dissatisfied, her research team will solve the problem immediately."

It was a rehearsed answer for a repeated question—but Mr. Chamberlain didn't appear satisfied by it.

"And where is this Aspen?" His gaze shifted about, as if expecting a wolf to leap out from behind the cocktail tables. "I certainly hear a great deal about them."

Yes, and it would be nice to *see* them in this moment, too, Emry thought—then Penelope swung back in with her bright smile.

"Oh, Aspen! *Such* a dear. Is it true they're writing a song for the troupe?"

Emry made a note to have Aspen grow this woman a flower later on. She was doing half of his pro-spirit propaganda work for him.

"Aspen and I are writing it," he gently added. "A show of what spirits and humans can do together—"

But Mr. Chamberlain and his stoic top hat were simply not having it.

"Then perhaps after writing your little song, you can work *together* to capture the evil lynx spirit mangling my roads in the Cima mountains."

Emry's composure faltered. He had prepared for many questions; he had *not* prepared for news of an evil lynx spirit.

A victorious glint sparked in Mr. Chamberlain's eyes, and Emry silently cursed himself. He must be more careful—Ella Sorman wouldn't so much as blink at unexpected tidings like this.

"Have you seen the roads yourself?" he asked steadily. In the corner of his vision, Damir gave a tiny nod of approval. He had managed to avoid admitting he didn't know about the issue. Admitting ignorance of an attacking spirit would spread around Mr. Chamberlain's social circle faster than pollen in spring.

"Not four days ago," the merchant blustered, clearly glad of the opportunity to complain. "Saw the trickster's work, too. Didn't see the damn lynx myself, but I was there for the rain it summoned. Not a cloud in the sky to six inches of mud underneath my wagons, all in a blink. And the road! My best driver swears upon Hara herself that the very *dirt* changed direction! Led them right into nowhere and delayed my shipment by a whole three days—"

"Oh, was that *your* shipment?" A young man at another table perked up, pulling away from Sage and Riley's attempts to charm him. "My manservant was trying to traverse the Cima mountains just the other day and described a driver who was terribly lost. He nearly got caught in all that mud himself."

Around them, more and more partygoers glanced over at their conversation in curiosity. Sage quickly cleared her throat and floated over, her pastel skirts swishing around her ankles.

"Well, you know Cima weather," she said with a friendly wave. "Always so terribly unpredictable, spirit or no."

Next to her, Riley snorted and tugged on her black coat. "And who wants to go to Cima, anyway? Not like it has anything but farms—"

Mr. Chamberlain glared at her.

"I mean"—she shuffled slightly behind Sage—"farms are great. So great. Love those...cows."

Mr. Chamberlain veered deftly back into complaining, his voice growing louder, more insistent. "If we are unable to resolve this Cima spirit issue, who are we to let these spirits into our cities? Our towns? They're overrunning our grand plaza at this very moment!"

Now Councilmembers were peering over, frowns dotting their faces as others began to quietly gossip about the conversation. Damir subtly checked his pocket watch, but Emry didn't need the silent signal. Spiritsong needed to clean up this mess before they went onstage—and the one troupe member who could easily put this all to rest wasn't here.

It was beyond time to call for them.

Emry picked up his own drink, but instead of taking a sip, he took a slow breath and connected to his magic. On his inhale, he focused, and on his exhale, he released, expanding his energy in a silent search for Aspen.

It slipped out of him and into the ground, seeking out the forest spirit's magic signature. After years of practice with Aspen, it had become easier to ignore the immediate result of this sort of search: rocks, dirt, weeds. His magic disregarded all of that as background noise and crept into the backstage area first. Up the steps, across the wooden platforms...

After feeling nothing there, he tentatively moved closer to the audience—but within seconds, the chaos there overwhelmed his senses, and he suppressed an outward grimace. The abundance of leafy decor and unfamiliar spirit signatures was far too much for someone of his middling skill. If Aspen were truly somewhere in the crowd, he had no hope of finding them—

Then a strange flash of anger briefly crossed Emry's path. Not his own anger, but someone else's, snaking up his magic like a vine whipping toward him. He snapped back to himself in surprise, nearly dropping his glass.

"Karic?" Damir murmured next to him.

"I'm fine." His grip on his glass tightened. He had never felt anything like that before. He'd have to ask—

The scent of mint and honeysuckle wafted through the air.

"Hello, Ms. Sorman!" Aspen called brightly as they passed her. "Oh—pardon the antlers, please. Cedar, if you could duck under the lanterns there..."

Penelope gasped in delight. Emry spun around in relief.

Aspen had arrived—and they weren't alone, either. Their human form, dressed in the same gray coat and shiny Guild pin that Emry wore, was flanked by two spirits of vastly different sizes. Upon their left shoulder, a flitting pigeon could hardly keep still. At their right, a massive elk did their level best not to tangle themselves up in the surrounding banners. Even from this distance, Emry could spot what set them apart from normal animals. Their little groves—the foliage that kept them alive—wrapped gaily around their talons and antlers in bright splashes of green. They had even decorated themselves for the festival with flowers, moss, and the occasional spotted mushroom.

Though in Emry's opinion, nothing could compare to the vibrant garden spilling out of Aspen's lute.

"Good evening." Aspen led the way right up to Penelope, smiling wide. "Are you enjoying the festival so far?"

After a knowing glance at Emry, they plucked two orchids from the lute on their back and handed one to each of the Chamberlains. Penelope immediately tucked the flower into her hair, joy radiating from her apple-red cheeks.

"We're enjoying it immensely! Aren't we, dear?"

Mr. Chamberlain cleared his throat, ready to parade about his grievances all over again. "We were actually just discussing—"

"The transportation issue in Cima," Emry cut in smoothly. "Of course, you've heard all about the lynx spirit playing tricks on the roads in the Cima mountains."

Aspen maintained their smile perfectly. Emry hadn't been the only one to attend the school of Ella Sorman.

"I'm afraid that happens sometimes," they said, a distinctly Cal-like tone taking over their voice. "Maybe the road was built too close to their grove, or something's forced them to grow closer to the road than usual. But after this festival, I'll be friends with half the spirits in the Cima mountains. Once we visit them, you won't have to worry about the roads ever again."

The young man near Sage tipped his hat. "How capital of you. I'll feel far better about sending my manservant out that way if you do make a visit. Won't you, Lewis?" He turned to Mr. Chamberlain, whose mustache fumbled the words as they came out.

"Well—that would be better, I suppose..."

Sage and Riley nodded eagerly in support of Aspen's plan.

"*So* much better," Sage said.

"Loads." Riley quietly stole the young man's drink and downed it.

Mr. Chamberlain's complaints slowly suffocated under the fresh chorus of positivity, and all around them, the partygoers gradually relaxed and turned back to their own conversations. After Penelope finally made her curtsies and dragged her husband off to talk to Karlson, all of Spiritsong formed a private huddle.

"What would I do without you?" Emry smiled at Aspen, then bowed to the elk and the bird. "Cedar, Pigeon. I'm so glad to see you've made it. I can't tell you how excited Aspen was to get your letters saying you'd attend."

"I pinned them on my wall," Aspen said proudly.

Sage popped up at Emry's shoulder, bouncing on her heels. "Out with it, Aspen. How many spirits are in the crowd? Have you checked the count with Cal yet?"

Riley appeared at Emry's other shoulder, a short, dark shadow in her black coat. Emry wondered if Damir ever got jealous of her stealing his somber style. "No, no, let me guess!" The drummer held up a callused hand in protest. "Three hundred. No—three hundred fifty."

"Close!" Pigeon answered with a thrilled chirp. "Four hundred."

"Four?" Emry gaped. That was nearly a third over what Cal had expected. He'd have to buy her champagne after this—and possibly several headache remedies. "Does Cal have enough—?"

"She planned for four and twenty." The flowers in Aspen's hair bloomed along with their joy. "I showed Cedar the tables and everything. Right, Cedar?"

The ancient elk carefully bowed their head to join the conversation. "I did indeed—"

But Aspen was far too excited to let them have a turn.

"I haven't talked to all of them, but there are at least four spirits from the Vornik underground rivers here," they babbled. "And Pigeon brought all her friends from Matlock, and *they've* already met with some new friends from Cima and northern Aviko. Do you think we can do this again next year? In case I don't get to talk to all of the spirits here?"

Emry sometimes wondered how Aspen got so many sentences out at once, until he recalled that spirits didn't actually need to breathe.

"We'll talk to Ella about it, but I imagine the Guild has other plans for us that don't involve creating new festivals."

"Oh, of course." Aspen charged ahead, losing none of their luster. "Whatever they think is a good idea."

"Well, whatever their next good idea is, I'd like to be there," Pigeon said firmly, hopping from Aspen's shoulder to Emry's to Sage's. "I told Lydia I want to see at least fifteen new places before I go back to sleep. Can you imagine it?" She flapped her wings. "*Fifteen new cities? Are there even that many out there?*"

Emry frowned. "Sleep?" he repeated. "Wait, I thought spirits didn't—"

"Spiritsong," Damir called gruffly. "It's time."

As committed as they were to their Guild tasks, every bard in the group let out a collective sigh of relief upon entering the backstage shadows, and it wasn't simply due to the cool air. Yes, the diplomacy work to foster spirit and human relations was important and all.

But back here was where the fun began.

"Gods, *finally*." Riley tossed aside her black coat to reveal an equally black waistcoat underneath. "Emry, Aspen, I'll grab your lutes for you. Sage—?"

"Let me check my makeup!" Sage hurried after her. "And yours, too. Last looks are very important—we're performing for spirits here."

"Come on, spirits don't even know what makeup is."

"Last looks can't hurt," Emry said diplomatically, folding up his coat and gloves. "Sage, I'm sorry. I've probably sweated off all the hard work you put in earlier—"

"Em?"

His shoulders immediately relaxed. That voice was more of a relief than all the shadows the backstage had to offer.

"Cal!" He turned, already reaching for her. "I thought you'd still be at the check-in tables with Zeke?"

He wasn't far off—she looked as if she had just arrived from the tables. A dirt-stained apron was still draped over her arm, her hands remained ungloved, and her hair was pulled back in simple twists to stay clear of the piles of soil. But her dress reflected her enthusiasm for the festival itself. Even in the darkness, he could see the deep green gems carefully applied from neckline to hem; a nod to both her Council status and the foliage of the festival.

Hara take him—every time he thought she couldn't possibly look more beautiful, she proved him wrong.

"Zeke can manage the tables for a moment." Cal took his hands in hers. The carved gold of her wedding band brushed against his fingers, and he took a moment to kiss her knuckles. The glittering green gems were lovely, yes—but he'd never tire of seeing that sparkling ring on her hand.

"Is everything all right?" he asked, searching her face for any sign of stress or worry, anything that would have dragged her away from her work. But the dark hall, all wood scaffolding and thick curtains, made it hard to make out more than a strange sort of anticipation crossing her features.

"Come with me," she said. "I'm afraid it's urgent."

CHAPTER TWO

EMRY

As Emry nervously followed Cal through the backstage labyrinth, he finally glimpsed the organized chaos that fueled the festival.

Every spirit researcher in Cal's employ scurried between crates and canvas bags stored in the halls, filling the dark space like overexcited shadows. They traded reports, fetched soil, scrambled for more paper and pencils... Each one looked harried and enthusiastic in equal measure, which came as no surprise to him. After all, the festival had been a joint venture between the Auric Guild and Cal's research department. What better way to gather information about the spirits than to invite them all to Vornik? It could only bode well for spirit and human relations, as Cal's presentations had deftly put it. So many spirits had come out of the literal woodwork in the last two years. The garden spirits in Matlock first. Then spirits traveling from all over the province to visit Aspen. Then even more appearing to humans in vineyards, forests, farms... After being woken up by Aspen's call to defend against the white wave, the spirits clearly weren't going anywhere anytime soon. It would only be neighborly to welcome them in some fashion.

But in this case, neighborly gestures involved mulch rather than a homemade pie.

"Mr. Whitlock?" Cal called to a man hunched over a clipboard, her busy stride maintaining its strict pace. "How are we faring on soil?"

Zeke Whitlock brightened and hopped to scuttle alongside her. "Still well-stocked. I checked not five minutes ago."

Now that Zeke was working for Cal and not Devrin Gray, Emry hardly recognized the man. All that nervous energy that had once encompassed him now flowed as excitement, which in turn bubbled up in his verbal report. The speed of his words, unfortunately, did nothing for Emry's nerves.

"I've also checked the questionnaires, like you and Aspen asked," Zeke rattled off. "We've interviewed about twenty spirits from the greater Vornik area. Then thirty from Matlock, fifteen from the Cima province, and over forty from the Selj countryside so far. None from Envis, but..." His smile thinned. "Perhaps we'll get lucky."

That wasn't nearly enough information to satisfy Aspen, but Emry couldn't focus on the spirit's follow-up questions. Cal hadn't slowed her pace nor had she hinted what this urgent situation was. It could only be about the festival, couldn't it?

His mind spun through increasingly ridiculous possibilities. The spirits were unhappy. They had all hated the Forsgren Quartet's performance and were complaining. No, no—the *humans* in the audience had decided they didn't want the spirits there. They were all just like Mr. Chamberlain, yelling and starting fights. Gods, that would be awful. His parents were standing right there and smiling, and if the entire festival had suddenly gone to rot, what on earth was he going to tell them—?

Wait, hold on.

"Mum?" He stopped in his tracks and grinned. "Dad?"

THE SPIRIT'S CURSE

But it wasn't just his parents. His sister Georgie stood right next to them—and Marley, too—

"You said..." He sniffed, vision blurred, voice wobbly, heart bursting. "You said you weren't going to make it here. You had a river route expansion—"

His family surrounded him and Aspen in seconds, a Karic tangle of curly hair, freckled arms, and grins bright enough to light the entire town square. Emry burrowed in and wiped tears off his cheeks.

An urgent matter, indeed.

"Surprise!" Marley laughed and squeezed the life out of him. "We tricked you!"

His mother, Tessa, managed to kiss his forehead in the loving mayhem. "A route expansion taking precedence over your festival? Darling, please."

"Shiro's beard, I'm glad the secret's out." Georgie lifted Aspen in a viselike hug, then did the same for Emry. "It was killing me not to mention it in my letters. Almost rowed down yesterday just to get the surprise over and done with."

Emry wanted to bombard them with questions. When had they gotten in? How was their trip? How long had they been planning this—? Then beyond the curtains, the noise of the crowd swelled, dragging him back to his duties. He hardly had time to spare as it was—he'd have to find his family seats before they—oh no, *seats*—

"But I..." He looked around wildly for Damir. "I'm so sorry, I don't have any seats saved for you."

Cal came to his rescue once more, catching hold of his hand and squeezing. "I wrote to Damir weeks ago. He already secured them front row seats."

In a rush of relief, he cupped her face and gave her a searing kiss. She giggled against his lips and pressed right back, surrounding him in a perfume of rich earth and flowers. A goddess, indeed. He had the best wife, the best family, the best Guild—

"Did everyone know about this?" He turned to Aspen. "Did *you* know about this?"

"No!" The spirit shook their head fiercely, unable to stop smiling. "No, I swear!"

That had been wise on his family's part. If Aspen had learned about it, they would have burst and told Emry about it ten seconds later.

Tessa raised her voice over the Karic family babble. "We couldn't wait to see you. Cal told us your...*magic*"—the word still being a strange one to apply to her son—"has greatly improved with all your practice." She touched his cheek. "And how healthy you look, my dear, without all that concert possession nonsense."

That much was true. Emry hadn't been possessed in years now, which was an objective improvement upon his health—but the motherly doting still made him blush.

"It's all Aspen, really," he demurred. "Best teacher I've ever had. Wouldn't be able to grow a single leaf on stage without their magic lessons, would I?"

He looked around for Aspen, but the spirit had dragged his father, Edward, over to the wing to peek through the curtains.

"I've talked to dozens of the spirits so far," they rambled, bouncing on their heels as they pointed at the crowd. "See, that's Pigeon over there, and Cedar. They're some of my best friends. Oh! And there's Tabby, from Halagrad. I just met her today..."

Emry joined them at the curtains to get his first peek at the audience—and nearly floated at the sight of the happy, buzzing festival.

Most days, the city of Vornik gave off an air of rigidity. Straight roads, towering columns, symmetrical brick facades—from the Council building to the Academy campus, it all smacked of order and formality. If Emry was being honest, he vastly preferred the tiered chaos of Tazlo and the winding canals of Senne.

But even he had to admit that the spirit festival had pleasantly softened Vornik's edges. The central plaza dripped with comforting shades of green. Emerald banners swaying on lampposts, sage ribbons fluttering from balconies, garlands wrapping around merchant and food stalls... Taken together, it would have provided enough verdant variety to rival a forest.

But Aspen had refused to stop the decorations there. Literal greenery crawled into every nook and cranny the plaza had to offer. Ivy blurred austere brick while climbing pothos broke the imposing lines of the columns. And every line and leaf seemed to lead back to the centerpiece of the whole affair, the part that Emry had the biggest hand in: the stage.

The wide wooden platform nearly sagged under the display of foliage that audiences had come to expect from a Spiritsong performance. Emry and Aspen together had made sure that lights and plants wound up and around the structure until one could hardly tell where the wooden boards ended and nature began. Just as the trio had hoped, as the sun set, the stage lights drew more and more attention, until the crowd naturally formed around it like moths to a lantern—humans and spirits alike, well over a thousand in total.

And the best part was having his family there to see it all.

"Incredible," his father said, his voice soft in wonder. "So very impressive. Tessa, do you see—?"

"I see it." She beamed and twined her fingers with Edward's. In an echo of her motion, Cal reached out once more for Emry's hand, her wedding ring clinking against his own band. He lifted her hand and kissed it.

"Very proud of you," he murmured. "You've outdone yourself."

"I simply brought the spirits here." She leaned against his shoulder. "I believe it's time to show them what you can do."

Aspen took his other hand, flowers blooming eagerly in their hair. Emry took a slow, steadying breath, then squeezed both their hands in return. Behind him, Damir quietly approached from the shadows.

"Karic family," he said in a low, professional tone. "If you could please follow me to the front row."

Emry drew back from the curtain and nudged Aspen. "We should go get Sage and Riley. Make sure they're not still arguing over—"

Another flash of anger sent him rocking back on his heels, and he grabbed the nearest column to keep himself upright.

"Em?" Cal said, but he couldn't respond at first. He was still trying to sort out the strange feeling.

The anger had struck again—a wave of that same emotion his magic had brushed up against before. Only this time, the anger was closer, flecked with other things. Fear, jealousy, ash, the sharpness of teeth...

He tried to grasp more of it, to understand it—but it was gone as quick as it had come, leaving nothing but confusion and Aspen's nervous, almost-painful grip on his fingers.

"What is it?" Cal's worried gaze darted between them both. "What happened?"

Emry could only look to Aspen for help—but they didn't say a word. Their eyes methodically roved across the audience once, twice... Then they dropped Emry's hand and shook their head.

"I don't know what it was," they said quietly. "Cal, please stay back here with Damir. Keep all the researchers backstage as well. Just to be safe."

Cal stiffened. "What are you talking about—?"

"Emry?" Sage and Riley melted out of the shadows, instruments in hand. "It's time to go on."

Emry checked the front row. His family was now in full view there, alongside Ella Sorman, Karlson, Councilmembers... They were safe and within arm's reach. And Cal would be safe, too, backstage with Damir. Whatever that was—if it had truly been anything—he and Aspen could handle it. Though he desperately hoped no sort of handling was needed. Not tonight.

He steeled himself, took his lute from Sage, and nodded. "It's time."

CHAPTER
THREE

ASPEN

Over the past two years, Aspen had learned to love the stage as much as Emry.

The only thing better than listening to the music they loved was sharing it with others—and walking from behind the brush of the curtain, emerging from shadow into light, felt like basking in the sun after a rainstorm. The promise of music washed the air clean, leaving nothing but joy between them and the crowd beyond the stage. Joy, brightness, and the vibrations of their clapping that Aspen could feel all the way up through the cobblestones.

Most days, they absorbed as much of the audience's excitement as they could and reflected it right back. Most days, they squeezed hands with Sage, Riley, and Emry—then paraded out with them shoulder-to-shoulder, their flower-filled lute on their back and their concert lute in their hands.

But today, something lurked beyond the excited faces and the echoes of the last troupe's chords. Something in the crowd stalked.

And Aspen couldn't figure out what it was.

There was simply so much of *everything* in the plaza. So many plants, so many humans, so many spirits. This was nothing like acclimating to an unfamiliar forest or a crowded street. Forests had their own hum, their own rhythm that Aspen could fall into easily. Even the humans' roads and towns had a tune of their own that they had long since learned to follow.

But here, every little thing teemed with life and called for the spirit's attention. The silent growth of all the plants, yes, and certainly the humans cheering. But their new spirit friends called out, too, adding a unique cacophony of their own. Brays, cheeps, bellows, whistles. While Aspen adored the sounds, the chaos of it all smothered their hunt for that brief threat of anger.

After a moment, they released their search, defeated. Whatever it was, it wasn't showing its face any longer.

If Emry had concerns—if he was trying to search for the one blot in the crowd, too—he didn't show it. He gripped his lute purposefully, shoulders back, spine tall. As he walked forward, he gave a delighted laugh at the sight of his family in the front row.

Aspen took a breath, then held onto that laugh and grounded themselves to it, winding it in their flower-filled lute like any other beloved seedling. As long as Emry was with them, everything would be fine.

"Evening!" Emry called, his projected voice immediately quieting the applause. "Have you been enjoying the festival so far?"

Shouts to the affirmative rang back. Somewhere, a cow mooed. Emry pointed in its general direction.

"I'm going to take that as a yes."

As the crowd settled back down, Aspen quietly reached out to the flowers near Emry. Prodding them with magic, preparing them to bloom...but it wasn't time to release their glow yet.

"We are truly thrilled to have such a turnout tonight," Emry continued. "We didn't know what to expect when setting up our very first spirit festival, and I daresay none of you knew what to expect, either. But we're absolutely ecstatic to see you all, particularly those of you who have traveled across provinces to be here."

"What's a province?" one spirit called out.

The humans in the crowd all chuckled. Emry laughed with them and fell back next to Aspen.

"My dear Sage has requested we start with Dawn's Reel. So, without further ado..." Emry looked at Aspen and grinned. "Here's Spiritsong."

For past concerts, the troupe often planned to make the audience wait for the magic they expected from Emry and Aspen. To hold for some chord or important pause, to keep the crowd holding their breath in anticipation of the show within a show.

This time, they had agreed not to hold Aspen back.

At the very first chord, the flowers around them burst to life, glowing in ripples that wreathed the stage in celebratory light. For Aspen, performing such a trick was as simple as extending a finger. It was as if the buds were just as excited to honor the music; they bloomed immediately and cast their joyful, shifting rainbow of light over the crowd's faces.

For Emry, such a display took more time. Without the benefit of Aspen possessing him, his magic had to stretch to slip into the channels the spirit had prepared, gradually lighting the flowers in a slow, steady rhythm. But by the end of the first song, the light was there all the same, both in the petals and setting off a glow in his eyes from the exertion. His light, his magic, and his music surrounded them, all gaining strength as the chords grew. It was everything Aspen loved, and even with an empty audience, their heart would have been full to bursting.

But their audience wasn't empty, not even remotely so. Their audience now had spirits—and they, too, loved the music.

Their fascination and joy echoed back through the flowers in a way that the humans' excitement never could. It traveled through roots and vines, all the way up to the lute strings under Aspen's fingers. Aspen had never absorbed this sort of energy—earthy, strong, *familiar*—at such strength before. For their part, they couldn't get enough.

They tried to give back that happiness as much as they could. They sang, showing off the words they had learned from Emry. They danced, showing off the steps they had learned from Sage. And their troupe mates twined their talents with every beat. Riley's drums, endlessly energetic, kept Aspen in perfect time; Sage's voice reached lofty notes that Aspen could only aspire to.

And Emry—Emry swayed the crowd like sunflowers tilting toward the sun.

Everything he did on stage looked effortless. His playing, his singing, his movement between troupe and audience. In one moment, he was spinning Aspen around, almost laughing through his song—then in another, he was serenading the crowd, entrancing them with his mere presence.

Aspen didn't know if Emry could sense the spirits' excitement like they did. The vibrations, the scent of a joyous spring. But that didn't matter—the bard had more than enough joy of his own, particularly when he sang to his family in the front row. On his knees, beaming, hand outstretched to briefly grab Marley's in sheer delight. Between just the spirits and the Karics, an entire forest could have grown on their enthusiasm alone.

For a brief moment, there was nothing like it. For a brief moment, they understood why Emry had once left home for this.

Then the music evaporated for the last time, as it always did. Aspen gravitated back to their troupe mates, dizzy and overjoyed and untethered, while Emry turned to the audience with an exhausted parting smile, his eyes rapidly dimming back to their normal dark brown.

"Thank you so much!" he called to the crowd. "You've been a wonderful audience! Don't forget to come back tomorrow for Karlson, the one and only Ella Sorman, and..."

As he spoke, Aspen gathered their magic back into themself, gently nestling it inside the lute on their back to regrow within the soil. Their hands flickered weakly around their concert lute, but that came as no surprise—the performance had taken much of their strength. It didn't matter. They would rest and recover within a matter of hours. Emry's store of magic would need a little longer, of course, but—

A spike of energy jolted their attention back to the audience.

Aspen quietly set down their concert lute and moved closer to Sage, their translucent fingers balling into fists. The magic was a sharp, angry thrum now, prowling underneath the pulse of the crowd. And it didn't shy away this time. It grew—closer and faster and angrier than before, welling and welling—

Until a shadow, claws out and teeth bared, leapt out of the crowd and onto the stage, barreling right toward Aspen.

CHAPTER FOUR

ASPEN

Aspen dove to escape the incoming blur, their palms slamming into the wooden stage. They flinched, not at any pain or the roughness of the planks, but at the clumsiness of their human form. These limbs weren't right, weren't *enough* in this moment. They closed their eyes and tugged on their energy, shaping their form into something bigger. Claws, thick fur, long teeth, four paws to stand on—

Then opened their wolf eyes to regard the attacker.

Even without such vision, they would have recognized the anger seeping from the spirit. It was the same anger that had haunted them before the set, watching from the chaos of the crowd. Now out in the open, the spirit had taken the form of a lynx, his body entangled in the vines and thorns that sustained him. Every sharp tooth, every claw bared shone sharply in the footlights.

And his gaze bore right into Aspen.

Good, they thought. The lynx didn't seem to care about anyone else—not on stage and not in the audience. As long as Aspen worked to lead him away, the humans had nothing to fear.

But they didn't know that. Shrieks rose from the front row. Behind Aspen, Emry pushed Sage and Riley toward the curtains.

"Get off the stage!"

"But Aspen—"

"We've got it handled!" That wasn't Emry, but Georgie, clambering up onto the boards. While others in the front row scrambled away from the commotion, she already had her boot knife in hand; behind her, Marley scrabbled eagerly to follow.

Aspen's focus faltered, hackles lowering. "Georgie!"

"Hara take me." Emry shoved his lute into Georgie's hands. "Hold this for me. Marley, get *down*!"

As Damir tugged on Sage and Riley and the Karic parents struggled to pull Marley off the stage, Emry grabbed an overhanging vine, twisted one end around his wrist, and snapped the other end on the floor like a whip. The lynx flinched and snarled, his attention broken for a split-second; that was all Aspen needed. They poured their magic into the surrounding plants, bidding them to grow thick and fast toward the lynx. Around their limbs, weaving in with the vines already wrapped around him—

With a yowl, the lynx's thorns shot up like knives, slicing the new growth to ribbons.

You, he called to Aspen, a silent wave of rage that only spirits could hear. *You did this!*

Did what? they tried to ask, but the question was useless. The lynx leapt, and they tumbled back together in a cloud of leaves, fur, and claws.

The fur and claws didn't last long. To evade the lynx's massive paws, Aspen shifted from one form to another. Wolf to bird to mouse back to wolf, ducking and dodging and blocking. They couldn't strike back, not here, not in front of the audience.

But their magic, so drained after the concert, began to sputter. The soil in their lute went dry and scattered across the boards, and inside the sound hole, the flowers shriveled. Spirits didn't need to breathe, but Aspen felt a gasp welling up in them all the same. A deep, urgent need for rest and sunlight—

Georgie's knife whiffed past Aspen and embedded itself in the thorns above the lynx's back. The spirit whipped around in surprise, and through his exhausted, flickering form, Aspen saw their way out—Emry, poised by Georgie, his hand outstretched.

"To me!" he shouted. "Just for a second!"

Aspen shoved the lynx away and bounded over to Emry, first as wolf, them stumbling to their feet as a human, hand reaching out—

Their fingers met, and Aspen could breathe once more, taking refuge in Emry's consciousness for the briefest of moments. Emry only had a drop of energy left in him—but fear and protectiveness churned the little magic that remained.

Let me help, he insisted—and Aspen was in no position to refuse.

Trap it, they said quickly. *Don't hurt it.*

Eyes and veins all glowing now, Emry grabbed a handful of hanging ivy, and Aspen shoved whatever magic they had left into the leaves. The vines launched from Emry's hand with more force than either of them could have managed alone, catching the lynx just as his form solidified.

No! the lynx tried, but he was too exhausted against the fresh attack. He writhed briefly against the ivy yanking him down onto the planks. His thorns twisted, his vines tried to snap the restraints... then he collapsed in defeat, a growl the only lingering evidence of his resolve.

Aspen slipped out of Emry and back into their lute, barely able to maintain even the outline of a human form. There was soil backstage, they thought weakly. They could go find it, then rest inside their lute for a while...

But the cresting energy at the front of the stage threatened to overwhelm them first.

Spirits had crowded the front row—a menagerie of animals, all with their hackles raised, feathers puffed, and teeth bared as their gazes darted between Aspen and the restrained lynx. Only a thin line of shaky researchers held them at bay. Save for the Karics and the brave researchers, the other humans had fallen back, watching the commotion—the spirits—with wide, fearful eyes.

Aspen's chest tightened. So much for a strong start to spirit-human relations.

They picked up their lute, glared at the lynx, and pointed to the curtains. "Let's get him out of here. Now."

～

THEY RETREATED into the first solid structure they could find—a neighboring tavern, already emptied out so that patrons and workers alike could hear the music.

"Sorry about this!" Aspen called to the perplexed tavern owner, who stood frozen behind the bar while Shrike landed on the floor with a foliage-shaking yowl. "We'll be just a minute!"

But their escape drew a much larger audience than they had hoped for. Cal defended the door, turning away Sage, Riley, and the Karics (which was only possible after she confirmed in her firmest voice that no one was injured). Several spirits had also perched at the tavern windows, reaching out to Aspen and each other in an avalanche of conversation.

Who is that? Pigeon demanded first.

Another bird beside her ruffled its feathers. *Bet you anything he's from the west. From Envis or whatever the humans call that place. Never liked those mountains myself. Nothing good can come of them.*

I don't know who he is, Aspen tried, hoping to calm them. *I promise, I'll tell you as soon as I sort it out.*

But both Cal and Aspen's attempts to shoo away their unwanted audiences failed. The gossiping spirits remained settled on the windowsills, and over at the door, Damir and Ella burst through Cal's barricade, matching storm clouds gathering over both of their faces. Damir's storm cloud, Aspen was used to—that was what his face looked like all the time—but Ella's contrasted deeply with the bright gold bands in her braids and her dress.

"I would like answers," Ella said imperiously, her long, silky skirts trailing on the grimy tavern floor. "*Now*, if you please. I have a mayor, a Council, and over a thousand people to explain this situation to."

Aspen only had a loose grasp on what a mayor was, exactly, but Ella's demands alone were more than enough to jolt them into action. They turned to the lynx, who huddled against the bar in a bundle of ivy. Amidst the flickering lamplight and the warm wooden furniture, he looked more like an angry shrub with teeth than a large cat.

Can you speak in their language? Aspen asked.

The lynx hissed. When Aspen didn't so much as blink in response, the hiss melted into a grumble, then into a low, sharp voice.

"'Course I can," he muttered aloud, his words tinged with a looping Cima accent. "Humans never shut up."

Huddled at Emry's side, Cal quietly took out a tiny notebook and began scribbling.

"Why did you attack me?" Aspen continued.

"You're Aspen, aren't you?" the lynx said. As he spoke, his ears flattened and the thorns around him grew longer. "You're the one who woke me up. You're the reason I can't go back."

Aspen stiffened. "Go back where?"

"It's not a *where*. I can't go *back*. I can't go back to sleep."

Cal stopped writing. Beside her, Emry frowned. "I beg your pardon?" he said.

"I don't expect you to get it," the lynx snapped at him. "Sleep. What I was before, when I lived in my grove. I can't do it anymore, and it's your fault." He turned back to Aspen, and the long tufts on his ears twitched. "Tell me how. Now."

Ella drew herself up, her expression just as muddled as everyone else's. "What is this creature talking about?"

But Aspen couldn't find the words to explain it—not to her, and not to the others. A cold dread had begun to take over their form, something they couldn't attribute to the draft in the tavern.

Cal tucked her pencil behind her ear and stepped forward.

"Sleep isn't quite the same for spirits as it is for humans," she explained. "The research on it is...nascent, to say the least. But consider it a form of stasis for spirits. A passive state where they simply exist and act as a source of energy to their grove."

That was the technical definition she and Aspen had agreed upon, yes—but her formal wording had never captured it exactly. For spirits, sleep came with an untethering of time, a steady silence. Aspen had lived in this stasis for years before waking, and their memories of that period were foggy at best. Seasons had passed, trees had grown and fallen, animals had come and gone...and all the while, they had tended their grove in quiet, solitary, peaceful bliss.

Sleep was the best word they had for it—and years ago, Aspen had pulled other spirits out of it.

"Before the wave," they said quietly, taking over where Cal had stopped. "I asked Cedar to warn the other spirits about what was coming. Cedar's message traveled farther than I could have expected. Our warning saved the spirits, but it—it woke them, too."

They swallowed. Waking had been just the beginning. Within years, the spirits were making friends, visiting, sending letters... And now, attending music festivals in droves.

But the lynx wasn't done. He bared his teeth.

"And what rotting good your warning did me. I couldn't stay in my grove anymore. Couldn't go back to the way it was. And the other spirits say *you* did it." The ivy holding him in place began to curl. "So *fix* it."

The humans all silently looked at Aspen, who would have welcomed any sort of sound to fill the space instead. The scratch of Cal's pen on paper, Emry's humming. Anything to distract them from the answer they held on their tongue.

"Aspen?" Emry said gently. They turned to him and forced themself to speak, not daring to say the answer to anyone else.

"I can't," they said. The lynx snarled; Aspen did their best not to flinch.

"What do you mean, you can't?"

"I don't know how!" they shot back. "I've never been able to go back to sleep myself! I don't even know if it's possible!"

In a blink, the lynx went from fearsome predator to frightened kitten hiding in the bushes. It shrunk back against the closest barstool, one paw raised. "You can't go back? At all?"

Emry stepped in, both hands lifted. After Aspen's brief possession, his movements were weak and unsteady, but his gaze was firm. "I understand you're upset, but just because Aspen doesn't know how doesn't mean it's impossible—"

"Can't go back to sleep?" another voice said, muffled by glass. All eyes turned to the window. Pigeon still perched on the windowsill, head tilted, with an assembly of other spirits flanking her—all of them staring at her in surprise.

"They said we can't go back to sleep!" she repeated.

Immediately, Aspen could feel the message ripple outward—from bird to bird, then across the plaza, sending up flares of emotion as the realization struck the other spirits. Confusion, surprise, anger, sadness—

Then the noise began, and no one else in the room needed magic to understand what was happening outside. Several humans hurried past the tavern, casting wary glances over their shoulders at the town square. Knocking soon rattled the door.

"Ms. Sorman?" someone called; Aspen vaguely recognized the voice of a Councilmember from the reception earlier. "Ms. Sorman, are you in there? What is going on? Something's upset the spirits—"

As the knocking grew more urgent, Ella stepped forward, her frown sharp. "If we let this continue, not even I will be able to smooth this out with the Council. How can we calm them?"

"I'll talk to the spirits," Aspen offered, though their mind was utterly blank on what words to use. "I'll go out there and tell them it'll—it'll be—"

A warm hand settled on Aspen's shoulder.

"That it will be fine, and we'll begin searching for a solution immediately," Cal said, her posture every bit as stoic as Ella's. "Both the Vornik and Matlock research teams are already here on the ground. I can debrief them tonight and launch them in the morning."

Emry's hand squeezed Aspen's other shoulder. "We've done it before with the wave and with the Matlock spirit well. We'll sort out this mystery, too." He managed a small wink in Aspen's direction.

Damir crossed his arms and nodded to the lynx. "And this one?"

The lynx growled in response. Aspen turned to him, their resolve bolstered by the hands on their shoulders. That spirit wasn't going to slink away in this mess—not after his disastrous spectacle onstage. "Him? He'll help us with our research."

"Help?" The lynx bristled. "How would I even—?"

"These are the answers you wanted, right?" Aspen glared at him. "If you really want them, you're going to help get them."

"But it's not my fault!"

"Being awake? No." Aspen pointed to the window. "But all this?"

Somewhere out in the square, a coyote yipped in fear, then another, and another. The birds had left to scuttle about in the air, leaving only Pigeon peering in, her feathers puffed in confusion and dismay. The knocking on the door grew louder.

"Ms. Sorman?" another human called. "Someone must speak to these creatures at *once*. Are the Karics in there?"

Everyone in the tavern swiveled back to Aspen and the lynx.

"You're helping us fix this and that is final," Aspen repeated. "What should we call you?"

The lynx shifted from paw to paw, then settled back on his haunches, claws sheathed, voice uncertain.

"Shrike," he finally said. "Call me Shrike."

CHAPTER
FIVE

EMRY

Emry couldn't fall asleep that night.

Despite his bone-deep exhaustion, his mind kept whirring. Replaying not the joy of the concert, but the chaos of Shrike's attack, the panic of the spirits in the square....

But most of all, he kept recalling Aspen. How afraid they had seemed in the tavern, how guilty and uncertain they had looked when talking to Shrike.

He had never seen them like that before.

At some point in the night, memories faded into dreams and disjointed sleep, leaving him groggy and sandy-eyed when dawn streamed in through the windows. With none of his party daring to venture too far from the spirits—any of the spirits—last night, the Guild had hastily booked him a room at a neighboring inn. It was a decent inn, at least, and he could likely requisition a good cup of tea for Cal before tackling the morning...

He tried to lift his head—then collapsed back onto the pillow with a pained groan.

He hadn't been possessed by Aspen in years, and his body had wasted no time in reminding him of the consequences. A headache thrummed behind his eyes, while a dull pain moved like sludge through his veins. And, naturally, the old aches in his knees had flared up, eager to join in on the sadistic fun.

Normally, Emry's use of his own magic during concerts avoided this sort of mess. Sometimes, he even felt stronger after his set—though he always attributed that to the exhilaration that came from a good performance. For the most part, he was able to keep his old pains down to the occasional flare.

But his pain management wasn't exactly prepared for lynx attacks before his encore.

He gathered his strength and turned onto his side—slowly, painfully—hoping to see Cal lying beside him. That would make him feel better; it always did. But the other side of the bed was still made, the duvet crisp and the pillow unmoved.

Hara take him. He would bet half his Guild earnings that Cal had stayed in the Academy library all night.

As he briefly gave up on further movement and let his pillow consume him, the door to his room opened a crack.

"Good morning," Aspen said, their tone indicative of the opposite. "I suppose you'll be wanting this?"

They pushed their hand through the opening with a small offering: the morning newspaper and a gray, pain-relieving moonflower. The dull petals did little to brighten the room, but Emry didn't care—to him, the flower was a tiny blossom from heaven.

"Please," he mumbled. Aspen slipped inside and helped him eat it, petal by petal. It still tasted bitter, as those flowers always did, but the taste was hardly his biggest problem right now. "Cal, is she…?"

"Yes." Aspen slouched. Normally, they came in as bright as the dawn when Emry woke up, particularly after concerts. But this morning, the flowers in their lute drooped, and instead of mint and honeysuckle, they smelled like rain. "She stayed in the library through the night. I tried to tell her to go to sleep, but…"

Emry sighed. As much as he wished he had been there to press the issue, he knew that wouldn't have helped, either. His wife was too stubborn. Generally, her loved her for it, but now wasn't one of those times. "We'll get over there to help her, then."

Aspen frowned. "Are you sure?"

Emry moved his legs and winced. "We'll get over there...eventually. Hand me that newspaper, please?"

Given their ability to greet the newsboy at the press house before dawn, Aspen had formed a habit of buying the paper for Emry and Cal before they had even woken up. But this time, the spirit hesitated in handing it to him. "Maybe you should rest first—"

"I appreciate the thought, but I can still read just fine."

He soon found it wasn't the effort of reading that worried them —it was the headline.

SPIRIT ATTACK AT FESTIVAL
Spiritsong Under Siege! Bards Fight for Their Lives!

Emry groaned and rubbed his eyes. Perhaps he should take Aspen's advice and bury his head under the pillow for a few days.

"I tried to tell the newsboy that it wasn't a siege!" Aspen fiddled with a loose thread on the duvet. "Cal said a siege involves armies and—"

"It's a figure of..." Emry sighed and folded up the paper. "Never mind all that, my dear. Let's just focus on helping Cal, shall we?"

Two hours and one cane later, Emry limped through the central Vornik plaza. It felt strange to walk through the bleary square when just hours ago, it had been filled to the brim with music and people. He half expected to hear the echoes of the concert against the columns or—less fortunately—the shouts of newsboys cluttering the place with their sensationalized headlines. Gods, Mr. Chamberlain and his ilk were going to have a field day with articles like that. He could almost feel their smug satisfaction poisoning the air—and their words would soon follow. Insisting that spirits didn't belong in their cities. That they weren't *civilized*. Why, simply look at the violence that took place during that naive bard's ill-advised concert...

Emry shook off the imagined conversation and kept moving through the square. Fortunately for him, the newsboys hadn't yet arrived to peddle their scandals. All he saw were a few morning travelers, coffee carts setting up for the day...and a huddle of spirits, all being interrogated by researchers who had slept about as much as Cal had.

"And you're sure you don't know of any older spirits in your area?" a familiar voice floated by—Zeke slouched on a bench, talking to Pigeon while clutching a cup of coffee. Around him, a dozen other birds perched, as if he were the bearer of the last breadcrumbs in the province. "Is there any spirit in Matlock who might have more information about sleeping?"

"Maybe, but..." Pigeon paused. "Some of the older ones died during that spirit well dig."

"Right. Of course." Lips pressed together, Zeke jotted a note down, then caught sight of Emry and Aspen and brightened feebly. "Ah. If you're looking for Mrs. Karic, she's in the—"

"Library. We know." Emry tried to sound confident, but his voice came out cracked and raspy. "Any luck so far?"

"Not yet." Zeke grimaced. "I've spoken to..." He flipped through his papers, and the bags under his eyes grew heavier. "Sixteen spirits across four provinces. Still no spirits from Envis, as far as I can tell."

"Did any of them leave after last night?" Aspen asked.

"Less than a dozen, by my count. Most are still here, your lynx included. I tried talking to him this morning, but..." He glanced over at the stage. Damir, Shrike, and a handful of spirits had gathered at the base of the stage, while Sage and Riley stood atop, setting up their instruments. Sage paraded about the front of the boards, while

Riley hunched further back with her drum and a coffee the size of her drum.

"We could teach them a song!" Sage turned back to Riley, trying to keep her tone bright and cheery for the spirits' sakes. "What about—what about the 'Sunlight Reel?' You know, sunlight for spirits!"

"Kill me," Riley said. "I mean, fine. Let's do it."

The audience of spirits all tried to sing along with Sage, their voices warbly and off-key in the morning air. Damir winced and rubbed both of his temples. Shrike curled up deep into the stage's shadow.

Zeke sighed and turned back to Emry. "We'll keep trying. I promise."

Aspen gave a small bow in thanks. "May I please borrow Pigeon for a moment?"

Zeke nodded and moved on to his next subject of interrogation—a goat with a crown of flowers around its horns. On the bench, Pigeon perked up.

"Borrow?" she repeated. "I thought humans borrowed objects."

"It's a figure of—" Aspen waved their hand. "I'll explain it later. Do you know where Lydia is?"

"At the library with Cal."

"Good. Could you ask Cedar and Brinna to meet us there?"

"Oh, the Alta who looks after Cedar's fane and tells all those stories?" Pigeon tilted her head. "I like her. Very grumpy. Lots of wrinkles."

"Maybe don't mention that when you find her," Emry croaked.

Once Pigeon had flown off, Aspen strode toward the carriage stop at a brisk pace. The pace, they had clearly learned from Cal, but it was their own nervous energy that fueled it.

"Hey." Emry patted Aspen's shoulder once they reached the stop. "We're going to figure it out. It'll be all right."

"I know." But the flowers in their hair remained furled.

They took a carriage to the Vornik Academy library, where Emry and his cane silently cursed how expansive the grounds had become. The city had clearly worked to re-beautify the campus after the white wave and various surges had torn up the ground, but he could still remember every uprooted tree, every shard of split earth.

And none of that could compare to the cracks in Cal's professional veneer.

"Our current records don't have any data on spirit stasis." She was already halfway through a lecture to Lydia when Emry opened the door to the study hall. "So, I'm working my way through the Alta records we haven't already reviewed. If you could help me search in section B?"

Lydia scooped up her notebook and pushed aside a lock of greying hair. "If I do, will you take a nap?"

Cal snorted.

Much like when Emry had once found her in the Tazlo library, she had gathered a haphazard stack of books and notes around her in desperate defense against her problem. But the chalkboard looming on the wall was ominously blank, and the circles below her eyes underlined her lack of progress.

Emry didn't know how to solve the spirit's sleeping problem—but he certainly knew how to help with Cal's. As Lydia greeted them and passed by with her task in hand, he limped his way down to Cal's desk.

"I haven't uncovered any—" she tried, but he held up a palm.

"Coffee first, my dear."

Together with Aspen, he placed three coffees and an iced bun wrapped in paper on the desk. She gasped and downed one of the coffees in one go.

"Gods, thank you." She slumped in the desk chair. "And is that—?"

"Cinnamon bun," Emry said proudly. He had picked out the largest one, still warm and dripping with icing. "Can't imagine you had any dinner last night, did you?"

She dove for the bun, but the overly sweet icing didn't have its intended effect—she somehow looked even more miserable than before. "I'm so sorry. I meant to come back last night and make sure you were all right."

Emry waved a hand, then immediately regretted it—such sudden use of his cane made his wrist hurt.

"Oh, I'm fine," he tried. "Aspen shoved a garden down my throat and now I'm right as rain."

Cal paused in tearing apart the cinnamon bun, her eyes narrowed. "You know I don't like you joking about that."

"I know, I know." So much for trying to lift her spirits. He leaned in and kissed her cheek, tasting a hint of the icing at the edge of her lip. "Really, I'm all right—I was only possessed for a few seconds. Just give me a day or so and I can help research with the best of them."

She tore off half the bun and handed it to him. "You don't have to help."

"Darling, it was practically in my vows." He nibbled at the pastry. He never had much of an appetite after concerts, but he hoped the icing's sweetness would cut through the pain-induced fog in his mind. "Any leads beyond Vornik's current records?"

"None." Cal carefully wiped her hands before turning the page in her journal. Unlike her typical, fastidious notes, these ones lay heavily smudged and slanted across the page. "So far, the Altas don't have any stories about spirits going to sleep. And if they do mention spirits being silent, they don't postulate on how they may have gotten that way."

Beside Emry, Aspen remained quiet, staring at the notes without reading them. For their sake, Emry cleared his throat and tried to sound positive.

"Aspen's asked Brinna to come here for a visit—maybe she'll have something for us. How can we help you in the meantime?"

He handed Aspen part of his cinnamon bun as he spoke. Spirits didn't eat, of course, but they always felt better being included in the meal.

"Well..." Cal glanced at Aspen. "I do have some questions for you, if that's all right."

Aspen nodded and sat cross-legged on a nearby desk, their scrap of iced bun in hand. Cal took a sip of her second coffee, then flipped to a fresh page. "When did you first wake up?"

"About fifty winters ago," they said, their gaze fixed on the empty chalkboard. "Someone came to visit my grove, and I just sort of... woke. I don't really know why."

"And how long had you slept until then?"

"Seventy winters, maybe. It's hard to count."

Cal made a note in shorthand. "And have you really never slept since?" she asked. Aspen started to fidget with the pastry.

"No. I—I never really wanted to."

"And you've never felt anything akin to sleeping? Any sense of... falling out of time, or losing awareness?"

They were silent for one moment—then their eyes welled.

"It's all my fault, isn't it?" they mumbled. "I bothered Cedar until they woke. I had them send the message. And now none of them can"—their voice cracked—"I didn't mean to hurt them! I didn't *know*!"

Emry reached over and took Aspen's hand, ignoring the ache in his arms and the icing on their fingers.

"It's not your fault," he said. "You did the right thing warning them about the wave. If you hadn't, they might have died."

"And just because you haven't found a way to sleep doesn't mean it doesn't exist." Cal took Aspen's other hand. "I've learned not to assume too many things in this world, particularly when it comes to spirits."

As Aspen gave them a weak smile, Lydia poked her head into the study hall, her glasses askew.

"You called for an...elk associate, Aspen?" she asked uncertainly. Behind her, Cedar towered over the bookshelves, just as unamused as they had been yesterday, Pigeon perched on their antlers.

"*Move*, you great lug." Brinna pushed past the elk and wobbled on down to the front of the room. The Alta hadn't aged a day since Emry's first meeting with her; the only thing that had changed was that they now had matching canes.

"I thank you for thinking I'm a source of wisdom in this city," Brinna continued, "but I'm not sure I'll be of any help in all this nonsense. I've got plenty of stories for you about surges and the like, but none about spirits taking a nap."

Emry's hopes sank. Next to him, Aspen's shoulders slumped. "None about sleeping at all?"

"Oh, plenty about sleeping spirits. Spirits ignoring humans, mostly. Just not the rotting *how* of it all." She adjusted her shawl. "Couldn't possibly relate. I fell asleep five minutes into the carriage ride here, and I'll do it again on the way back."

"Any luck with you?" Aspen asked Cedar. The elk spirit gave a huff.

"It is as you suspected," they said. "I asked around through the night, but there is no spirit here who has been able to return to sleep, and no spirit older than I who might have more information."

Aspen stood, slipping away from Emry and Cal's grasp.

"Then we'll look through the books here," they said. Their own words seemed to give them resolve; the flowers in their hair bloomed stronger as they spoke. "And if they don't have anything, we'll— we'll travel around and find other spirits and ask. We'll do whatever it takes."

Something about the phrase pricked a worried, selfish pang in Emry's chest. He was just as willing to find answers, of course—but Spiritsong had responsibilities in the city lined up for after the festival. Their joint song to debut, soirees to host, this new spirit-human mess to mop up. Surely, there was a better way to find a wise spirit than to blindly cavort across the province, as Aspen was suggesting...

Wracking his foggy brain for any helpful thoughts, he looked up at Cedar, who barely fit in the door, and Pigeon, who was whispering something to Lydia.

"I already apologized to Aspen for gossiping," she said. "I can't help it, I like talking to the other spirits! They're my friends!"

Emry smiled. Apart from Aspen, Pigeon was the most social spirit he knew. Back in Matlock, she had been adept at finding and forming her own social circle—pinpointing not just every garden spirit in the city, but the location of Devrin's illegal dig into the spirit well.

A thought finally broke through his haze.

"Pigeon's good at finding things," he said. The others looked at him in confusion, and he quickly jumped to clarify. "Finding spirits, I mean. Maybe she could locate an older spirit, like how she located the well in Matlock?"

Cal faltered. "I appreciate the idea, Em, but it took several days for her to find the well. To go about feeling for an older spirit, anywhere across the provinces..." She turned to Pigeon. "Wouldn't that take months?"

Pigeon flapped her wings in indignation. "Excuse you! I was half-dead when my friends and I searched for that well!" She looked at Aspen and Cedar, her beady eyes glinting. "Lend me some of your magic and I'll show you what I can do."

CHAPTER SIX

ASPEN

Pigeon could spread commands as efficiently as she could gossip, and by midday, every spirit in the city had gathered back in the festival plaza.

"Oldest ones up here with me!" Lydia called, waving her arms to sort the meandering shuffle of spirits. "Cedar, Pigeon, up here. The rest of you, form a circle around us—yes, that's it! Good work, good work."

Despite the Matlock researcher's friendly encouragement, the circle was slow to form. Animals of all shapes and sizes gradually took up half the square with their irregular formation, while Cedar, Pigeon, and a smattering of older spirits waited impatiently at its center. Aspen was tempted to join the spirits at the center and get the process started quickly—but they refused to run this experiment without the lynx spirit that had started this whole mess.

"Shrike?" they called, searching for the spirit's signature: mountain air and seething annoyance. Fortunately, the search didn't take long. Between Shrike's sour energy and Damir's equally sour frown, Aspen could have pinpointed them both from across the city.

"There you are," Damir grumbled as soon as Aspen approached them at the edge of the plaza. "Look, I realize no one here values my contributions, but I do, in fact, have better things to accomplish than cat-sitting."

Shrike hissed at that. Damir hissed back, then ran a hand over his face and pulled out his pipe. "See? Look at what this is doing to me. I'm unraveling."

On the contrary, Aspen thought that Damir looked no different from his usual buttoned-up figure, with his all-black attire and his moody blonde hair. But they knew better than to disagree with their musical manager when he was in such a state.

"You're freed from cat-sitting," they said, then turned to Shrike. "I'm glad you're still here."

"Didn't have much of a choice." Shrike licked his paw, refusing to meet Aspen's gaze. "The big antlered one told me the little bird would track me down if I ran. Said she can find anyone in any city."

Aspen made a note to grow flower crowns for Cedar and Pigeon later.

"She can and she has." They drew themself up. "And you're going to help her do it again. Go join the circle."

Shrike stopped licking his paw. "I'm not joining that stupid circle."

"Yes, you are." They added an edge to their voice. "This was *your* question. You either help or you don't get your answers at all."

Damir gave a subtle nod of approval—but Shrike didn't cower.

"I can find my *own* answers, then."

Damir shot him a look. "Oh, really? You've got your own dedicated cadre of spirits, researchers, and libraries in those vines of yours?" He puffed on his pipe. "Go join the circle, hairball."

Shrike flattened his ears and padded toward the other spirits. Aspen made a note to throw in a flower crown for Damir, too.

THE SPIRIT'S CURSE

When they joined Shrike back at the growing circle, they found that spirits weren't the only ones to have gathered in the plaza. Humans—including the Karic family—had clustered together on the fringes, no doubt drawn in by the headlines that had finally made the rounds through the city. Some people, like Georgie and Marley, waved to Aspen and gossiped to each other about the spirits' various animal forms. Others hung back, wary and quiet.

If only Mr. Chamberlain could take a cue from the latter.

"Ms. Sorman," the man argued loudly as he followed Ella down the sidewalk, his voice floating all the way to Aspen. "That spirit cannot be allowed to stay in our midst. That *thing* is the trickster from the Cima mountains."

Next to Aspen, Shrike gave a low growl and shrunk in on himself.

"It has proven to be a great danger," Mr. Chamberlain continued. "Not just to the people of Cima, but to the people of Vornik." He glanced at the other observing humans and raised his voice even higher. "I know Councilmembers! I'll talk to them! I'll make sure that spirits cannot enter this city again—"

Now the spirits were facing him, too. A rumble went through them, and Pigeon immediately flapped her wings. "What do you mean, cannot enter—?"

Aspen was swift to send a message, a single word, through the ground to any spirit that would listen: *Wait*. Ella was still here; Ella would help fix this.

"That is entirely unnecessary," she responded flatly to Mr. Chamberlain, maintaining her steady pace toward Aspen. "I can assure you, the Guild's spirit representative has this situation under control."

Aspen swallowed. Their grasp of the humans' language might still be lacking, but that sounded an awful lot like she was referring to—

"Aspen?" Lydia called. "I believe Pigeon's ready for you. She'll await your signal."

As every spirit eye in the plaza turned to them, Mr. Chamberlain puffed himself up, his cheeks now ruddy.

"And what precisely are you planning on doing to rectify the situation?" he demanded of Aspen.

They froze between indignation and panic. No matter that they had no idea what *rectify* meant—they didn't have anything to offer Mr. Chamberlain or the spirits. They had nothing under control, and certainly no sort of signal or plan. And all the eyes staring at them—there were so terribly many, and if they didn't say something smart and dignified in the next few seconds, every single one of them would be disappointed—

"The solution is quite simple, Mr. Chamberlain." Emry stepped up beside Aspen, a pleasant smile on his face even as the grip on his cane was tight. "Shrike has agreed to assist Aspen in this new research venture. He won't be in the Cima area to disrupt transportation lines or cause any harm for the foreseeable future."

"In fact"—Cal took Aspen's other side—"if you remain in the plaza, you'll be able to witness this research venture for yourself. Aspen needs only a moment to confer with their new associates on the process."

Aspen tried not to slouch in relief. They had no idea what they'd do without Emry or Cal. If it had been left up to them, they might've told off Mr. Chamberlain with some words they had learned from Georgie.

"Yes, that's exactly it." They latched onto the lifeline Emry and Cal had thrown them. "If you'll all give me a minute with, um, my Pigeon associate..."

They hurried over to Pigeon, who had settled on Cedar's antlers once more to preside over the cluster of older spirits. Visually, they looked no different from the others. A long-clawed badger sat on her haunches, glancing nervously at the humans on the fringes. Next to her, a proud hawk preened its feathers in veiled impatience. And in the center:

"Hello there." Aspen bent to greet a single bright dandelion in a pot, held nervously by a young boy. The sight was unusual, even for Aspen. They had only seen spirits manifest as plants out in the forest—here in the city, animal and human forms were far more convenient for mobility.

"Dandy said he could help," the boy said, keeping one eye on Cedar's lurking form at all times. "He's very old."

Somewhere beyond the circle, Mr. Chamberlain scoffed. "Shiro's beard. They've got a rotting *weed* assisting their research."

Aspen set their jaw and ignored him.

"How old are you?" they asked, both out loud and silently to the dandelion spirit. They felt a sweeping gaze, as if the flower was reaching out and assessing them in turn.

"Twice as old as you, you whippersnapper—"

"Excuse me—!" Aspen started, but Pigeon swooped in over their head.

"All right, all right, let's see what we've got," she said, sounding for all the world like an avian Lydia. She landed first on the badger's paw, then on the boy's shoulder. The boy gave a giggle.

"Right," she finally said, then in quick, silent communication: *I've got it. You older spirits all feel a bit similar.*

Cedar's eyes narrowed. *I am unsure if I appreciate that.*

No, no, it's a good thing! Pigeon landed on the cobblestones in front of the group. *If everyone lends me their strength, I should be able to search for a similar...* She tilted her head. *A similar...*

Signature, Aspen supplied.

Whatever that is. She pecked at the ground. *Hm. Do you feel those mountains to the west?*

Aspen couldn't exactly feel them, but they vaguely recalled the maps of the Vidanyan river routes that Emry had shown them a few times. Tazlo was in a mountainous area, and the eastern Cima border had its own mountain range, but those weren't the ones Pigeon was referring to. The mountains she was targeting lay far to the west, at the very edge of the province.

Aspen frowned. They knew Pigeon was talented in searching for things, but those mountains were at least a day away as, well...as the pigeon flew.

Are you sure you can search that far? they asked.

Only if everyone helps.

What are we waiting for, then? the hawk cut in. *We've got everyone here.*

The badger clicked her claws together, still surveying the crowd with a twitchy nose. *It is an awful lot of us, don't you think? We should probably do this quickly.*

But Aspen didn't give into the spirits' impatience or their nerves. They weren't going to begin without Cal's say-so.

They glanced around. Cal hadn't gone far—she stood just outside the edge of the circle, flanked by her own support group. While the researchers behind her guarded emergency bags of soil and jugs of water, Emry stood with her, rubbing comforting circles between her shoulder blades.

"My love," he murmured. "Deep breaths."

"I can't take deep breaths, I'm about to witness"—she fumbled with her pencil and scooped it back up—"witness a spirit ritual that has never been done before and may never be done again. Hara take me..." She finally caught sight of Aspen and gathered herself together. "How exactly will you be sharing your energy? Will you be using the rain like in Matlock?"

Aspen squinted up at the sky; not a single cloud marred the perfect blue above. "I don't think we'll need the rain this time," they said, gauging the road under their feet. "The ground should be all right. Are you ready?"

Cal finally took a deep breath. "Yes. Of course. Ready when you are."

Aspen nodded and sat down in the middle of the circle. The silent gesture was enough to quiet the other spirits, until the only sounds in the plaza came from the hum of the surrounding city. It was strange, having a barrier of spirit energy between them and everything else. If they closed their eyes and only focused on the group's array of magical signatures, they could pretend they were back in the forest again.

But there was no time to savor the situation. They steadied themself, then sent a tremor of energy through the ground—not to help Pigeon, but to center the spirits' attention on them.

I'll go first, they said. *I'll lend my strength to Pigeon so she can start the search. Once you see what I'm doing, follow my lead.*

They hoped their voice didn't shake too much. Cal wasn't wrong when she had said this had never been done before—but Aspen figured that if they spoke loud and confident like Emry, it would turn out fine.

Or, mostly fine.

Don't give too much, they added. *Only what you can.*

They closed their eyes and focused, trying to understand the sort of signature Pigeon was looking for when it came to finding an older spirit. Cedar, Dandy, the badger, and the hawk all had a sort of a…oh, what was that word? Cal had used it last week, something about mushrooms—*mycelial*. Aspen liked that word. A *mycelial* feel to them. A feeling that burrowed deeper, earthier than just soil and decaying leaves. It was hard for them to imagine a spirit even older than the ones sitting around them—and perhaps one didn't exist.

But that was for Pigeon to discover.

They relaxed into the cobblestones and pushed their energy forward, through the rock and the underlying soil. It met with worms and roots and bones until, finally, it reached Pigeon, who soaked it up like parched earth. They had to pull back quickly, keep a close eye on what they shared, lest it become too much.

Now you try. They nudged Shrike beside them.

Shrike reluctantly did the same, their energy much thinner than Aspen's—then three more spirits shared, then a dozen. Before long, it was difficult for Aspen to feel their own tether amongst all the others.

They weren't sure how much time passed after that. The hum of the city ebbed and flowed; the sun's rays slowly shifted from warming one shoulder to the other. The only constant was Mr. Chamberlain's impatient complaints peppering the air.

"How much longer is this going to take?" he said sharply to Ella. "I have business to attend to. I cannot simply sit around watching dangerous creatures meditate—"

A sharp *crack* snapped through the earth. Mr. Chamberlain gave an undignified yelp.

Aspen opened one eye. With so much spirit energy underground, weeds had crept up around the stones, and the flowers placed so carefully for the festival now sprawled across every available surface. Around Pigeon, paving stones had split under the force of the new growth, but she paid the rocks no mind. Instead, she tore at the flowers, placing them on more even ground with her beak and talons to create a map. Petals formed the rough shape of forests. Vines and stems formed river paths...

Cal grabbed Zeke's arm. "Help me draw out the map. Quickly, before it blows away."

As the researchers approached, Aspen closed their eyes again, focusing once more on giving Pigeon the energy she needed. Even if they couldn't see the map forming, they could feel its feather-light presence growing bigger and bigger, while Pigeon's flaps and hops grew more and more frantic—

Until she leapt into the sky, breaking her connection to the other spirits.

"I got it!" She fell back down with an exhausted, graceless plop. "I—I think I got it. Rotting hard to sort out exactly where it is, but it's out there."

Aspen scrambled up, hope surging through them. "You really found one? An older spirit?"

"A *very* old one," Pigeon corrected proudly. "Older than the soil, it felt like. If any spirit knows about sleeping, it's got to be that one."

She hopped over the tiny mountain range she had pieced together and pecked at a wide gathering of white petals. Cal swallowed; Aspen looked up.

"Where exactly is that?"

She compared her own drawing to the map on the ground, then conferred quietly with Zeke's notes. Zeke grimaced and nodded in a confirmation of her fears.

"Envis," she said. "The spirit you found is in Envis."

CHAPTER SEVEN

ASPEN

"So we go to Envis after the festival ends," Aspen said confidently. "I don't understand the problem."

They had regrouped back in the same tavern as the night before, holding court at the largest table by the hearth. The owner, a gracious smile pasted on his face, handed out mugs of beer while keeping one nervous eye on Shrike in the corner. For Aspen's part, they kept one nervous eye on the door, where a light commotion preceded Ella Sorman's entrance.

"No, there is no need to arrest the spirit," she said haughtily to someone out of view. "And no, I'm not aware of any new legislation regarding spirits. Mr. Chamberlain is sorely misguided, and I don't mind you printing those exact words. Now, if you'll *excuse* me."

She shut the door on the journalists hounding her, took a steadying breath, and approached the table with her usual poise. "Well? What have you decided?"

Aspen thought it was obvious. "We're going to Envis, aren't we?"

"Are we, now?" Ella pressed her lips together and sat at the head of the table, her tone flat. "Envis will love to hear it."

Aspen sat as well, now thoroughly confused. "I don't understand. Can we really not go?"

They turned to the others, but no one leapt to explain. Emry toyed with his mug, then sighed and handed it to Riley. Sage fidgeted with her skirt. Cal stared at her notes as if the answer would materialize on the page.

In the end, it was Ella who pushed the conversation.

"Damir?" she said. Damir stiffened and cleared his throat.

"Envis takes an…isolationist approach to most things," he said. "It's been like that since the war. After refusing to ally with Vidanya, they've refused most everything else since. Apart from a bit of trade, they rarely welcome people from outside their borders."

Aspen bit their lip. Damir never spoke about Envis much, but it seemed that the province's isolationist approach extended to the spirits residing there as well. Zeke hadn't yet found a single Envisian spirit through his festival questionnaires. And the gossiping spirits around Pigeon—they hadn't trusted the mountains in the west, had they? The mountains that, for better or worse, kept Envis tucked away from the other provinces. Even now, they could feel the spirits' worry simmering low out in the plaza, as encouraging as thunder in the distance.

"Envis doesn't have to *welcome* us, exactly," they pressed, trying to stay positive. "They just have to let us in for a few days. Just so we can ask the spirit a question."

Damir's voice echoed bitterly in his mug as he drank. "Try telling that to their border guards. Until a few years ago, the place didn't believe spirits existed."

Aspen fidgeted. "Well, that's not so different from what the humans here used to think."

"Trust me," Damir muttered. "The folks in Envis don't enjoy being proven wrong."

Aspen withheld an impatient sigh. They knew where the old spirit was, and they were *going* to talk to it. There was no point in giving up just because a few humans might be grumpy about the whole affair. If Aspen had given up at the first sign of irrational human emotion, Cal and Emry would never have gotten back together.

"Then I'll go by myself," they announced. "I can be there and back in a few days. If I stick to the forest, they won't even know I'm—"

Ella was quick to dash that plan.

"I'll *not* let you go alone," she cut in. "If the headlines out there are any indication, we must act quickly and as one. We have a connection to Envis, and we will use it."

Her gaze settled on Damir; he immediately flinched.

"No."

"Mr. Nedrov—"

But Aspen had never seen Damir so pale.

"I am *not* a connection to them," he hissed, though his Envisian accent betrayed him. "They don't want to see me. They haven't written in—"

Shrike gave a loud huff and uncurled from the shadows, stretching every one of his claws over the wooden floor. Somewhere behind the bar, the tavern owner cringed.

"If you're not going, then I'll go." He headed straight for the door. Aspen leapt to follow.

"What? If I'm not going alone, you're not going alone, either—"

"You said it was *my* question, didn't you?" Shrike said smugly. "Then *I'll* get it done. Rather than just sitting around and listening to stupid humans talking."

Damir shoved his chair back, now even paler than before. "You go into Envis unsupervised, hairball, and we'll have another rotting war on our hands—"

Shrike took one more step. Aspen threw out a hand, and a tangle of vines sprouted up over the door. The poor tavern owner gave a sad, tiny whimper and left the room.

"He won't be unsupervised," Aspen said firmly. "We'll go together."

Emry locked eyes with Cal, then stood. "Of course. And we'll both come with you." He turned to Damir. "If it's not safe for you to go into Envis, you don't have to join. We can handle this ourselves—"

Damir gave a barking laugh. "You three? Handle it yourselves? *Gods*." He passed both hands over his face and gave one long groan. Then, with his voice still muffled by his hands: "Fine. All right, I'll go."

Aspen brightened. "Really?"

Damir dropped his hands. "We'll leave after the festival, but we are not"—he pointed out to the plaza—"bringing the entire flower gang out there. I draw the line at leading tree caravans."

"Of course not," Cal jumped in. "We'll ask that they disperse after the festival, and I'll communicate our findings back to my research team here."

Sage raised a tentative hand. "What about the concert?"

Next to her, Riley had slowly gathered everyone's mugs together as they had moved their attention to Aspen. Damir scowled and snatched his mug back. "I said, we're leaving after the festival—"

"No, not *this* concert." Riley snatched it back. "The concert in a few weeks at Sumac Hall. The one Spiritsong is headlining before our tour."

Emry shrugged. "That's weeks away. We'll be back in time for that." He turned to Aspen. "Won't we?"

Aspen swallowed. Their past outings—to Matlock, to Senne, to other cities to perform—had been as straightforward as Emry's shrug. A few days there, a few days back. Aspen had no inkling of what the roads within Envis might be like nor how deep in the forest the spirit resided—nor even if that spirit had what they sought.

But with so many eyes on them, there was no time for doubt.

"Of course we'll be back in time." They summoned their courage and stood. "We'll leave after the festival."

Damir raised his arms half-heartedly, then dropped them. "That's what I said."

CHAPTER
EIGHT

EMRY

The remaining two days of the music festival passed far too quickly.

While the rest of the city resumed their festivities the following morning, the day itself was, tragically, naught but a sleepy haze for Emry. After all the excitement of the concert, the attack, and the spirit wrangling, his pain and exhaustion kept him firmly in bed from morning to sundown. He couldn't even convince Cal to relax and sleep in with him as a consolation prize.

"Darling," she tried weakly as Emry wrapped his arms around her waist. "I'm supposed to meet Lydia for a report this morning."

Emry stubbornly buried his face into her warm shoulder, savoring the softness of her nightgown and her lingering perfume. "But you didn't hear the doctor yesterday. He proposed an experimental treatment that might heal me instantly."

Cal let her head fall back on the pillow. She knew where this was going but was helpless to stop it. "And that is?"

"Kisses." He pressed his lips to the back of her neck. "And staying in bed."

She bit back a smile. "Did he write a prescription for it?"

"Yes." He feebly reached for her wedding ring on the nightstand. "See, right here."

Cal rolled her eyes and curled into his arms—for all of twenty minutes. Then absolutely no form of protest would keep her from venturing outside.

"She said she had to 'inform the others I was alive' or something," he later complained to Tessa and Georgie when they came to visit him. "And reassure people there won't be another battle on stage tonight."

"I don't know," Georgie mused, glancing hopefully through the curtain at the plaza below. "The chaos was sort of fun. I've always wanted to know if I could take a bear in a fight."

Beside Emry's bed, his mother gave a tired sigh.

After they left, Damir was next to visit—and he was significantly less enthused by the chaos.

"Chamberlain refuses to shut up," he muttered, tossing the latest newspaper onto the bed. "Ella's about ready to strangle him with her bare hands."

"I'd pay good money to see that." Emry scanned the headlines and the splashiest articles. They contained the same mixture of gossip as yesterday: *Spiritsong Set List Scuttled! Are Spirits Safe?*

By the end of his reading, Emry wanted to steal the *S* type away from the printing press.

"About Envis." Damir leaned back in the same chair Tessa had occupied an hour ago. "Tree kid and hairball aren't going to like this, but when they get to the province, they'll have to pretend not to be spirits. At least for the first day or so."

Emry folded the newspaper, trepidation now mixing with his aches. He knew little about Envis himself, but the bitterness seeping into Damir's words—both now and last night—told him more than enough. "Is Envis...violent toward spirits?"

"Not that I know of."

"And they do know spirits exist now, don't they? They must have learned about the wave and heard about what they did—"

"Oh, they've heard. They're just..." Damir fiddled with his pipe. "Seeing spirits wander around their town isn't exactly the same as hearing stories from over the mountains. Best not to risk spooking them if we don't have to."

Emry tried to sit up in confusion, but barely made it off the pillow. "You mean the Envis spirits haven't made any appearances yet?"

Damir shifted in his chair, his tone rougher than before. "I don't know."

Emry tapped his folded newspaper in thought. Such a lack of spirits didn't make any sense to him. Every other province had spirits up and moving about—Zeke's questionnaires had confirmed it. And with such dense mountains and forests in Envis, it had to contain hundreds of spirits, at least. Surely, Damir would have heard something by now...if he was still in communication with Envis, that is.

He tried to choose his next words carefully. "But...you *have* spoken to someone in Envis recently, haven't you? You said they'd heard about the wave—"

Those were the wrong words; Damir launched out of his chair as if it were on fire.

"I have to go," he said quickly. "Just tell tree kid not to grow any antlers across the border and we'll be fine." A brief pause at the door. "Rest up, Karic."

He swept out of the room before Emry could close his mouth.

Emry's string of visitors eventually petered out, allowing him to rest again—and on day three of the festival, he finally escaped the confines of the inn. After scrubbing the pillow wrinkles off his cheeks and stretching the last aches out of his legs, he bounded—well, walked gingerly—to the plaza. Ready to enjoy the music, finish his glad-handing for the Guild, have a beer or two with Karlson and the others...

But just like the stubborn newspaper headlines, the nervous undercurrent from the first night still lingered in the plaza.

The music, naturally, was beyond compare. He stood with his family in the front row for Karlson and sang along to Ella's set. Danced with Cal, clinked beers with Sage and Riley...but it was hard to revel in it all when questions still wound so tight within the audience. The humans in the crowd kept glancing at the surrounding spirits and jumping at sudden movements. Similarly, the spirits clustered close to each other, whispering in between sets and keeping one eye on Aspen throughout the night. Emry could almost feel their thoughts rippling under the cobblestones. Aspen would fix this; Aspen would go get their answers for them and help them go back to sleep.

So, the following morning, he roused to support Aspen and stood before a carriage ready to take him to Envis. To a strange spirit in a strange forest across strange mountains.

He'd done stranger things in the last two years, he supposed.

"You be safe, all right?" Edward set his hands on Emry's shoulders. His family had never strayed far during the festival, and the morning of his departure was no different. "Keep to the roads and watch the weather. And if there's anyone in Envis who's finally interested in building a decent river route through those mountains, would you mind talking to them—?"

"No." Tessa pulled her husband away. "No, he is *not* going to advertise for you. Hara take me..."

Georgie nudged past both of them and gave Emry a hug that lifted him off his feet. He suppressed a wince; the pain was worth it.

"Here." She handed him a thin package wrapped in cloth. "Take this with you."

Emry didn't have to open it; he knew what it was by its heft. "Your dagger? Georgie, I couldn't possibly—"

Georgie glanced over at their parents, then leaned in. "This isn't a concert tour to another city. You're headed into the mountains. The old forest. You need to take something."

Emry huffed; there was no use taking that *something* if he didn't even know how to use it. He tried to push the package back toward Georgie, to no effect. "And *you* need to take something to fend off all the suitors for Marley."

Marley gasped and slapped Georgie's arm. "Did you tell him about—?"

Emry grinned over Georgie's shoulder. "She sure did."

"But you said you wouldn't!"

He briefly savored their squabbling—he didn't get to hear it often, after all—then he turned to the waiting carriage, where Damir paced and checked the luggage. His manager seemed no more eager to return to his home province than he had several days ago. The place he no longer talked to, the place that hadn't written to him in who knew how long…

Emry rubbed his chest, his heart tugging in empathy. He knew how hostile a homecoming could feel. Years ago, he thought that feeling would never go away.

Then his mother kissed his cheek, pulling him out of his thoughts. "Look after Cal and Aspen for us? And write to us when you've returned?"

He gave her a tight hug, lingering for just a moment in her warmth. "I will." Then he pulled back and smiled. "Love you to Weir and back. I'll try to plan another concert in Senne soon, all right?"

It took several more goodbyes, hugs, and goodbye hugs to even reach the carriage—but there was one last party to see off before he could board.

"And you're quite sure you're comfortable staying with the spirits here?" Cal huddled with Sage and Riley by the door, fidgeting with the pendant at her neck. Riley had barely more than a sleepy blink to offer in response, but Sage nodded eagerly.

"I already spoke with Alta Brinna. We'll stay with Cedar and Pigeon to speak with other spirits and continue the research here."

As Emry joined them, her eagerness faltered. "But you won't be gone long, will you? Ella's determined that we set up tea with every single Councilmember in the city—"

"What, all of them?" Emry said. Riley groaned in miserable confirmation.

"But if you and Aspen come back soon"—Sage did her best to brighten up her words—"we could divide them up a bit! Get them all excited about your song instead of a spirit attack. We...*will* debut the song at the next concert, won't we?"

Gods, the song. Emry leaned against the carriage door in thought. Spiritsong was indeed supposed to debut his and Aspen's co-written song in a few weeks. There was no getting around it—he'd have to hammer out the rest of the lyrics during the trip.

"We'll try to get back as soon as we can," he said. "And we'll work on the song in the carriage. Won't we, Aspen?"

He and Cal turned back toward the inn. Much like last night, Aspen had a very different audience to tend to now. A large crowd of spirits had met them at the doors, muddling their path out.

"I was going to go back to my grove today," a badger said, pacing outside the inn. "What if I can never sleep in it again? There aren't any other spirits near me. I won't have anyone—"

"We'll return as soon as we have an answer for you, I promise," Aspen tried to soothe her. "We might be even back within the week."

"And if there is no way?" a hawk asked indignantly. "If we're stuck out of our groves and the humans chase us out of their dens? Where will we go, then?"

"They won't—"

But others chimed in as well, wringing their paws and worrying aloud over their futures. Pigeon hovered anxiously at the forefront of the crowd. "Please tell the humans we don't mean to hurt them. We just want to know how to sleep again."

Emry leaned to the side to peer behind the crowd, where a cluster of humans had gathered around a newsboy advertising the latest rag.

"No violence at the festival last night!" he called. "But will peace last? Read one Councilmember's doubts on page four!"

Emry grimaced; behind him, Riley cursed and Sage huffed. Talking to the humans was already an uphill battle, and those warmongering headlines attracted far more eyes than Cal's thorough—and extremely *informative* and *helpful*—brochures on welcoming spirits. The sooner he and Aspen could return to guide the city away from this mess, the better.

"I'll be back soon!" Aspen called to Pigeon, drawing Emry's attention away from the dramatic newsboy. The spirit, having no luggage other than their grove lute on their back and their concert lute in their hands, now hurried toward the carriage. Behind them, Shrike approached the vehicle as if it were going to eat him.

"I won't fit in that," he snapped, this thick fur puffing up around his vines. Aspen handed Emry both lutes and shrunk into a neat little terrier shape. Without their grove on their back, it was nearly impossible to tell them apart from a normal dog.

"Then fit," they said to Shrike in false cheer. "Just like we practiced."

As they hopped into the carriage, Shrike grumbled and shifted more clumsily into a smaller cat form, shrinking his vines until they were barely visible amidst his long fur. His shape wasn't quite that of a house cat—his massive paws and tufted ears still conveyed a wild sharpness—but he could pass for a normal animal.

At first glance, at least.

"Welcome to the team!" Emry matched Aspen's false tone. Shrike laid his ears flat and slinked past him into the carriage.

Over the next two days, the carriage bore them toward the Envisian border with uncharacteristic efficiency, thanks to Damir.

"If we're going to do this, we're going to do it quickly," Damir said briskly. He folded up his map of Envis, where he had carefully planned a direct route to the town of Beldam from the mountain pass, and glanced at Shrike. "Besides, if we waste any more time, I might get a thorn to the neck before we even get to the pass."

Emry couldn't disagree on that. Shrike hadn't proven to be the easiest traveling companion over the past two days. The lynx's incessant grumblings jarred his every attempt to work on lyrics for the new song. Complaining first about the state of the roads—many still bruised and uneven years after the wave—then the lack of forest in the hills, the lack of hills in the forest...

Their mood turned out to be contagious. Aspen—now back in their human form—ran out of their favorite embroidery thread on the third day, leaving them tapping impatiently on their hoop. Damir couldn't get comfortable enough to nap. And Cal snapped her book shut after reading the same page three times.

"Envis," she muttered, parting the curtains to glare out the window. "Could the spirit be any farther away?"

Emry frowned. "I thought you'd be more excited about this. New spirits, new data..."

"New data?" She rubbed her forehead. "Darling, the data from this festival alone will take me years to parse. I never thought I'd say this, but I don't *need* any new data right now—"

The driver whistled and the carriage slowed to a halt. Cal brightened.

"We're at the border already?" She peeked out the window again. "We made excellent time, Damir."

"I'd say you're welcome, but"—Damir adjusted his position against the carriage wall for the twentieth time—"I'm not inclined to lie to you."

"What's happening?" Shrike demanded.

"Nothing. The driver is simply giving the border guards my letter from the Council." Cal smoothed her skirts. "We'll be through the border and into the pass in just a moment."

A moment passed. Then another, and another. Just as Aspen was beginning to fidget, the carriage door opened, revealing their very confused driver.

"Mr. Nedrov, this, ah—this border house. It is meant to be guarded, correct?"

Damir sat up. "What do you mean?"

"Well…" The driver fiddled with his hat, then stepped aside and nodded down the road. Damir clambered out of the carriage.

"Stay here," he ordered. Everyone promptly followed him outside.

The cool, open air flowing down from the mountains acted as a refreshing reminder that this border between Vidanya and Envis was a natural phenomenon. The jagged Fennskill mountain range neatly divided Envis from the other provinces, requiring very few humans to actually enforce the distinction.

But *few* didn't exactly mean *none*—and the little guardhouse at the side of the road was completely empty. Door ajar, no horse or carriage nearby. Nothing but birdsong and the whistle of the wind accompanied their footsteps on the road.

"Perhaps they're between shifts?" Emry tried. Damir merely snorted.

While Aspen checked around the house, Damir cautiously slipped inside—but neither he nor Emry could find any sign of trouble. Just supplies, a half-filled log, and a few handwritten notes.

Cal immediately reached for the log and notes; Damir reached for her.

"Mrs. Karic, I wouldn't—"

"Trust me, they'll be none the wiser." She checked the log first. "Strange. The last entry is from months ago." She looked around at her feet and drew a line in the gathering dust. Their footsteps had been the first to grace the floor in ages. "Seems like no one's been here since then."

She set down the log precisely where it had been, then sorted through the other notes, flitting through supply tallies and betting records until she landed on a list that made her pause.

"Isn't this where we're headed?" She handed the grimy paper to Damir. The note contained a simple list of towns, each one of them crossed out. Beldam was in the middle of the list.

Emry suppressed an instinctual shiver. "Why are they crossed out?"

"No idea." Damir stared hard at the list. "They're all north of... well. They're in the north." He quickly crumpled up the list. "Tree kid? Hairball? Anything out there?"

Aspen's silhouette passed the window. "Not yet—"

"What's this?" Shrike said. He pawed at a scrap of paper stuck in the grass by the door. Cal plucked it off the weeds and wiped off the dirt.

"Lovely." She set her lips in a thin line. "Helpful."

Emry peered over her shoulder at the words.

House Closed
Head South for Guides

"Guides?" Shrike sniffed the air toward the mountains. "We don't need guides to get in. We just follow the path the humans made—"

"Absolutely not." Damir shut the door to the guardhouse. "They're not talking about human guides, but information. The roads into Envis are treacherous on the best of days. If the guards happen to get any non-Envisian folk looking to jaunt their way over the mountains, they're supposed to advise on which roads are safe."

"I can keep the roads safe," Aspen tried. Damir shook his head.

"No matter how capable you are, I'm not going to place all our lives in your hands."

Shrike growled in frustration, but remained staring down the wide open road. Emry took a deep breath of the fresh air, hoping it would fuel his thoughts. He had little knowledge of the mountains themselves, but he *had* been this northwest before—with his family, on river route business years ago. Georgie had been testing her skills by opening a local, independent route contained within Envis. It had been built so Envisian hunters could traverse the mountainside more quickly...and eventually, so Envis itself could warm up to the idea of cross-provincial routes.

The path had succeeded on its first aim, and utterly failed on its second.

"Damir, may I see that map?" Emry asked. Once Damir fetched it from the carriage, Emry laid it against the wall of the house. "There's a..." He squinted at the lines. "Yes. There's a self-service river route for hunters just near this pass. It's not official, exactly, but it should still be runnable."

"Are you sure?" Aspen said, a few flower buds blooming excitedly in their hair. Cal stiffened and set a tentative hand on Emry's arm.

"Dearest, last time you said something was runnable, we almost drowned."

"No, no, I helped set up this route myself," he pressed. "It'll be safe, I promise. If we take the route as it forks north, it should land us within walking distance to Illev, just east of Beldam."

But Cal wasn't convinced. "We should do whatever our Envisian guide thinks is best," she deferred. Damir ran a hand through his hair, gaze shifting between Aspen's pleading expression and Shrike's slow inching down the road.

"Fine," he huffed. "All right. Let's go in the Karic way before I change my mind."

CHAPTER NINE

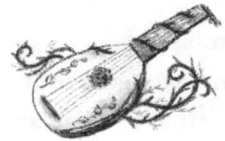

EMRY

For Emry's plan to work, they had to abandon the carriage and proceed on foot along a deer path, tugging only the barest of their luggage to the river route.

"Cal, my love," Emry said, staring at the large pack at her feet. "If you could think just a *little* smaller—"

Cal gave him a flat look. "This is the smallest suitcase I have."

"But we've only got the one boat!" He turned and sighed. "Aspen, are you absolutely sure you need your second lute—?"

"What? You're bringing *your* lute!"

As Emry passed a hand over his face, Damir strode past him, his tiny pack already slung over his shoulder. "Please, bring as much as you like," he muttered. "With any luck, we'll sink before we get to Beldam."

By the time they had whittled down their belongings and trudged to the cave, it was well past midday, and Emry was more than eager to escape the summer heat penetrating the tree canopy.

"The path starts here," he explained as he tugged branches away from the cave entrance, "until the elevation allows us to take the river the rest of the way. Should take about three hours or so."

He stepped back to let his companions have a peek at the narrow cave boring a hole in the foothills. It lacked the grandeur of Tazlo's waterfall entrance and Vornik's sinkhole stairs, but his excitement rose all the same. The cave offered more than just cool shadows—it promised a descent into a beautiful cave system, and deeper within, the low rush of steady, moving water.

A sound Emry dearly missed.

He wasn't the only one excited about the underground river. As he took the provided lantern at the entrance and led the way, Aspen practically skipped down the path behind him.

"I think you'll like this," they said to Shrike. "The boat's very relaxing once you get used to it."

Next to them, Cal snorted, then tried to hide it with a cough. And when they reached the river, she gave the inky waters a wary look.

"Three hours, you said?" She pulled her coat tighter around her. Emry finished checking the boat—in decent shape, thank Hara—then handed her one of the cork vests by the dock.

"It's a perfectly smooth route." He kissed her forehead and draped his coat over her shoulders, layering her in warmth. "I promise."

Eager to have this ride over and done with for Cal's sake, he handed the other vest to Damir, rolled up his sleeves, and helped everyone into the boat—

Well. Almost everyone into the boat.

"You're not serious." Shrike remained stubbornly on the dock while he watched Aspen shift into owl shape.

"Well, we're not going to fit in the boat any other way." Aspen settled comfortably on Cal's shoulder. "Have you not taken other forms?"

"'Course I have," Shrike snapped. He padded up to the edge of the river, pawed the surface—and with a huff, slid under the depths as a fish draped in riverweed.

THE SPIRIT'S CURSE

"See? It's not so bad," Aspen said brightly. Shrike spat a tiny spout of water up from the surface, then reluctantly hovered near the oar.

Once the boat was loaded—and adamantly refusing to sink under the weight of their luggage—Emry maneuvered it into the slow, shallow current, using the boat's lantern and Aspen's owl vision for guidance. Fortunately for him, the route hadn't changed from when he had first rowed it years ago. Its path wasn't the fastest nor the most efficient, but it did little to jostle the boat and gave them small gifts as they went. A bright sinkhole to light their way now and then, an occasional dock for him to rest at. Halfway through, it rewarded their progress with one of Emry's favorite sights: a wide, expansive chamber, a crack in the ceiling letting in a single, dusty beam of light.

He looked up at the sunbeam and gently slowed down the boat. The light wasn't the same as a romantic cluster of glow-worms, but it would have to do—it was practically a crime for him to ignore the acoustics of a chamber like this.

"Hey." He turned to Aspen, ignoring Shrike's impatient circles around the boat. "Want to give our song a test run?"

Aspen hooted in delight. "Could we, please?"

Emry smiled. *Song* was a forgiving term for the smattering of verses they had written so far. He often blamed the writing delay on his abundance of Guild events—but truth be told, half the delay could be attributed to Aspen's indecisiveness.

"It want it to be happy," they had said weeks ago. Then, when the weather changed: "I'd like for it to be sad." Then, when they finished one of Cal's novels: "Can it be romantic, please?"

And every time, Emry had laughed and pulled out a fresh sheet of paper. "One song can't be everything, Aspen."

"Not everything!" they'd protested. "Just a *few* things."

As a result, he had only a few words to offer the river.

You can feel it in the roots below

As sure as rain and the river's flow
That spring is gone, it's time for her to leave you

She stole away into the night
   No kiss left by the candlelight
Just flowers from the garden she once grew you

As he'd hoped, the chamber seemed to enjoy the sound, tossing it joyfully around the sunbeam and between the stalactites above. Behind him, Aspen hummed an echo of the song, and Cal hugged him from behind.

"I quite like it so far." She kissed the back of his neck. Emry closed his eyes and smiled.

"I'm glad," he said—though he was already revising the lyrics in his head. Something about the flower part didn't sound right. Flowers were too happy of an image when singing about someone leaving. He needed something different, something more bitter...

But once they slid out of the chamber and back into the darkness, he couldn't keep ruminating on the words. Ahead, the walls shifted, sparking his memory of the path that lay beyond them.

"The split in the route is just up here," he called back to Damir. "Aspen, you see it, right?"

Aspen stayed silent for longer than he liked. "Which way did you want to go?"

"The righthand path. That'll get us to Illev."

"Stop the boat if you can." Urgency spiked their voice. "There's something up ahead."

Emry dug his oar into the silt once more, forcing the boat into a turn around its new anchor. Aspen launched up from Cal's shoulder and flapped their wings once. A trio of glowing bubbles—tiny, ephemeral spirit shields—floated away from them, illuminating the cave in a cold white light.

The source of their concern lit up in equally cold shadows.

A cascade of thorns and roots blocked the righthand fork to the river, creating a line of grumbling white water where the path should have continued into darkness. Still in their fish form, Shrike dove near the bubbles, then returned and circled around the boat in a frustrated waiting pattern.

"Damir?" Emry said. "What are we looking at?"

Damir stared at him. "Me? There's a spirit flying above your head, your wife can classify hundreds of plants by memory, and you're asking *me* what this mess is?"

"You're from Envis—"

"Like that rotting helps!" He leaned back and sighed. "Whatever this is, I've never seen it before. Not above ground or below."

Cal gave a hum. "Could you get us a little closer?"

Emry tried to guide the boat closer, but the rush of water at the blockade buffeted him back. Aspen dove and yanked a few strands of vines out of their lute with their beak.

"Here." They handed one to Emry. "We can pull ourselves closer."

As an example, Aspen tossed out their own vine toward the wall of thorns, where it latched with a quick knot. Emry threw his a moment later—not as strong, of course, but he made do. Together, they pulled on the vines and dragged the boat closer to the roots, allowing Cal to squint at them in the lantern light.

"I'm sorry, but it's difficult to identify them from here. Some look sort of familiar…"

"Wait!" Shrike leapt, his voice briefly cresting the waters. "There's a"—he flopped back into the water and buoyed himself up again—"there's a spirit!"

Cal shifted the lantern higher to cast more light on the strange growth. While the roots stretched down from the ceiling, briar clustered in thick, deep patches on the walls; some of the thorns there stretched to the length of Emry's hand. He swallowed and held onto Cal's shoulder, ensuring she didn't lean too far.

"There's a spirit in this growth?" Cal asked. "Up here?"

Aspen landed on the edge of the boat. "Not here, exactly. It's farther away. I don't know how to explain it, but..." They clacked their talons on the wood. "It feels like the spirit we're looking for."

"That's not possible." Cal lowered the lantern in surprise. "We've hardly made it into Envis, and Pigeon's map pointed us much farther in. Days in, by my estimate."

Another splash from Shrike. "I don't like it!"

"You don't like anything," Damir muttered to the water, then pointed to the growth. "Can you get all this out of the way, tree kid? We can't go left."

"Are you sure?"

Damir's voice hardened. "Yes."

"Well"—Aspen shifted in place—"I don't want to bother the spirit so soon, but I think I could..."

Off to the side, Shrike leapt up once more in an impatient spray. "Oh, come on. I've got it."

Aspen's eyes widened. "No, wait—!"

But Shrike had already reached out. In front of the boat, the thorns shrank, and the roots parted. Emry started to lift up his oar—

Then with a sharp, angry creak, the thorns grew back twice as fast and twice as thick.

"I don't think it liked that." Aspen froze; the boat lurched. "No, it didn't like that at all—"

Emry swore and snapped off the vines tethering the boat to the blockade. "Left it is!"

But the ancient spirit wasn't content to let them leave peacefully through the darkness of the lefthand path. The lantern's wild swinging illuminated the spirit's presence in flashes: briar patches snaking along the walls, vines lashing out just over their heads.

"Can you tell it to rotting *stop*?" Damir shouted at Aspen, but the spirit had taken human form and was busy tossing more bubble-like shields out in front of the boat, desperately illuminating the path as the lantern sputtered.

"Shrike?" they called. "A little help—?"

Shrike darted past the boat, beelining away from the commotion as fast as his fish form could carry him.

Emry tightened his grip on the oar and steered the boat away from the vines as best he could. The current moved faster here, but if he could just hit a smooth patch of water, he could try reaching out to the growth himself. Make it all shrivel up, or shove it away somehow—

One of the vines started to wrap around the boat. Cal shrieked.

"*Absolutely* not!" Emry whipped Georgie's knife out of his boot. Cal was *not* going in the water today, not when he promised her—

He slashed at the vine just as the boat tilted. The growth ripped under the arc of the knife, but his momentum carried him too far. In one moment, he hovered over the water, desperately throwing the oar to Damir, the spray below giving him a taste of what was to come—

And in the next, he plunged into the current, the chill shoving the air out of his lungs.

Confusion briefly muddied his panic. This river had been cold years ago on his last run, but the ice that now pierced his bones was nigh unnatural. He could barely move, barely even think of fighting to the surface. He flinched and sank instead. Surely those vines would follow him underwater, finish off their attack in seconds…

But nothing came. Thin shadows whipped above the water, both angry and lost, darting along the surface but never breaching it.

Emry didn't question his luck. He fought against the cold and kicked feebly along with the current, searching for the boat's shadow. He had to find the boat before the vines found him, but his lungs burned, aching for the shield lights that hovered just above the surface—

Another, thicker shadow blocked the light, then plunged into the water; fingers wrapped around Emry's wrist a moment later.

"I've got him!" were Aspen's first words as soon as Emry breached the surface with a gasp. "Help me get him back in!"

Together, Cal and Aspen dragged him into the boat in a sopping heap. Cal's hands shook as she draped Emry's coat back over him. "Gods, I am never taking a boat again in my life—"

Aspen turned to the front of the boat. "Damir, go!"

"I'm *trying*!" Damir shouted—but he could barely keep the boat from smashing into the walls. Every second they stayed above water, every turn they made without flipping over, was a near miracle. More than a few times, Emry clutched Cal tight, convinced the boat would launch her straight into a patch of briar—only for them to veer away at the last second.

"Give me that oar!" he finally tried, reaching for Damir with a shivering hand.

"No!" Damir elbowed his hand away. "You almost drowned!"

"We're all drowning if you don't hand me that rotting—"

Sunlight finally glimmered up ahead, rapidly washing out Aspen's glowing shields. A sure promise to the end of the darkness— and the beginning of whatever else Envis chose to offer them.

"Where's this route taking us?" Cal shouted above the churning water. Damir didn't answer, but the sunlight spoke for him. The now-exposed river rippled past dark trees, thick undergrowth, shadowy canopies—then dropped them unceremoniously into a wider waterway, calm and steady. Emry took grateful gulps of the warmer air but could hardly do more before something else loomed over the river:

A village.

At first glance, its architecture seemed to mimic many of the towns he had seen in western Vidanya. Tall stone buildings clustered close to the river, draped in flowers and ivy, practically leaning to peer into the water. But there was something about the darkness of the windows. The lack of people along the pathways, the stillness of the river itself—

"There!" Cal pointed. "The docks up ahead. Damir, stop there."

Emry forced himself back to the task at hand. "I can tie the boat down—"

He shivered violently against the wind. Aspen yanked up a handful of river weed from the water.

"*I* can tie it down," they started—then looked up at the bridge. "Who's that?"

They all followed the spirit's gaze. Up ahead, a willowy teenage girl hailed them from atop a stone bridge, waving both arms, then pointing wildly to the dock on the left.

"South dock!" she called, her voice skipping across the water like a pebble. "Use the south dock!"

A man appeared at her side a moment later, looking down in confusion. Relief shot through Emry. Finally, some people who could help them out of this mess—

But next to him, Damir cursed.

"What?" Emry shivered once more. "Do you know them?"

There was no time for an answer—the boat was already angled toward the dock and coming in fast. He discarded the question and braced himself for the landing, determined to be useful.

"I've got it, I can help with the—!"

He stumbled onto the dock, got tangled in his own coat, and banged his shin on a bollard. Beside him, Shrike leapt up onto the planks, shifting from fish to cat form in a smooth, graceful blink.

"Have a relaxing ride?" he asked smugly. Emry glared at him.

"Are you all right?" the girl called from the bridge. Cal stepped onto the dock with all the grace Emry couldn't muster.

"Do you have a blanket?" she called back to the girl, then hurriedly tugged Emry's coat tighter around him and checked him for wounds. "We'll have to get you changed and in front of a fire—"

"I've got something!" The girl was now sprinting down the steps to the dock, holding out a shawl while a basket of flowers swung from her elbow. "This is all I've got, but..."

Damir disembarked with a huff; she stopped in her tracks and stared at him.

"Uncle Miri?"

The man from the bridge quickly followed her to the dock, holding a basket identical to hers. "Iris! Iris, hold on, we don't know who—"

When he caught sight of Damir, he froze as well, his face shifting from concern to trained, furrowed stoicism.

"Damir?" he barked. "What in the rotting hells are you doing here?"

Emry and Cal both swiveled to Damir, who sighed and turned back to them.

"Well." He tossed the oar back into the boat with a clatter. "Welcome to Raven's Rest."

CHAPTER TEN

ASPEN

ASPEN BRIEFLY HOPED that a place called Raven's Rest would live up to its comforting name—if not for ravens, then at the very least for a few soggy humans. On their friends' behalf, they longed for a fire, some blankets, perhaps that mulled wine that Cal seemed to like so much...

But Raven's Rest did not bestow such things easily. On the dock, Damir and the taller man stood in a glaring standoff, Iris glancing uneasily between them. To make any sort of headway, Aspen had to hide the flowers in their hair, clear their throat, and do their best to imitate Emry's charm.

"I'm afraid we ran into a bit of trouble with a spirit in the river route." They smiled weakly and nodded to Emry, who shivered on the dock. "Do you happen to have a fire going?"

Well, it was a poor imitation of Emry, but it seemed to work. Iris remembered the shawl in her hand and rushed over to the ailing bard.

"Yes! Yes, of course." She stood on her toes to toss a corner of the shawl over Emry's shoulder. "The gathering hall's already got a fire going for Harvey. Papa, can they—?"

But said Papa hadn't yet relinquished his silent battle with Damir.

"Well?" Damir piled onto the girl's plea. "Not going to let us in, Nik?"

Nik scowled. "'Course I'll—"

"Leave us stranded on the dock and I'll write to Yvette about it."

"Yvette?" Nik seemed to grow taller. "Why threaten me with her when you haven't bothered to write *me* for years?"

Damir set his hands on his hips. "Oh, like *my* mailbox has been overflowing these past—"

"The fire in the hall!" Iris shouted in forced cheeriness as she clambered up the steps, her wavy blonde hair tangling around her face. "It's just this way, if you'll follow me!"

Aspen took Emry's free arm—the other one having been claimed tightly by Cal—and carefully led him up the stairs, checking for any limping or blood. "Are you sure you're—?"

"I'm fine," Emry tried to reassure them through chattering teeth. "Throw me by a hearth and I'll be good as new." He stumbled on one of the steps and winced. "Just, um—how far is it, exactly?"

"Just up the road and past the square!" Iris charged away from the bickering men, her pace more of a skip than a stride. For her part, she seemed terribly excited to have sodden, injured guests. "I'm Iris Nedrov. Apprentice leader of the Rest."

Aspen had never heard of such a thing before, and judging by Cal's confused expression, neither had she. "And who's the...*leader* leader?" they asked.

"Papa is!" she said brightly. "He's the leader of Raven's Rest. Or... what's left of it."

Emry's limping pace gave Aspen the chance to take in the village and sort out what exactly that meant. All the buildings still seemed to be present. Narrow stone roads branched south from the wide river, letting tall, skinny houses dot them like leaves. Colorful leaves, too—each house had been lovingly painted in winding patterns of flowers, vines, and little black ravens. Together with the planter boxes that adorned every window, they formed a charming union of villagers' art and nature's work.

But while the nature was still there, the villagers were nowhere to be found.

The emptiness of it all unsettled Aspen more and more with every step. They could feel no other footsteps, hoofbeats, or wagon wheels vibrating against the earth. No chatter came from the houses; no one peeked out to assess the newcomers. And the flowers in each planter grew wild and haggard, alive only due to rain and sheer stubbornness.

Aspen looked to their right. Between the buildings, they caught glimpses of the river, and beyond that, the cluster of houses that populated the north side. They squinted—the window boxes and gardens on that side of the river appeared strangely thick with overgrowth. And was that ivy covering all the rooftops? They tentatively reached across the water in confusion, into the northern half of the Rest, hoping to feel something friendly, something human—

They were met with a sharp tangle of thorns and a low, fearful, distinctly mycelial aggression.

Aspen quickly yanked themself back and huddled closer to Emry. That presence was not just angry, but familiar. They had felt it in the cave, in Pigeon's search... That was what they were looking for. The old spirit—the *very* old spirit—lived somewhere beyond the north side of the village.

And it was not at all happy to see them.

Aspen glanced behind them at their surly followers—Shrike, Damir, and Nik—wondering if Shrike had sensed that presence across the river, too. He must have; he trailed at a stiff pace in his smaller cat form, his wary gaze roving over every corner and alleyway.

Oddly enough, Damir was doing the same thing.

"Nik, what in the rotting hells has happened here?" he

demanded, voicing the same question that was on Aspen's mind. "Where is everyone?"

"Headed south," Nik grunted as they entered a silent, weed-strewn plaza. Now that they had reached the waning sunlight of the open area, Aspen could see the family resemblance between the brothers. Though Nik was far more bearlike in comparison to Damir—dark, shaggy hair, unkempt beard, the bulk that came from thriving in forest winters—they both had the same bumpy nose.

And looking at Iris, so did she.

"They all went to Tail's End, Warwick, and Dav," she cut in, flicking an impatient gaze at her father's curtness. "It's just me, Papa, Harvey, and Otto left."

Damir's confused expression only deepened. "But *why*?"

Nik's face darkened. "Based on your trouble in the cave, it sounds like you saw why."

Only Emry's shivering kept Aspen from skidding to a halt.

"Wait, the spirit did this?" they asked, trying their best to keep moving despite their fright. "It chased your villagers away?"

Nik gave the barest of nods, his lips pressed thin. Aspen swallowed. This was far worse than Shrike's trickery on the roads in Cima. This was—this was *unheard* of. No spirit in Vidanya would do this sort of thing, would they? Spirits didn't need empty villages. Spirits didn't need villages at all.

Moving faster now, Aspen helped Emry past a splintered, wooden platform in the center of the square—a nightmarish echo of the grand stage they had performed on days ago. They wished the other spirits were with them to see all this. Pigeon, Cedar... Their presence would help block out the silence a little, fill in the village's vast, empty spaces.

Tentatively, they reached out once more: not to the north, but due east, back toward the mountains and Vidanyan border. If Pigeon could feel them and catch their worry, perhaps she could send along a few friends...

But the river had exhausted them, and their connection quickly fizzled out somewhere in the dark trees. There was no use trying it tonight. Best make sure the humans made it to morning first.

Ahead of them, Iris yanked on the door to a gathering hall, a spacious building that presided wearily over the vacant plaza. Its facade was drenched in paint and flower boxes, gray stone hiding behind the patches of color. As a bleak bit of comfort, the hall's interior tried to be just as welcoming. Cozy wooden furniture encircled a flickering hearth, while toward the back, a wide bar nestled under soaring rafters.

But this place was meant to house seventy people, not seven—and as such, the crackling fire seemed to be mourning its loss rather than comforting those it still had.

"Take a seat by the fire." Nik pointed them gruffly to the hearth. "Iris and I will fetch some blankets."

All the humans headed straight for the fire—but Shrike growled and hung back in the plaza.

"I'm not going in there," he muttered low so the others wouldn't hear. "Don't need the fire. I'll just stay outside."

The words bent Aspen's patience. Shrike had already abandoned them once in the tunnel; they weren't going to let him do it again.

"You're coming inside," they ordered. "You're not going to slink off. Not now. Not with..." They checked to make sure the humans were far enough away, then tilted their head north. "Not with *that* so close."

The shadows across the river seemed to grow at their words. Shrike flexed his claws once, twice...then huffed and padded inside.

When Aspen reached the hearth—a looming piece, each stone bigger than their lute—Emry had already been tucked into a chair by the fire, almost boneless in his relief. Next to him, Cal sorted through a pile of men's clothing Iris had brought her.

"My dear." Emry burrowed under a blanket and tried his best not to shiver. "It doesn't have to match—"

Cal folded and set aside a baggy tunic. "Says the man who refuses to wear anything other than neutral tones."

"I own colors!"

"Respectfully"—she patted his knee—"you think gray is a color. Now, please move closer to the fire so you don't catch a cold."

"I've got it." Aspen pushed Emry's chair closer to the hearth, but he wasn't alone in soaking up the warmth—he had neighbors in the armchair opposite him. An old man napped deeply, his feet kept warm by an enormous shaggy dog. They snored in unison, remaining blissfully ignorant of both the newcomers and Damir's string of impatient questions.

"How long has the village been like this?" he asked, pacing stiffly behind the armchairs. Aspen decided this jumpy demeanor was an ill-fitting look on their manager. They vastly preferred confident Damir—or even grumpy Damir at this point.

"What happened to the guardhouse at the border?" he continued. "And why are you two still here, if everyone else has left?"

The old man in the armchair snuffled.

"You three," Damir reluctantly corrected himself. Iris pointed to the dog.

"Don't you want to count Otto?"

Nik sighed and rubbed his brow. "Iris, the yeda, if you please."

After she ducked through a door by the bar, he sat down at a long table, several safe paces away from Damir.

"S'been like this for a few months," he said, his voice as gravelly as an old road. "Yarrow took Badger Falls and Illev—"

"Yarrow?" Aspen said. That wasn't a human name, as far as they knew.

"The spirit," Nik clarified. "It came from the north. Grew over Badger Falls and Illev first. Hit Beldam in a matter of weeks. By the time it came for us, folks were already leaving."

Cal looked up from the pile of clothing. "The crossed-out towns on the guardhouse list. Were they all...?"

Damir's jaw set as the realization set in. "The border road through the pass. It doesn't lead to any towns anymore, does it?"

Nik didn't meet his gaze.

"No living towns." He straightened. "But Raven's Rest isn't dead yet. Not while we're still here."

"Got the—!" Iris burst out from the door and banged her knee on a crate behind the bar. "*Ow*, Shiro's beard on fire—got the yeda!"

She hurried over with a tray of bread, butter, and hot tea, her skirt swirling around her ankles. Unlike Sage's pastel riots, Iris' dress stuck to a low palette of ochre and brown—but all around the edges, someone had embroidered delightfully bright flowers and little ravens. Aspen would have to ask her for the pattern at some point.

"I'm sorry, but what is yeda?" they asked. "Is that a sort of bread?"

"It's..." Damir began—but when Iris eagerly cleared her throat, he silenced himself and gestured to his niece.

"It's an Envisian welcome tradition for strangers." She proudly set out cups at the long table. "It means you're safe here and we won't harm you. If you drink and eat, it means you won't harm us." She set her shoulders back and gestured to the food. "The Rest has been doing it for hundreds of years, and we're not stopping it now."

Nik's expression briefly warmed with pride.

Cal and Emry slowly joined Aspen and the others at the table, all gathered together except for Shrike. For all his deflecting, Emry hadn't been wrong about just needing a good fire. He had changed into dry, albeit loose, clothes, and already looked almost himself after his dip in the river. He seemed to notice Aspen's scrutiny, for he briefly squeezed their hand before passing the bread to Cal.

"See?" He winked. "Good as new, right?"

Aspen would have felt far better about the whole thing if it wasn't the ancient spirit that had sent him into the river.

"The spirit that fought us in the tunnel," they said. "I don't know how, but it's in the northern part of the village, too."

Cal watched them over her teacup. "And you're...quite sure it's the one Pigeon found?"

Aspen hesitated—they didn't want to bring such news to what

was supposed to be a peaceful meal—but they couldn't hide the truth from them.

"It's the one we're looking for."

Damir stared wearily up at the rafters. Emry muttered a curse into his teacup. Nik looked between them, his frown deepening.

"Looking for it?" he said. "Pigeon? What are you talking about?"

As both a distraction for themself and an attempt not to offend their hosts, Aspen subtly handed their bread to Cal and redirected the line of questioning. Somehow, they didn't think Nik—nor anyone else in the Rest—was going to appreciate their mission to talk to the ancient spirit right now.

"You said Raven's Rest isn't dead yet," they ventured. "How? What have you been doing about Yarrow?"

Iris brightened. "Papa and I have been looking for ways to stop its growth, while Harvey handles all the raven messages. He's been sending letters to Tail's End, Warwick, and Dav for us. Telling them how things are going and asking for supplies now and then."

Nik grunted in agreement. "We've been keeping it from crossing the bridges into the south side of the village. Burning the growth away, ripping it up." He swirled the dregs of his tea. "Haven't been able to do more than that so far."

"But don't worry, Uncle Miri." Iris cleared the empty cups, then stopped by the hearth to make sure the blanket adequately covered both Harvey and Otto. "Papa and I will figure out something soon."

She swept off toward a back room, leaving Damir staring hard at Nik. Nik didn't say a word until the door had swung shut behind his daughter—then he leaned forward, returning Damir's stare.

"Look, *you* try to keep a teenager in line—"

"It's not that, it's—well, it *is* that, but..." Damir rubbed his eyes, then dropped his hands onto the table. "I had no idea, Nik. About any of this. You didn't write, you didn't tell me anything—"

"What's the point in writing?" Nik said in a very Damir-like hiss. "I already knew what you'd say."

"Knew what I'd say?"

Nik pointed down at the table. "I don't need a letter saying *I told you so* when my entire village is packing their bags."

Damir snorted. "As if I'd just write that."

Emry and Cal both gave him a look.

"Fine!" Damir threw up his hands. "You know what? I did! I *did* tell you so. I told you spirits were real years ago. Did you really not believe the news until Yarrow came knocking at your door?"

Nik's cheeks went ruddy. "I believed it—"

"Liar."

"And what have *you* done?" Nik stood. "What have you brought into the Rest? Half-drowned strangers and—and"—he pointed back at Shrike—"and another *spirit*."

Aspen stiffened. Shrike backed away with a growl, his tame cat disguise falling apart. His fur grew thick and puffy, the vines around his torso sharpened—

To distract Nik, Aspen quickly stood and grew a wide pink flower in the palm of their hand.

"*Two* spirits," they corrected him with forced sweetness. "Thank you."

Nik stared at them. "Two—?"

Back by the door, Iris gasped. "I knew it! I *knew* I saw flowers in your hair at the dock!"

Emry got up from his chair, hands raised and his blanket falling off his shoulders.

"Mr. Nedrov," he said, his tone far more even than Damir's. "I realize you've run into trouble with a spirit, but I promise we're not here to do any harm to Raven's Rest. Not us humans, and not Aspen or Shrike, either. But..." He glanced at Aspen. "Now that we are here, perhaps there's a way we can help you. We're technically here to talk to Yarrow—"

Iris dropped a dishtowel in surprise. "You want to *talk* to it?"

All at once, Nik seemed to loom larger over the table. "No. No, that will not be happening."

Aspen winced. They knew this wouldn't go over well.

"But you see," they leapt to explain, "we want to ask it about going back to sleep—"

"You won't be asking it anything," the village leader boomed. "I won't have any strangers, human or spirit, giving that *thing* an excuse to get any closer than it is."

Cal stood. "Mr. Nedrov, it's important that—"

But Nik had already snatched up his cup and begun to wash it angrily behind the bar.

"Bad enough having one spirit in the area," he muttered. "Now we've got three. Hara drag me to dust..." Then, more loudly: "I don't care what you're here for. All of you will head down to Warwick tomorrow. Cousin Yvette's down there"—he looked pointedly at Damir—"and she can house you for a few days. Just until you work out the fastest route back to Vidanya."

Aspen's argument ran dry on their tongue. Of course Nik didn't trust them, but they couldn't just leave. Not now, not when they hadn't even tried to get answers for the spirits.

Call pulled the blanket back up over Emry's shoulders, then stepped out from behind the table, taking a poised stance Aspen had seen many times during her work.

"Mr. Nedrov," she repeated firmly. "I am an accomplished spirit researcher in Vidanya. What Mr. Karic has offered in terms of help was no empty gesture. We have conversed and reasoned with hundreds of spirits across the border. Let us use our abilities and knowledge to assist in keeping Yarrow away from your village while Aspen and Emry pursue the answers they seek. I assure you, we have won over many spirits before and we can do it again."

Nik continued to storm—but Iris looked up at her like she was the sun.

"A spirit researcher!" She turned to her father. "She can help fight it back!"

Nik's words were punctuated by ceramic clinks. "Don't need a Vidanyan researcher. This is an *Envisian* problem and *Envis* will fix it—"

"And our *Envisian* solutions haven't worked," Iris shot back in a tone far beyond her seasons. "You didn't even write to Uncle Miri about it, and he's just as Envisian as you."

Damir gave a smug hum. Nik set down the teacup, stared at it for a long moment, then passed a hand over his face.

"Is three days enough?" he said, determinedly not looking at his brother. Cal hesitated.

"Allow us a week, at least—"

A new voice entered the fray. "A week? What, only a week with my dear boy Miri?"

The old man by the fire had woken and shed his blanket. Wrinkles deepened all across his face as he smiled broadly, first at Damir, then the other guests in the hall.

"What a joy it is to see new faces." He waved dismissively at Nik, the firelight dancing in his eyes. "Ignore that grumpy old man. A week, a month, you stay as long as you like." He spread his arms wide. "Welcome to Raven's Rest!"

Aspen determined they liked that welcome far better than Damir's.

CHAPTER
ELEVEN

ASPEN

Harvey Woodside, keeper of the raven tower and adoptive grandfather of everyone in Raven's Rest, had no reservations about the new strangers in his village—humans and spirits alike. He took on the mantle of tour guide with near-gleeful aplomb, ushering them back to the boat for their luggage, then guiding them down a nearby road.

"The birds'll be glad to see you," he told Damir, his grin brighter than the lantern in his hand. "They never forget a face, you know."

At Damir's feet, Otto reflected Harvey's joy. He wound first around Damir's legs, then tried to jump on the other visitors in turn. After almost knocking Emry over and chasing Shrike down the road, he finally pawed at Aspen's sleeve, his round eyes half-hidden behind a gray fringe. Aspen buried their hands in Ottos' fur; the dog's tongue-lolling excitement made it easier to ignore the dark, looming presence persisting on the other side of the river.

"It's nice to meet you, too," they said, beaming at the sweet face. "I very much like your fur. How do you keep it so soft?"

But Otto didn't linger for the compliments. With a happy bark, he galloped back to Harvey and Damir, who were busy filling the street with conversation.

"And you all have been here? Alone? For *months*?" Damir ran a hand through his hair. "And what's he rotting thinking, letting Iris stay here?"

Harvey shrugged. "Iris insisted on it herself. She is to inherit—"

"Iris won't inherit—Otto, stop licking my hand—Iris won't inherit anything if they both get swallowed up by leaves!"

Harvey turned to smile at Emry and Cal, the lantern light shining through his wispy white hair and highlighting the bird-shaped buttons on his vest. "Is this how he is with you? Expressing affection through quibbling?"

Damir rolled his eyes. "I am *not*—"

"Yes," Emry called back. Harvey chuckled and patted Damir's shoulder.

"Good to know you haven't completely changed, Miri."

Damir shoved his hands in his pockets and shot a glare back at Emry.

After a bend in the road, they stopped at a patch of cottages that grew under the shadow of Harvey's workplace: the raven tower, a surprisingly squat stone structure riddled with holes and ivy. Aspen immediately itched to venture inside—even out here, they could feel the hum of over a dozen sleeping birds—but Otto bolted right by it, and Harvey didn't give it a second glance.

"You'll stay in the cottage next to mine." He pointed to the house on the left. "Hope you don't mind the sound of ravens in the morning."

The two cottages nestled close to each other in the shadow of the tower. Harvey's cottage on the right had clearly been a sort of gathering spot once. The path up to his door was well-worn, and the scattering of mismatched chairs on the porch waited for guests who used to linger there. For stories, Aspen imagined, or a glass of wine.

The cottage next to it had been loved in a different way. It had no welcoming chairs, but its entire facade was neat and orderly, down to the precise, symmetrical vines painted on the porch columns. And even after months of neglect, dust seemed to avoid its planks and windows…and so did Damir.

"Oh, no." He stepped back. "We are *not* staying in Yvette's place."

Harvey hid a laugh. "It's only for a short while—"

"No." Damir shook his head fiercely. "She'll know. I don't care if she's days away in another village. If I misplace anything, if I so much as—as chip a teacup, she will find a way to manifest in the room and—"

Beside him, Emry yawned, his head resting on top of Cal's. "Is there a bed in there?"

Harvey nodded. "Sure is. I try to keep some of the houses orderly in case—"

"Wonderful." In a blink, Emry was inside. Damir hurried to follow him in.

"Don't touch a thing, Karic! Not until I can memorize exactly how it was before we came in!"

Cal watched both men leave, then let out a long breath and curtsied in Harvey's direction. "I assure you, despite how they act, we all appreciate you letting us stay here."

"The pleasure is all mine." He grasped her hand warmly. "Other than the birds, I haven't had neighbors in far too long. If you need anything, my dear, please let me know."

Once Cal disappeared, he turned to Aspen and Shrike—and though his back was hunched, he gave as deep of a bow as he could.

"It's an honor to have you both here, no matter what Nikolai says." He held a hand out toward Aspen. His grip was strong, but his eyes betrayed the sadness that wound through him like so many vines. "I truly hope you can help us."

Aspen wanted to promise the old man the world. That they'd convince Yarrow to leave and summon back all his villagers, so he could have a full porch again. But they had never even fathomed the looming presence that now lived beyond the river—and Emry had always told them not to make promises they couldn't keep.

"We'll do our best," they said. Harvey nodded, whistled to Otto, and shuffled into his cottage, humming as he went. Aspen turned to the other cottage—Yvette's apparent stronghold—but behind them, Shrike was headed not inside, but toward the untended yard beside the house.

The last thread of Aspen's patience with him broke.

"Oh, no you don't." They held out a hand, and a fence of thick bushes grew right in front of Shrike's nose. Shrike yowled and rounded on him.

"What now?" he hissed.

"What do you mean, what now? I'm not going to let you keep doing this—"

"Doing what?"

Aspen gestured toward the yard. "Going off on your own! Pretending like you're not with us! Back in the cave, you ran off and it could've gotten the humans killed—"

"The humans?" Shrike repeated with a cold laugh. "I don't care about the humans, and they don't care about me. We're square."

"That isn't true!"

The lynx sat back on his haunches. "Oh, so you're saying they like me? That taller man wanted to kill me as soon as he saw through my stupid disguise."

Aspen wouldn't go that far—but they also couldn't claim the humans particularly liked Shrike. They took a deep breath and gathered themself together.

"Look. It's just a week, and we're supposed to be the spirit ambassadors here." As much as they wished otherwise. "Give the humans a chance and work with them until we can talk to Yarrow."

Shrike's eyes narrowed. "And if Yarrow doesn't know how to go back to sleep?"

Aspen couldn't entertain the thought just yet. That was one

promise they *had* made to the spirits—that they would answer that question.

"It will. And as soon as we know, you can—I don't know, go off to your grove and ignore everyone again."

Personally, Aspen thought that sounded awful. A quiet grove, with nowhere to go and nothing new to see? No spirits or humans to talk to? They couldn't do that. Not when they knew what life outside the grove could be like.

But spirits, they supposed, were just as varied as humans were. Cedar's stoic pride could hardly be compared to Pigeon's friendly chattiness, which ran in the opposite direction of Shrike's spiky obstinance, the badger's anxiety, the hawk's impatience...

And they all wanted to go back to sleep, just like Shrike did.

They reluctantly drew back the bushes.

"You don't have to stay in the house with us," they said. "But please don't go far from the garden. In the morning, we'll put together a plan and get your answers. All right?"

Shrike stared at them, then flicked the nub of his tail. "All right."

And with a nod, he slunk into the darkness of the garden.

CHAPTER TWELVE

EMRY

To Emry's dismay, unplanned swims in icy rivers did not get along well with his old possession aches.

After retrieving his cane from the boat—thank Hara it hadn't fallen into the river with him—he had hobbled behind Harvey last night, gritting his teeth against the unevenness of the cobblestones and thinking of the warm bed at the end of the walk. A long sleep, a few blankets, and Cal snuggling against him would truly make him as good as new, just like he had promised Aspen.

But at dawn, the ravens had other ideas.

Emry grumbled, threw his pillow over his head, and tugged the blanket over Cal's ears, trying to block out the incessant cawing outside the window.

"How many are out there, d'you think?" he mumbled. "A thousand?"

The blanket wasn't enough; Cal grabbed his nightshirt and buried her face in it. "A hundred thousand."

"A legion." Emry's dramatic words were muffled by the pillow.

"Blotting out the sky with their wings. You'll have to save me from them."

"I already saved you from drowning. I cannot possibly do more." Her smile betrayed her cold words; Emry kissed her forehead and pulled her closer.

"At least Harvey let us stay the night before we get devoured by his ravens," he said, but it was only half in jest. After all of Damir's warnings, he had feared Envis would chase them out with pitchforks.

Though given Nik's reaction last night, he supposed it hadn't been entirely out of the realm of possibility.

"Do you really think we'll need just a week to sort out this mess?" he asked. "Like you told Nik?"

Cal groaned. "I've no idea. But three days was hardly sufficient, either. We just need enough time to show him that he can trust us. That we can help." She pulled the blanket back over her head. "Now, if those ravens could just let me *think* for a minute…"

Eventually, all the cawing was too much for Emry to ignore. He let go of Cal, shuffled over to the window, pulled back the curtain—and found that Harvey didn't actually command a legion of birds like he had assumed. He found only twenty or so creatures zipping happily in and out of the nearby tower. None of them had missives tied to their legs; they were simply flying to greet the dawn and each other.

Cal wandered over to his side, her blanket now draped over her shoulders like a grand, regal cape. "I should ask if any of them travel beyond the mountains." She rubbed her eyes. "If they do, we should inform Vidanya we're alive. See if Zeke can send over a summary of his reports from the festival."

"I don't think the poor bird can carry back a briefcase of files for you."

Cal blearily slapped his arm; he kissed her cheek.

"But yes, we should write." He nodded out the window. "Tell them all about your heroics in the tunnel."

She grimaced, as if she didn't want to remember it. "Apologies to the Karics, but I'm never letting you on a boat ever again."

She pulled the blanket tighter around her shoulders. Despite it being a plain, simple cloth, Emry rather liked the look of it. He should buy her a real cape sometime, a nice one. If she wore it to work, the other researchers would bow at her feet.

Frankly, for all her help yesterday, *he* should bow at her feet.

"What, you don't want to tell your associates all about how you saved me?" He slid his hands around her waist and peppered her neck with kisses. "Pulled me right up out of the frigid waters and whisked me away to safety?"

"I recall Aspen doing most of the pulling—"

"Ah, but I only had eyes for you."

She sighed and attempted to cover his mouth with her hand. "Darling, you're terrible—"

"Am I, though?" He took her hand and kissed the inside of her palm, watching victoriously as her eyelids fluttered at the gesture. "I don't think I am."

ONCE THEY BOTH finally made it downstairs to write the letter, they first stole a moment to admire how charming the little cottage was. Cal ventured onto the porch, taking in the fresh morning mist, and Emry wandered about the main room. Last night, he had only been aware of stairs, then a room, then a bed. But now, he could see that this cousin Yvette had clearly loved and cared for the place before her departure. Every coat on the rack had been carefully mended, the hearth swept to perfection. And sketches of various family members —all of varying quality, from portraits to children's drawings— dotted the walls. Emry squinted at one of the more polished sketches and smiled. Even against the wrinkled paper and faded lines, he could tell who was in the drawing: a less harried Nik, a younger Damir, and a far younger Iris. Iris, all chub and blonde curls, balanced in her father's arms, while Damir leaned against his older brother's shoulder. Funny—he was actually smiling in the sketch.

"Rotting stove." Damir's voice jangled in from the kitchen, followed by a series of thumps and bangs. "See, *this* is why I don't…"

His complaints trickled away into mutterings. Emry's smile faded, and he carefully straightened the frame on the wall. Damir would never express it, but it couldn't have been easy coming home to an empty village—even one that hadn't written to him in years.

Emry considered the pencil and paper in his hand, then wandered into the kitchen.

"Need any help?" he asked, though he already knew the answer.

"No." Damir waved him off. "I'll be fine."

Emry took a seat at the kitchen table and made a show of starting his letter-writing, mostly to let Damir get used to his presence. Then, after a minute or so, when Damir had paused and Emry had a few lines on the page: "I'm sorry your return home was like this."

He expected his manager to be equally dismissive of the apology. Instead, Damir leaned against the counter, eyes looking anywhere except for Emry.

"Didn't mean to return home at all. Not yet, at least," he added. "Wasn't going to ignore them forever."

Emry raised his eyebrows.

"I wasn't!" Damir insisted, folding his arms. "I just…they hadn't written. They didn't want me to come back."

Judging by Harvey's welcome last night, Emry didn't believe that to be entirely true. "How long has it been?" he asked.

"Hasn't been since…" Damir scowled and returned to fumbling with the stove, his words choppy. "My last letter was soon after the wave. Told them about spirits being real, asked them to check the fanes here. Just to see, you know? Just to—" His cheeks reddened, and he cut off his own words. "Stupid request on my part. Nik was still Nik. Stubborn as a rotting mule."

"He didn't believe you?"

THE SPIRIT'S CURSE

Damir's jaw set. "No. He didn't."

All of his hurt settled on the word *didn't* like a bitter, stagnant pool. Emry didn't need to ask what Nik's letter had said; he had received a letter just as cutting, once.

"And you didn't write after that," he finished for Damir, who huffed.

"Didn't write, didn't visit. Kept telling myself I was too busy." He gave a humorless laugh and gestured sharply to the window. "And now all this. A spirit attacking the village and I had no idea because Nik was too *stubborn* to admit he might have been wrong!"

His voice rose, as if he were trying to shout at Nik from across the village—then he slumped into an uncharacteristic slouch, flat and defeated.

"I just wish I had known. About Yarrow. About all of it."

Emry wished he knew about a lot more than Yarrow. A dozen more questions nearly tipped off his tongue: about Nik, about Raven's Rest, about Damir's hidden interest in spirits...

But more questions wouldn't help his manager now. Instead, he set aside his pencil and kept his voice steady and reassuring. "Even if you had known, you couldn't have fought off Yarrow yourself."

"I could've done *something*," Damir snapped, then softened again. "I happen to know a few spirits myself now. Maybe we could've...I don't know. Gotten here earlier."

"But we can do something now," Emry asserted. "We've done it before, just like Cal said. We'll sort this out, get the Rest back on its feet, and all go home together. And Nik might..." He hesitated here, on the words he himself needed to hear years ago: "I know you won't believe me, but it's possible your family regrets what was in the letter. It's possible they want to talk about it more than you think they do, and it's just their stubbornness getting in the way." He smiled. "And yours, too."

Damir almost smiled at the words—then gave a noncommittal grunt, smothering any other emotions in his throat. "Wish you'd be more cynical sometimes, Karic."

"Why?" Emry folded up the half-finished letter, his grin widening. "That's your job."

After leaving Damir to continue warring with the stove, he met Cal in the mist and headed over to the tower, where Aspen waited eagerly for them.

"Harvey's already up there!" they called, their voice too loud in the morning fog. They had as much energy as the ravens did that morning, while beside them, Shrike licked his paw in a clear show of apathy. "I've counted twenty-three ravens so far. Do you think he's given all of them names?"

Emry nodded to the door. "Why don't you go on and find out?"

Aspen bounded up the spiral stairs, Shrike following at his leisure. Emry held the door open for Cal and followed at a more... ache-friendly pace. He didn't need his cane this morning—not yet, at least—but these creaky stairs were certainly going to test him.

Above, Aspen was already interrogating Harvey. "So, how many are there, really? And how do you pick their names?"

Cal matched her pace to Emry's and lowered her voice. "If Aspen wants to adopt a raven, my answer is no."

"What, you don't want a raven tower in our garden?" he teased —but as soon as he passed a window, his smile vanished.

The northern side of Raven's Rest was gone.

In the chaos of landing at the dock, he had only gotten glimpses of the houses on the other side of the river. And when he had reemerged from the gathering hall and stumbled toward a warm bed, he hadn't seen anything other than dark shapes in the north. He had assumed it was much like the southern side: empty, sad, a little overgrown.

But here, in the daylight burning through the morning fog, he could see the entirety of Yarrow's handiwork. The vines that smothered every rooftop, the dark briar that filled every street. There was no question as to why the villagers had retreated south—there was simply no space for humans left.

And this wasn't even the only town taken over by the spirit.

"Nik said all of them were like this?" he asked. "The towns further north?"

Cal stopped at his shoulder, her response quiet. "I checked my notes against what he said last night. Every single town on the border guard's list is gone."

Emry suppressed a shiver and kept walking. An attack like this would have headlined every paper in Vornik—*should* have headlined every paper in Vornik.

But it was an Envisian problem, and Envis had resolved to fix it. Until now.

Next to him, Cal pulled her travel notebook out of her pocket. Her marked page had the list of towns jotted on one side, right next to a host of notes on Yarrow's behavior from last night. When she had offered her spirit research services to Nik, she hadn't been bluffing. Emry had every confidence that she could gain Envis' trust—that she could genuinely do something to help within the week, like she had claimed.

But Emry feared he had...exaggerated his own potential contributions, to say the least.

"Cal..." He tried to gather his thoughts just as her dress gathered dust from the steps. "I'm not quite sure what to do here."

"What to do?" She looked up at the platform ahead. "Well, I can't say I've often sent letters via raven, but I'm sure Harvey will show us how to—"

"No, no, I mean. What to do with all...this." He gestured back to the window. "Aspen can talk to the spirit. *You* know all about them. But..."

He had nothing of value to offer. His magical abilities had done nothing to stop Yarrow's attack in the tunnel. And music—well, that would do just as much good here as a broken oar in a flood.

But he didn't have to voice anything else. Cal twined her arm around his, her eyes going soft.

"You know," she mused lightly, "I recall a certain bard wisely coming to me for help with a talking lute a few years ago."

Emry avoided her gaze. "Well, it wasn't entirely on purpose."

"And I recall that same bard bringing us to Devrin Gray for answers about the wave."

He snorted. "A load of good that did in the end."

"*And* that bard convinced Ella to listen to us before it was too late," Cal pressed. "And protected people when they needed it most. He's united spirits and people, saved my life, saved *Aspen's* life..." She brought his hand up to her lips and kissed his knuckles. "We wouldn't be here without you, Em."

He quietly returned the gesture. "And I wouldn't be here without either of you."

They finally made it to the top platform, where Emry was surprised to see a distinct lack of birdcages. The ravens roamed freely throughout the tower, gliding from alcove to peg to Harvey's shoulder.

"And they really don't fly off?" Aspen asked. Harvey chuckled as he fed one of the ravens, the pockets of his wool vest filled with birdseed. As a breeze filtered through the windows, his wispy white hair fluttered and settled.

"And abandon free dinners for life?" he said. "No, these are smart birds. They know paradise when they see it."

One of the ravens landed on Aspen's outstretched arm and cawed. Next to them, Shrike slunk off into the only thing that counted as a corner here—a space between two small crates.

"They're beautiful birds," Emry said. The raven on Aspen's shoulder practically sparkled in the morning light. Eyes gleaming, beak shining, feathers bearing a hint of iridescence. If he could just buy Cal that regal cape, then have a few of these ravens perched on her shoulders at all times... She'd be running the entire Council within a week.

Perhaps she could be convinced into getting just a *tiny* tower for the backyard.

"This one's Joslyn." Harvey stroked the bird's beak. "She can get your letter to Vidanya. She's one of the few who still knows any routes beyond the mountains."

Emry nudged Aspen's shoulder. "She's a bit bigger than Pigeon, isn't she?"

"Only because Pigeon likes being small." Aspen's eyes dimmed. "I tried reaching out to her last night, you know."

Cal looked up from her notebook. "All the way past the mountains? Did it work?"

"No." Aspen gingerly touched the raven's beak. "I don't have a circle of spirits to help me. I'm not sure if I can even reach the mountain by myself."

Emry could only assume that Shrike would be of no help in this regard.

"Here." He handed the letter to Aspen. "Want to write anything to Pigeon before we send this?"

Aspen brightened and immediately borrowed Cal's pencil to jot down a few extra words at the bottom of the paper. While they wrote, Emry wandered over to the window near Harvey, focusing not on the northern village ruins, but the forest beyond them. From this distance, the trees seemed to trap shadows a little more than the south, as if Yarrow was hoarding nighttime for itself. The sight was decidedly less than welcoming—but if they were going to do something to help, as he had promised Damir, the first step was to walk into that forest.

"How will we find Yarrow's grove?" He turned—but Cal was already next to him, placing her journal on the stone sill. She had flipped to a new page covered in dots and squiggles.

"Aspen felt Yarrow's presence in both the tunnel and the northern side of the village." She bit her lip in thought. "But it can't possibly be everywhere. Look at how far it's spread."

She dragged a finger from point to point, each one labeled with abandoned town names. Harvey sidled up next to her, his wrinkles converging into a frown.

"Well, those are all correct," he mumbled, rubbing at the white stubble on his jaw. "But before it took Illev, I heard tell of some growth in Ragisk, over this way. And farther north of that…"

As he pointed out blank spots on the page, Cal took back her pencil from Aspen and filled in the map, until the swath of Yarrow's growth reached the edges of the paper.

"It's just so strange." She paced around the platform with her journal, her voice a mix of fear and fascination. Shrike duly avoided her path, crouching closer to a crate with a basket of flowers on top. "I've never heard of a spirit taking over a house, much less a village. And the fact that it grew through multiple towns… Harvey, do you have any Altas nearby?"

"Oh, do you?" Aspen echoed. "Their stories were so helpful before."

Harvey faded at the question. "Not for generations. I might still have a few stories knocking around up here"—he tapped his own head—"and if you go down to Warwick, my old neighbors might have one or two. But for a real Alta, you're best off heading back to Vidanya."

"Is that where you got all this?" Shrike pawed the basket of flowers. One of the petals landed on his nose; he blew it off.

"What, all that?" Harvey laughed. "No, no. That's all from Iris."

Cal picked up the basket. In the sunlight, Emry recognized it as the same one Iris had been holding when she had met them at the dock. The basket was nearly bursting with berry vines and the remnants of small white flowers, most of them already withered from their time out of the soil.

"Yarrow's plants," Harvey continued. "You can find those wherever that spirit is growing. Nik and Iris regularly go to the bridges and pull 'em out. Not sure it helps much, but…" He rummaged around in the basket and pulled out a handful of berries. "My birds can't get enough of these."

Several of the ravens around him squawked, forcing him to dole out the berries like candy to children—but Cal and Aspen were still focused on the basket.

"Actually, Shrike is right." Cal frowned as she sifted through the foliage. "These are Vidanyan plant species. I've seen several of these grow just outside Vornik, where we've been tracking spirits."

Aspen held up a withered flower; it immediately brightened in their hand. "Foxhill yarrow. These grow all over the forest south of Tazlo."

"And these berries!" Cal pulled one out; the ravens all stared greedily at her hand. "Several farmers have been trying to adapt them to their farms since they grow so...fast."

She fed the berry to the closest raven and grabbed her notebook once more.

"*That's* how Yarrow is spreading so quickly," she said, flipping faster and faster through the pages to get to a fresh one. "Here in Envis, these are invasive species. This one"—she held up a vine—"has an immense root structure. It all but chokes out the plant life around it. And this one here!" She took the yarrow flower out of Aspen's hand. "It secretes a scent from the leaves to keep other plants from growing around it. And *this*—gods, the amount of seeds it can emit in one year, enhanced by the work of a spirit? I'm surprised the forest can harbor anything other than these plants at this point."

Her excitement far outweighed the positivity of the situation, but Emry smiled anyway. He did, after all, owe his life to her discovery of such things.

"And you said Nik and Iris have been pulling these off the bridges?" he asked, toying with one of the vines. Even with his small amount of magic, he could feel it—the eagerness of the vine to find soil, spread, and grow.

Harvey grimaced and rolled up their letter. "The bridges and parts of the northern village, if the weather's good enough. They want to try and see what Yarrow's doing off in the northern forest. Though I've been telling them not to go near those trees—the paths are bad enough as it is."

With a practiced hand, he secured the letter to Joslyn's leg, sent her off into the sky, then pointed north. Everyone gathered with him at the window.

"Those roads used to go up to Illev and Beldam, you see," he continued. "But no one's maintained them in ages. Can't even get to the towns still untouched in the northwest. Ravens are the only way to reach 'em these days."

Emry squinted out at the forest, focusing on a few lines he could barely make out. "And those roads?"

Harvey waved a hand. "Oh, those have been lost for far longer. Used to lead to a few fanes we've got around here. Damir was the last one to visit them."

Of course—the fanes Damir had wanted his family to check on years ago. Emry tapped the stone sill in thought. He might not have any scientific discoveries to make—but he knew what to do at a spirit fane, at least. All three of them did.

"How about we try to clear the road to one of the fanes?" He looked at Aspen. "Talk to another spirit first, bring an offering, and see what they think of Yarrow? I could bring my lute, if you think that'll help."

If the spirits there weren't as ornery as Yarrow, at least.

"Oh. Yes!" Aspen's eyes widened at the idea. "Yes, of course—"

Behind them, Shrike snorted.

"We don't *need* to talk to anyone else first." He pawed at a petal on the floor. "Let's just walk into the forest and go to Yarrow itself."

Cal glanced down at him. "Do you really think that's wise, given how Yarrow treated us in the tunnel?"

Shrike's ears twitched; Emry clapped Aspen on the shoulder. Was his plan the smartest one? No. Was it the only one they had? Yes.

"All right," he said proudly. "Time to make a new friend or two."

CHAPTER THIRTEEN

ASPEN

ASPEN THOUGHT Emry's plan was brilliant. Talking to the spirits would be easy. All they'd have to do is feed Emry another few moonflowers before the walk and then they'd—

"Go into the forest?" Nik repeated. "All the way to the fanes?"

Aspen nodded eagerly.

"Absolutely not."

Well, perhaps not everyone thought Emry's plan was brilliant.

After leaving raven tower, Aspen's cohort had yanked Damir away from Yvette's cottage and over to the river, where they found Nik and Iris inspecting the westernmost bridge for invasive growth. Nik stood staunchly at the base of the bridge, arms folded. He was dressed for gardening work—thick gloves, muddy boots—but the outfit made him no less intimidating.

"Yarrow attacked you only *yesterday*," he said. "What makes you think it'll let you reach the fanes in peace?"

Damir impatiently checked his pocket watch. "Well, we can't very well talk to the spirits in the forest from here, can we? We have to brave the trees at some point. Ideally before we lose any more daylight."

Iris eagerly lunged for her cloak. "I'll go with them! I know the way to the—"

"*Absolutely* not." This steeled Nik even more. "You finish with your garden, then head inside for breakfast. No one's going into that forest today."

Aspen had many things they could say to that—but so did Damir, and Cal, and Emry, and Harvey. All of them launched into several arguments at once, while Iris stormed off and crouched beside a planter box at the side of the river. Otto came up and licked her hand; she didn't acknowledge him.

"Haven't broken the habit, have you?" Damir seethed to Nik. "Can't let anything happen unless it's your idea—"

Nik glared. "I only let *good* ideas through. Unlike that time you bought that stupid wagon and—"

"That was one time, and it was twenty years ago!"

Aspen quietly slipped away from the bickering. The humans would go around in circles for a few minutes more, at least. Adding words of their own wouldn't help the argument.

But perhaps they could help Iris a little.

"Is this your garden?" they asked, reaching out to the planter with their magic. The plants here didn't feel familiar, like Yarrow's invasive flowers did, but they seemed healthy enough: well cared for, well spoken to.

Iris nodded, her arms wrapped around her knees. "Thought maybe keeping some Envisian plants around could help fight against Yarrow." Her gaze flicked up to the forest. "Not that they did any fighting out there."

"I'm sure they did fight." Aspen crouched alongside her. "It's just hard for humans to see it. Could you tell me about them?"

She methodically listed out the plants, touching their leaves and petals as she went. Though Aspen only recognized a few of the classifications, the recitation seemed to help Iris. She gained energy as she went, and by the end, she had unfurled and was pulling up a few tiny weeds as she spoke.

"I've named all of them, too," she said proudly. "This one's Katya. This one's Maria. And this one—see the thorns?" She pushed aside a leaf to reveal a row of tiny protective spikes. "I've named her Yvette."

Aspen had a feeling Yvette would be quite proud of this development.

"Katya and Maria. Are they named after villagers as well?"

Iris' voice softened. "My friends. Katya's family went to her cousins in Warwick. Maria's in Dav with her parents."

She continued weeding in silence, while Otto licked her cheek and leaned his fuzzy bulk against her side. Quietly, Aspen loosened the roots of the weeds, making them easier for her to pull up. At fifteen years old, most humans would consider Iris nearly grown, but she was still a child—and human children weren't meant to grow up in silent places like this. Not even animal children grew up like this. Wolf pups had litters to play with and learn from; deer often had twins.

Iris didn't have anyone.

"Do you think..." she finally said. "Do you think there really are spirits at those fanes you want to visit?"

In truth, Aspen didn't know for sure—Yarrow's presence spanned so much of the forest that it was almost impossible to feel anything else. But they couldn't let Iris down, not now.

"I'm sure there are," they said confidently. "I've been to hundreds of Vidanyan fanes with Emry and Cal. We almost always find a spirit to talk to."

Iris brightened. "If they are there—could I talk to them, too?"

"Oh. I think they'd—"

But her excitement was growing again. "I'd go talk to them every day if they want! And clean their fanes and everything. I'd take care of them, I promise. Do you think they'd like that?"

Aspen knew what *they'd* think, if they lived at such a fane. "I'm sure the spirits will love that."

Behind Aspen, a shadow shifted. They glanced back; Harvey had been watching them both from the bridge. The old man seemed to think for a moment, then turned back to Nik and Damir's argument.

"I just said," Damir retorted, "I didn't visit last year because I was—"

"Feeling superior, yes—"

"Nikolai," Harvey cut in, his single word like a solid block of stone; the force of it stopped both brothers in their verbal tracks. "Raven's Rest does not have time for this nonsense. You will allow Damir and our guests to find what they seek at the fanes, and as leader of the Rest, you will secure provisions and accompany them. Now."

Nik balked. "But—"

Iris was already grabbing her cloak and fastening it at her neck. "I'm going! If Papa's going, I'm going!"

In a silent gesture of finality, Harvey whistled to Otto and shuffled away. Nik glared at Damir, then barreled past him toward the gathering hall.

"Four hours," he barked over his shoulder. "Four hours in that rotting forest, then we're out."

W͟H͟E͟N͟ ͟H͟E͟ ͟A͟N͟D͟ Iris returned with Harvey's requested provisions, they lost no time in guiding the group over the bridge and through the northern ruins of the Rest. To Aspen's relief, the angry presence that had lurked there upon their arrival had retreated—but it had left all of its growth behind. Yarrow flowers fastened doors shut; creeping vines broke through windows. And the farther they trekked from the river, the thicker it all grew. Once they reached the forest, Aspen could hardly sense anything else. The briar smothered the undergrowth, the saplings, the moss, while long thorns grew above it as a protective shield. And the *silence*—the silence was what bothered Aspen the most. A healthy forest was a loud one. They expected bugs, birds, constant rustling in the brush from creatures big and small.

Not this. Not faint birdsong and wind rattling dry, dead branches.

Aspen sighed and kept going. They had hoped this old-growth forest would feel...different. Comfortable, like their aspen grove back in Tazlo, or a warm, welcoming tavern in Senne. But all around them, the trees silently writhed against the invasive growth. Against the spirit that wasn't supposed to be here, the thorns that bled the earth.

Ahead of Aspen, the humans could feel it, too, even if they didn't realize it. As soon as they entered the murkiness of the forest, their shoulders hunched, and Emry's tawny face took on a gray tint. While he glanced back nervously at Aspen and chewed on the last of a moonflower, Cal bent down to inspect some of the yarrow spilling over the edge of the path.

"And this growth truly spreads all the way to the other towns?" she asked Nik, careful not to touch the bloom. Nik's gaze remaining on a constant, wary swivel.

"In patches. If you see growth this thick close to your village, it's too late." He glanced back at Raven's Rest, barely visible between the trees. "Usually."

Cal added another note to her map. "Shouldn't have sent Joslyn out so soon," she murmured to Emry. "I'll have my own report for Zeke by the end of the day."

She straightened and kept walking, continuing her conversation with Nik and making more marks in her notebook. But her map was already too large as it was—Aspen couldn't imagine having a grove that widespread. They'd have to pick a few different trees to live in, then move about from time to time to monitor the growth elsewhere...

Which meant that Yarrow could truly be anywhere in the forest right now.

They quietly slowed down and fell into step alongside Shrike. "We need to sort out where Yarrow is."

"That's what I've been *saying*—"

"No, not to talk to it." Aspen nodded to the humans. "To make sure it's not going to threaten them."

"Oh." Shrike shuffled. "Well, I'm not like Pigeon. I don't think I can find it—"

"I'll do it. It's just..." Aspen hesitated. "Could you lend me a little energy?"

A breeze rustled the dead leaves overhead. Shrike regarded the foliage for a moment, then stopped and sat on the path. "Fine. Take some."

Aspen quickly sat and tugged on the offered energy. It was reluctant, to be sure, but it was there, and Aspen quickly bound it to their own. As a result, their energy whipped much farther through the forest than their last attempt to reach out. They felt their way back to the river first—nothing there, as they suspected—then rippled up the mountain, over boulders and steep slopes. The forest there held several pockets of Yarrow's presence, as if it had many little groves, little strongholds it clung to. But it could only live in one of them at a time—where was it, where was it...

Ah. Northeast, up at the peak. Yarrow simmered strongest there, a dark cloud in Aspen's mind. They pulled back, not daring to go closer, and opened their eyes to check the humans' direction. Nik and Iris were leading the others due west on a level path—not near Yarrow's current stronghold at all.

"We're clear," they said quietly and stood. "Thank you."

Shrike shook out his fur and resumed his trodding. Aspen took another look at the trees, shifted into wolf form, and padded alongside him.

Though Yarrow's presence didn't linger in the west, its tangle of growth certainly did. Before long, the humans couldn't make headway through the thorny path without the spirits' assistance.

"Can I help?" Emry gestured to the edge of the sprawling briar. "I might not be able to clear much, but—"

"I'll go first," Aspen said quickly; Emry's face fell, and they bit

THE SPIRIT'S CURSE

their lip. "But...you can clear out what we don't catch. Make sure no one trips on anything."

As promised, Aspen and Shrike went first, carefully nudging the growth aside and breaking foliage only where needed. With Yarrow so far off in the northeast, nothing here retaliated—no thorns poked at them, no vines lashed out. But Aspen still slowed their pace to a deliberate crawl, unwilling to take chances with the humans so close to the growth.

The group soon fell quiet, listening only to the wind and the sparse birdsong overhead. At first, the methodic progress was a distraction from the silence, but before long, Aspen grew impatient and grumpy. If they were going to spend most of their allotted four hours clearing rubbish, they needed *someone* to talk to.

They glanced over at Shrike.

Why do you want to go back to sleep so badly? they asked—silently, so as not to draw the other humans closer to their work. Shrike jumped at the sudden question, then drew himself together.

What?

You just want to go back to sleep and ignore everything, Aspen said, trying not to sound accusatory and failing. *Why?*

Why? Shrike repeated, his eyes narrowing. *Why do* you *want to stay awake?*

Aspen could hardly fathom the question. *Because—because there's so much to do! The humans have all sorts of friends, and festivals, and—and art, and books—*

So your life is all parties and books? Shrike stopped. *Have you thought at all about what happens after that?*

Aspen stopped alongside him. *After what?*

After they go. Shrike twitched a tufted ear in the humans' direction. *After you've been to all the festivals hundreds of times. After you've read all the books. What then?*

The weeds under Aspen's paw shriveled. They had thought about that part, of course. They knew that Emry and Cal and the others had lifespans. All animals did.

But it wasn't pleasant to think about. In fact, it made horrible, awful things curdle in Aspen's chest, deep in the soil inside their lute, and so they had, well...shoved it into a corner of their mind to gather dust.

But Shrike pressed on, dragging those thoughts out of the corner.

It's not going away just because you want it to, he said. *None of it is—the good and the bad. It'll all keep going and going and going unless we can find a way to go to sleep. To get rid of the curse.* He turned to the path ahead, his golden irises softening. *If the spirits at the fane aren't already awake...don't wake them up.*

But—

Shrike looked them in the eyes. *Don't do it.*

Aspen wanted to tell him it wasn't a curse. That humans, *their* humans, were wonderful and the best, and—

"Aspen?" Emry called. "Did I clear enough of it over here?"

Aspen stared at him for a moment. At him and Cal, holding hands, walking along the path. At two spring blooms who had about forty seasons left—a fraction of Aspen's life so far.

Every bloom in their lute furled tightly.

"You're perfect," they called back to Emry, then took a shaky breath and looked at Shrike. *All right. If they're not awake, I'll leave them be.*

Thank you.

But there was still some part of Aspen that deeply hoped a waking spirit lay ahead. Another friend to make, another being they could talk to about all this. What would they say to it first? They'd ask about Yarrow, of course. How the spirit dealt with all this strange growth, with being surrounded by another spirit's grove. But they desperately wanted to ask other things, too—like if it recalled Damir's visits from seasons ago. Or if it enjoyed living in an older forest. Or if it ever spoke with the spirits at the other fanes. Perhaps it could write to Aspen in the future, just like Pigeon and Cedar did. It could take care of Raven's Rest, after Iris and Nik and—

Cal set a hand on their shoulder. "Is this the place?"

Aspen looked up. They had been so lost in their thoughts that they hadn't realized the path had come to an end. The thorns continued ahead of them, crawling first over plain, matted grass, then over a single statue in the center of the clearing.

It took them a moment to sort out the shape of the statue: a fox, poised on a rock, with one paw lifted. Its features weren't just worn by time and weather. Lichen blanketed its paws, yes, and the chiseled details of its fur were all but gone—but Yarrow had completed the work of obscuring the fane. Thorns twisted up and around the base of the statue, while yarrow flowers and vines ensnared the rest of the clearing. No one—no human or deer or any other creature—could possibly approach to honor the spirit now.

"Godsdammit," Damir muttered, then glanced sheepishly at Iris. "Sorry."

Iris paid no attention to the swear. She gazed at the statue in fear, the emotion betraying her young age. "Is the spirit all right in there?"

"Don't worry, I'll talk to it." Aspen quickly sat on the bare patch they had just cleared. "I'm sure it's fine."

But as soon as they reached out, they flinched, their whole being freezing in place. They couldn't sense a spirit in the grove at all—only the dead tatters of one.

Its lingering magic, cold and corpse-like, lay across the soil, keeping what remained of the grove alive. But Yarrow had embedded itself into every corner of the place—not just overtop within the thorns, but deep underneath. Burrowing far below the other spirit's energy, as if it were hiding from something. From the sun, from the shadows. From what it had done.

"Aspen?" Emry crouched next to them. "Is everything all right?"

Aspen couldn't respond. They reached shakily for the closest remnant of the fallen spirit instead. If there was something left, perhaps they could try to revive part of it. Tend to it. Honor it, at the very least.

They brushed against the magic, and memories shot through

their head. Not their own memories, but the dead spirit's, jolting through them in panicked flashes. They saw thorns creeping in from further up the mountain. Shadows that didn't belong, cold that wasn't right for the season. Confusion simmered first, then fear and a horrible choking sensation—

A furry head knocked hard into their shoulder, ripping them out of the memory.

"*Don't,*" Shrike hissed. "It's no use. They're gone."

Iris now clung to Nik's arm. "What's gone? What happened here?"

"Aspen," Cal said gently, now crouched beside Emry. "If we need to leave—"

"No." The word came out louder than intended. "I have to..." They looked around at the dark forest, wiping tears off their cheek. There had been other paths, hadn't there? Other fanes to find. "I have to check the others."

Shrike's ears twitched. "There might not be a point in—"

But Aspen was already in the air.

Flying while carrying their lute was never ideal—it was far easier to take any bird shape they liked and leave the instrument on the ground—but the other fanes were too far away for them to fly like that. They took the largest shape they could think of, clumsy and wide-winged, and dove toward the next fane with their lute in tow. There was no time to clear a path or check on Yarrow's position this time. They just had to know.

They landed in front of the second statue, a bear with its back hunched under the weight of Yarrow's thorns. Aspen touched the ground: also dead. Like the fox, its final, terrified memories lay scattered over the meadow.

The third one was an owl, eyes hidden by white flowers. The fourth, a stag, berries dripping from its antlers. All of them were gone; the torn scraps of their magic slashed and layered over Yarrow's presence.

When they landed back before the fox in human form, they had no words to offer the others. Their chest was empty, the space still reverberating with the spirits' final moments.

But Shrike was filled with words.

"They're dead, aren't they?" He paced angrily in front of the clearing. "All of them. Yarrow took their groves, just like it took the humans' dens."

Damir stared at the statue, glassy-eyed. To Aspen's surprise, Nik silently set a hand on his shoulder—and Damir threw him off with a sharp, angry flinch.

"*Don't*," he spat, his words as seething as Shrike's. "Don't pretend you're sorry for me. Don't pretend you believed me." He ran a hand through his hair, blinking hard. "If it's dead, we should leave. We should leave now and—"

"Leave?" Shrike hissed. "Why? There aren't any answers in the village."

Aspen turned to him. "There aren't any answers here, either."

"Exactly." Shrike's eyes narrowed. "The only answers are with Yarrow itself."

The fox's fears merged with Aspen's own. "No. We're *not* going to find it right now, not with the humans here—"

"Then what else are we going to do?" Shrike snapped. "Wait around and let it do *this* to us? We talk to it now, get our answer, then leave this dead forest forever."

Before Aspen could stop him, Shrike began ripping up the thorns around him. *Yarrow!* He sent the call into the soil. *Yarrow*—

The earth rumbled. Damir cursed and lifted the lynx off the ground, away from the thorns. "The hells you will—Iris, run!"

For once, Nik didn't argue with Damir's command—he pulled Iris down the path. "Let's *go*!" he shouted to the others. "All of you!"

As Damir tossed Shrike back onto the path, Aspen reached for Cal and Emry. "Stay close to me. I can—"

Thorns wrapped around Cal's ankle and yanked backward. She collapsed to the ground with a shriek.

"Hold on!" Emry grabbed her arm, his magic immediately

leaping to fight the thorns—but it beat uselessly against the powerful growth, a sunbeam against a stone wall. Aspen reached forward and severed the restraint in one angry motion.

"Keep going!" They pulled Cal to her feet, grabbed Emry's hand, and ran.

Aspen had been in hostile forests before. Storms, fires, even surges, they could weather. But they had never run through trees that fought like *this*. Branches whipped out toward them, roots lifted to trip them. It was all Aspen could do to keep the ground before their feet level, keep the humans moving onward and outward, toward the river glimmering through the trees—

But ahead of them, just before the path wound into sunlight, Shrike had met with worse luck.

"Aspen!" Iris called, tugging on the lynx's front leg alongside Nik and Damir. "Help!"

Vines curled all around Shrike, entwining themselves in the growth that formed the lynx's grove. He thrashed and yowled in deep, vibrating fear, but Yarrow was too fast for him to counter.

"Emry, you take the other side," Aspen ordered, skidding to a halt beside Shrike's left flank. "Hold still, we've got you!"

As Iris and the others hurried away, Emry pulled out his boot knife and hacked at one of the vines.

"Come on, come on...."

Yarrow's growth quickly surged back. Shrike gave another terrified yowl; Emry cursed.

"Hara take me." He grit his teeth and brought the knife down again with a shout. "Let him *go*!"

The knife flashed with a white light as it whipped through the vines. The brambles slithered back with an audible hiss, sending Shrike lurching toward Aspen in relief.

We'll throw the rest of it off together! Aspen grabbed his fur. *One, two—*

With a final push, they both cast aside the last of Yarrow's hold and rushed from the shadows into the light.

CHAPTER FOURTEEN

ASPEN

THE LAST RESIDENTS of Raven's Rest maintained their frantic pace into the sunlight. Past ruins, across the bridge, into the square. Only briefly did Aspen stop, skidding to a breathless halt at the southern end of the bridge. If even a single leaf appeared over the bridge, they swore they'd tear it all down to—

But nothing happened. Yarrow let them retreat across the river, watching them with a deep, almost laughing sense of smugness and patience. Smugness, in that these little spirits had dared address it. Patience, in that these humans lived for so few seasons. What were they, compared to an immortal being?

Aspen didn't realize they could hate another spirit so much.

After checking the second bridge, they met back with the others in the gathering hall, where Harvey had made them promise to report back.

But the group had nothing to bring in except dirt, scratches, and ugly words.

"I told you so!" Nik had already rounded on Damir, one angry finger pointing north. "We ended up taunting the damn thing, just like I said!"

Damir's gaze hardened. "We didn't taunt it—"

"The rotting *cat* spoke to it!"

Shrike flinched at the loud words but made no retort. He hadn't said a single word since being rescued from Yarrow, and hadn't even growled when crossing the threshold into the gathering hall. Now, crouching by the doorway, he briefly looked as he had when cowering in the tavern in Vornik: small. Small and scared.

Aspen swiftly stepped in front of him.

"He didn't mean to anger it." They tried to adopt Cal's firm tone of voice. "He just wanted answers, like all the other spirits do. He didn't do anything to encourage Yarrow to hurt us. Yarrow chose to do that on its own."

Shrike blinked at them. Damir turned to Harvey, who hadn't moved since opening the door for them.

"Yarrow seems to have a penchant for hurting spirits," he said, his voice quiet and dark. "The spirits at the fanes are dead—all of them. Aspen confirmed it."

A mourning pall fell over the room. By the bar, Iris stared hard at the teacups she was arranging. At the hearth, Emry silently tended to a scratch on Cal's ankle. Aspen plucked a moonflower for their lute and handed it to her.

"Does it hurt?"

"Hardly." Cal took the flower anyway, her smile fragile. "I daresay my nerves are more bruised than anything else. Em?" She reached down and gently ran her fingers through his curls. "Why don't we have some tea?"

Emry didn't meet her gaze, his voice thick. "It almost took you away from me."

"But it didn't—"

"It almost took you, and I couldn't *do* anything." Eyes shining, he rapidly shook his head and got to his feet. "I'm sorry. Tea—yes, tea will help."

In a quiet, somber shuffle, they gathered around the teacups Iris had set out but didn't so much as touch the handles. Aspen made sure to sit between Emry and Cal; Shrike slowly padded over and crouched by the edge of the table.

Harvey, seated between Nik and Damir, was first to break the silence.

"I'm sorry, Miri," he said wearily, then added: "To all of you. If I had known you were heading to a grave, I wouldn't have pushed you on it."

"Couldn't have known," Damir said, his voice overly gruff, eyes distant. Slowly, everyone's attention settled on him.

"Damir," Emry ventured, still holding Cal's hand tightly. "I know you were interested in the fanes here, but I admit I never expected you to be one to...honor spirits."

"What, you mean buying out every greenhouse in Vornik for your concerts isn't honoring Aspen?" he tried weakly, then waved the words away. "I know. I didn't, at first. Wasn't until mum and dad...well."

The brothers didn't meet each other's gazes.

"I went to the fox fane one day," Damir continued, aimlessly flicking his pocket watch open and closed. "Don't know why. It was the closest, I suppose. I didn't expect anything. Maybe just a few minutes to clear my head, shout at the trees. That sort of thing."

Aspen leaned forward. "Did the spirit speak to you?"

"Not in the obvious sense. It grew a flower. A lily." A humorless smile briefly crossed Damir's face. "I ran back and took it to the others. Swore up and down that a spirit still lived in the fane."

Nik shifted uncomfortably.

"I visited the fanes for years after that," Damir continued. "Talked to the spirits. Occasionally got flowers in return. I thought maybe they would remember me if I came back. Maybe I could talk to them, with Aspen's help. Truly meet them, somehow." He grimly stowed his pocket watch. "But Yarrow's taken them, just like it took the villages."

"Have you...ever seen this before?" Iris looked up at Cal—but it was Shrike who answered first.

"Never heard of it before," he said. "Humans trying to kill spirits, sure. But spirits hunting their own?"

Emry cracked a tiny smile. "Well, there was that little business with a certain lynx jumping up onstage and—"

"I wasn't trying to kill—!" Shrike huffed and curled up, his vines growing thicker around him. "We went to the spirits and they're gone. Nothing more can be done about it."

Iris, however, had one last question. "Did they suffer?"

This was directed not to Cal, but to Aspen. They opened their mouth, wanting to lie, wanting to say no. But they had seen other spirits pass more quietly and more fully than this. Like the spirits torn away by surges, or the spirits that had withered away in Matlock. There were no tortured traces of them left; no scrap left over from their murder by another spirit. Nothing like what they had just seen.

"I'm not sure," they finally said, settling on a bleak half-truth while trying to hide the fear in their voice. "It's like Shrike said. I've never seen anything like this before."

Damir spun his teacup. "I have."

Iris' eyes went wide. "At our fanes—?"

"No, not nearly so close." He took a reluctant sip of his tea, then slouched over the table. "Back during the war, before I left Envis. Vidanya had come to the province for an alliance talk."

Realization dawned on Nik's face. "When you went north to Sheck's Run."

Damir nodded. "I was sent as a representative of the Rest to attend the talks. Middle of spring, mind you. Best weather Envis has to offer. But three nights in, a winter storm swept through the area. The following morning, the town's fane was covered in Vidanyan plants. Same as what we saw today. Flowers, thorns, the lot of it." He gave a cold laugh. "At the time, I thought it was a sign that Envis should ally with Vidanya. Couldn't have been more clear to me. But, due to other politics and such rot"—he shrugged—"the talks fell through. Envis sent the representatives back and remained isolationist through the war and beyond."

Cal, still leaning close against Emry, already had her journal open to find Sheck's Run on her map. "That could have been Yarrow's first victim," she said, placing her finger on a dot at the very top of the page. "The Vidanyan representatives could have accidentally brought in those invasive species on their carriages, their shoes...all Yarrow had to do was propagate them." She grabbed her pencil. "Did you see anything else? Any other anomalies while you were up there?"

Damir shook his head. "Nothing else after that. I left after the talks ceased, young and stupid and angry that Envis was ignoring what was going on beyond their borders. Went and joined the war effort soon after, intending to report back to the Rest if any threat started to come their way." He glanced at Emry. "Ended up working for one of the Guild musicians attending the Envisian talks as a diplomat. A young up-and-comer named Ella Sorman."

Emry smiled. "Yes, I might've heard of her."

"I went back to Vidanya with her, thinking others outside Envis might believe in spirits. I was proven wrong until Aspen appeared." The corner of Damir's mouth quirked up. "When Ella told me Aspen healed her wrist after that surge, I almost didn't believe her. Thought she was playing a cruel trick on me."

Aspen reached back into their lute and plucked the first flower they could think of—a white rose, its petals soft and perfectly formed. They offered it to Damir.

"Thank you for thinking of us. Even when the others didn't."

Next to Damir, Iris stared at the flower, her expression still mired in gloom. "Whether or not we thought they were there, those spirits are—*were*—our neighbors. Practically villagers of the Rest." She turned a determined gaze on her father. "We need to know why they were killed."

Cal swallowed. "We'd have to talk to Yarrow again for that."

"Again?" Shrike said. "I barely said two words to it today."

Nik's face darkened. "And two words was more than enough."

Aspen grew a tiny vine around their finger in thought. As much as Nik would hate to hear it…Iris was right. Yarrow still held the answers to both her question and Aspen's.

"They just weren't the right two words." They fidgeted with the vine. "I don't know how we should do it. But if we want answers —*any* answers," they added, glancing at Shrike—"we have to try to talk to it again."

The tea in the gathering hall offered them no ideas—only warmth and steam as a boon against the bleakness. But as they all trudged back to the cottages, Harvey was already hard at work on fighting the gloom.

"Tell you what," he said bravely, as if the news about the spirits hadn't made him hunch over further. "Come on in and I'll fetch you some good beer. I've got a few glasses' worth sent up from Warwick. We can toast to the spirits." He lowered his voice as he shuffled into his house. "And think a little more on that plan to talk to Yarrow again."

As soon as Harvey was gone, Emry turned to Cal, his hand on the small of her back.

"Really, how is that ankle?" He anxiously checked it again, even as he himself was beginning to limp. "Did it hurt at all on the walk here?"

"Em, it's fine—"

"Why don't you prop it up on a chair, just to be safe. And I'll make you some more tea. Damir—?"

"Go on, I'll get the kettle going," he muttered. "S'long as it doesn't burn me this time."

The humans all filed into Harvey's cottage—but when Aspen went to follow them, Shrike cleared his throat.

"Hey." The lynx sat awkwardly by the garden, shifting his weight from paw to paw. "Can we...?"

Aspen nodded and stood patiently, waiting for the next words to come.

"Just wanted to say thank you," Shrike said to the cobblestones rather than Aspen. "For saving me. And...for not blaming me for Yarrow's attack."

Aspen held themself very still. Remain casual, they told themself. Don't spook them off now that they were saying something nice.

"It wasn't your fault," they reassured him. "All you did was say its name."

"But if I hadn't—"

"Yarrow attacked us without reason in the cave, and they attacked without reason today," Aspen said firmly. "We'll just be more prepared next time."

"Prepared. Right." Shrike pawed at the ground. Murmurs and light laughter tinkled inside the cottage. "What's um...what's beer, exactly?"

Aspen brightened. "Want to come in and find out? It smells a bit like bread."

Shrike's gaze lingered on the door, curiosity sparking—then he shook himself.

"Maybe later," he said, and padded toward the garden. Aspen let out a breath. They hadn't seen it coming, but gentle words from Shrike were a nice surprise. Perhaps the best thing to come out of the day, if they were being honest.

"Tree kid?" Damir poked his head out onto the porch. "Got any of those moonflowers for Karic? Keeps complaining about Cal's ankle when his own damn leg's about to fall off."

Aspen sighed. Now that, they should have seen coming.

"I'll be right there!" Moonflowers already dripping from their lute, they retreated into Harvey's cottage.

CHAPTER FIFTEEN

EMRY

EMRY CLOSED his eyes against the sun.

"All right." He held up a finger as he posed his question. "Damir. If Damir could shape-shift into an animal, what would it be?"

"A bird of some sort," Cal mused.

"A horned owl, then," Aspen said confidently. "They always look angry." They paused. "Do you think Damir's always been angry?"

Emry shrugged. "Could always ask Nik."

"Nik would just say yes."

All three of them hummed in sleepy agreement.

To recover from the chaos, pain, and beer of the previous day, the trio—well, mostly Aspen—had decided that a morning of basking was in order. After visiting the ravens, then ensuring Shrike still lurked close by in the garden, the three of them set out a blanket in the yard and simply...laid back for a while.

Well, *Emry* laid back for a while. The other two couldn't bring themselves to remain still.

After moving to the shade under the apple tree, Cal—who had

declared she'd turn into a cat, if given the chance—filled page after page of her notebook with her observations on Yarrow so far. Sketching out the various plant species it used, estimating distances between the affected towns—then complaining that none of this data would properly fit in a letter to Zeke for analysis and filing.

"If there were three more Joslyns, maybe," she grumbled, "I could get Mr. Whitlock's opinion on Yarrow's growth rate. Or how fast it might travel between its—what did you call them, Aspen?"

Aspen—who had no need to declare what animal form they would take—sat cross-legged near Emry, weaving flower crowns. "Strongholds."

"Yes, that."

Emry laid an arm over his face to block out the morning sun. The thin blanket underneath him allowed blades of grass to poke him in the back, but the light summer warmth still melted away his remaining aches. If he were an animal, he decided, he'd like to be a lizard, basking on a rock. "Cal, I thought you said your team had plenty of data already from the festival."

"But this is *different* data."

He opened one eye. "Oh, that different data you didn't want on the way here?"

Cal bit back a smile. "You're incorrigible. Eat another moonflower petal, please."

After he reluctantly did so, he checked on Aspen, who held up their half-finished crown. Unlike the colorful ones stacked by their knee, this one held dark green foliage braided with purple leaves and black flowers.

"You think Damir will like this one?" they asked.

"I think it's impossible for Damir to like anything."

Aspen hummed. "You're right."

Soon, the others' industriousness began to itch at Emry, and he eventually pulled over his own notebook and flipped to his list of song lyrics. He only had a matter of days until they were supposed to leave Envis, and he had made just as much progress on his and

Aspen's song as he had at getting answers from Yarrow. Or protecting Cal. Or generally being helpful.

Which was to say, he had done absolutely nothing of substance and he hated it.

He leaned back on his hands and watched Aspen weave. Even though it had been their idea, all the flower crowns and the basking didn't seem to be helping their mood—their shoulders and finger movements were just as tightly wound as Emry's worries.

Perhaps Emry couldn't fight ancient, immortal beings—but he could lift a spirit's spirits, and that had to count for something.

"Aspen." He lifted his notebook. "Want to go over the song one more time? I was wondering if you could help me with some of the lyrics."

His gamble paid off. Aspen immediately tossed aside the flower crown and clambered over, sunshine gathering in their expression. "Yes! Yes, please. Where did we stop last time?"

"Down here. But I wanted to revisit the lyrics up here first. I'm not sure the flower part is working. Tell me what you think of this..."

As soon as he began singing, Aspen finally relaxed, almost puddle-like on the sun-warmed blanket. Under the tree, Cal smiled and gave Emry a small nod of approval.

THE FOLLOWING morning brought even more sunshine through the hope of happier news: Joslyn the raven had arrived from Vornik with a fresh message in tow.

"Joslyn!" Harvey waved the bird down. "Over here! No, not directly to Mr. Karic—he's not the one with the berries in his pockets. Come along now, come on..."

Once the bird had been properly compensated with fruit, Harvey met the trio on the porch, a tightly rolled letter in hand.

"I imagine you'll want to respond to them right away"—he held out the roll—"but Joslyn will need a bit of rest before flying off again."

Damir stood at the doorway, squinting against the morning sun, his blonde hair sticking up at all angles. "When she flies back," he mumbled, "can she take me with her?"

Emry unrolled the letter and got a peek of Sage's handwriting. "What, and miss out on all the fun of murderous spirits? Where's your sense of adventure, Uncle Miri?"

Damir glared at him. He ignored it and began reading the letter.

Dear Emry,

Are you absolutely sure we shouldn't come over there and join you? I don't like this pattern of spirit attacks, and I can't say Ella likes it much, either. If Mr. Chamberlain or anyone on the Council hears about this, they'll throw a fit. At least Karlson hasn't heard about it, yet. He's near Cima, trying to talk down Shrike's reputation there, and—

Emry kept scanning the contents, searching for that happier news he had hoped for.

Pigeon and Cedar are still here with Lydia, conducting research and reassuring the other spirits that Aspen will have answers for them soon. Riley's trying to downplay Shrike's attack at every event, and Mrs. Chamberlain attended my soiree yesterday, bless her. But her enthusiasm alone won't be enough to sway the others, not when they're—

He kept searching.

Do you know when you and Aspen will return to Vornik? Have you sorted out the rest of the song? I met with a journalist last night—she's more than eager to write a piece on the song when you're back and ready to debut it.

THE SPIRIT'S CURSE

It wasn't good news, exactly, but it did draw his thoughts back home, to the happier tasks that awaited him there. Even though it had only been days, it felt like weeks since he had last been on stage. Did Raven's Rest even have a stage? He hadn't seen one yet, unless it was on the other side of the river...

But when he asked Harvey as much, the man just stared at him.

"'Course we do. You walk right by it to get to the gathering hall."

Emry blinked. "What, that old platform?"

He had assumed the sagging wood square was for market day or village announcements, not music. The very thought of it was almost as depressing as their spirit discovery yesterday.

"Darling, can I—?" Cal reached for the letter.

"Of course."

While he wallowed in visions of the sad stage, she scanned the letter, her eyes moving far faster than his had. "I'll work on a reply. Slowly, of course, for Joslyn. Do you know what you'd like to say back, Aspen?"

Aspen's form flickered, and they fidgeted with the flowers in their pockets. "I'll, um—I'll think about it."

They hurried off toward the raven tower, shriveled flower petals drifting from their lute. Cal met Emry's gaze in worry, but he held up a hand.

"Give them a few minutes. They'll be all right."

A few minutes passed, then an hour. Emry and Cal made tea for three and wrote out their responses to Vornik. An hour after that, Aspen's tea and paper both lay untouched.

"I promised Iris I would meet her at the river." Cal glanced out the window. "But I should check on Aspen first—"

"Let me." Emry kissed her cheek and gathered the cold teacups. "We'll meet you at the river, yeah?"

He briefly considered bringing Aspen's teacup to the tower—but there was nothing so disheartening as cold tea, so he left it behind and creaked up the tower steps. Sure enough, Aspen was still there, sitting on the top platform and feeding birdseed to the ravens.

"I think they like me," they said weakly. "Wish I could ask them what birdseed tasted like."

Emry grimaced. "Crunchy, I imagine." He sat across from Aspen, careful to avoid any bird droppings. "Still thinking about your letter?"

Aspen's face fell. "I...I don't know what to write. We haven't even spoken to Yarrow yet."

"That's all right. We'll think up a plan and speak to it." Emry tried to sound encouraging for the spirit's sake. "Once we get it talking, it won't take long to sort out if it has our answers or not."

But that didn't seem to encourage Aspen at all. They simply sat, gaze distant, empty hand still held out to the birds. When they next spoke, their voice was almost a whisper.

"What if I can't bring back any good news to the other spirits? I've never had anyone depend on me like this. I don't..." They wiped their eyes. "I don't want them to feel cursed like Shrike does. If they do, and I can't help them, I'd just be a failure—"

Emry took Aspen's hand. "You're not a failure," he said. "Yes, they all look to you now, but as soon as they asked for answers, you went and crossed an entire province to get them. You've braved forests and spirits and—and carriage rides with Shrike to help them. You're doing your best, and I won't have you say any mean things about yourself, all right?"

Aspen's smile briefly returned at that. Emry wiped a tear off their cheek, then stood.

"I'm sure the ravens are delightful company, but how about you come join Iris and Cal at the river? We can think more on your letter there."

When they arrived, both ladies already stood at the water's edge, inspecting the flower boxes there as if it were a pleasant promenade spot and not a backdrop to village ruins. And to Emry's surprise, they weren't alone: Shrike had left the garden and joined their outing, lying low in the shade at an awkward distance.

"Morning, Shrike," Emry said. "Talking a stroll with the ladies?"

"I just thought they were going over the bridge into the forest," Shrike retorted.

"Ah, so you wanted to protect them?"

"*No*—"

"That's very kind, thank you, Shrike," Cal said loudly, then smirked at Emry and continued her inspection. "Iris, what about plants with deeper roots? Ones that stretch further vertically?"

"Like these?" Iris nudged one of the blooms in the planter. "Variegated rue. Rotting difficult to pull out. I swear, half the roots are as tall as I am. But if you think they could block Yarrow..."

Emry joined Cal at the planter, their silhouettes rippling gently in the river just beyond his feet. "You didn't tell me this was a defense strategy meeting."

Cal tested the planter's soil with her finger, then wiped the dirt off on her traveling cloak—a plain brown thing borrowed from Iris. "If we do really plan on confronting Yarrow directly, I'd rather not leave the Rest defenseless." She nodded to the water. "I'm not sure why, but the spirit hasn't tried to cross the river, apart from its attempts across the bridges. The water seems to be what's keeping the south side of the village safe so far."

"But you don't think it's enough."

"I hardly know if anything is enough." Cal pressed her lips into a line. "But yes. If the water ceases to be sufficient protection, we could create a deep underground barrier to block Yarrow's progress."

Aspen crouched by the planter and ran a hand above the flowers; they all followed the direction of their palm like it was the sun. "An underground barrier with just the rue?"

"The rue and the dwarf rowan." Cal pointed to the trees planted in regular intervals along the water. "Its roots are wide where the rue's are long. Together, they could form a grid of sorts—but only if there's a spirit here to make sure they don't entangle themselves to death." She paused. "And we happen to have two and a half spirits with us."

Emry looked up. "Am I the half?"

Cal patted his arm. "It's a compliment, my love."

Aspen jumped to their feet, buoyed by the plan. "We'll do it." They turned to Shrike, who snuffled and padded over in silent acquiescence. "Where should we start?"

Emry gauged the length of the river. Raven's Rest wasn't particularly large, but doing this sort of...root-weaving down its entire length would take several days.

And ideally, he'd be leaving the village by then.

"Why don't we start with the bridges and the narrower parts?" he suggested. "Then tackle the other areas if we have time?"

They began at the eastern bridge, the one Iris had waved from upon their landing in the Rest. The planted rue and rowans stopped just by the dock, giving the spirits—the two and a half spirits—a good starting place.

Emry just wished the *half* could keep up with the other two. The rue and rowan struggled under his grasp, both difficult and unfamiliar—though that didn't surprise Cal when he mentioned it.

"These varietals don't grow in Vidanya," she reassured him. "Of course you're not familiar with them."

But even when he did get the hang of them—how their roots felt in the soil, the resistance they gave to being manipulated—his work was still far clumsier than the spirits'. The growing grid of roots quickly confused him, muddling beyond his human comprehension, while Shrike and Aspen made quick paces ahead, weaving roots together like they did it every day. Which, Emry supposed, they did.

He slowly untangled and re-tangled the roots in his patch, wishing he could be quick and decisive, like when he had chopped at the roots holding back Shrike—his boot knife had made quick work of it then. But slashing roots was counter to Cal's grand plan, and after a few more minutes of struggle, he stood, wiped dirt off his hands, and joined her with an exhausted sigh.

"The other two will have to go on without me," he said, gulping from the waterskin Iris held out to him. "Afraid I make a better bard than a gardener."

"My cousin Vera made a better gardener than a bard," Iris said. "You should've heard her at festivals. They let her sing early on, so they had time to drink and forget about it later." She brightened and nodded to the gold pin on his waistcoat. "But *you* must be good. You said you were part of the Eric Guild—"

"Auric Guild."

"—and I haven't heard you sing anything yet. Could you? Just this once?"

"Oh, here we go," Shrike muttered by the river. Emry shot him a look.

"Come on, you technically heard our concert in Vornik before you attacked us. Was it really all that bad?"

"He knows it wasn't!" Aspen called from farther down the river. As they focused on growing the roots below the road, all manner of plants grew above ground as well, thriving on the infusion of magic. A spiral of vines from Iris' planter spread across the cobblestones, its tiny thorns ticking against the cobblestones in a steady rhythm. *Click, click, click...*

Emry started tapping his foot to the beat. He could sing their new song to this. They had recently tweaked the lyrics, after all, and it needed to debut somewhere. A riverside was as good a place as any.

> *You can feel it in the roots below*
> > *As sure as rain and the river's flow*
> > *That spring is gone, it's time for her to leave you*
>
> *She stole away into the night*
> > *No kiss left by the candlelight*
> > *Just one thorn from the blooms she always grew you*

He pulled Cal toward him and swept her into a dance—a simple three-step, their paces cut short to fit the narrow road. But Cal didn't seem to mind. She giggled and turned, her plain cloak floating out behind her as she moved. Emry couldn't help but admire the grace of such a sight. It didn't matter what she wore or where she was—she always shone a bit brighter than everything around her. With her, the song always flowed out more easily.

> *She cannot stay, you know that well*
> *No prayer will pull her gray farewell*
> *Out from your palm, the hand that she once held to*
>
> *But if you grow through the Sun and snow*
> *The burnished leaves and the bones below*
> *She'll dance back to your arms just like she used to*

He was so focused on Cal, it took him a moment to see the music's effect on the others. Aspen had stopped to watch them, smiling and dangling their bare feet above the water. But nearby, the flowers still grew, bursting out of their planters in joy. Shrike even had to bat a few of them out of his way as he pretended to ignore the music.

When the song ended, Iris clapped loudly.

"You're nothing at all like Vera. And far better than those traveling singers that used to come through from Illev." She dangled her feet above the water next to Aspen. "Do you think you could you play that for the others on our stage? I think it needs a good song."

Emry gave her a strained smile. That poor stage needed far more than a good song.

"Happy to, if you want." Not that there was much of an audience to play to if she insisted. Some townsfolk. A dog. Yarrow, if it chose to listen from beyond the water...

The shadowed northern forest drew his gaze.

Yarrow was accustomed to aggression, wasn't it? All it knew of Raven's Rest was Iris and Nik pulling and burning its growth. And the newcomers to the Rest were hardly better: tromping through caves and pathways, pushing aside and breaking its work. What if they tried something different, something Yarrow was utterly unfamiliar with? Something that Emry and Aspen had done a hundred times?

He turned to Cal, still holding her hand. "What if we sang to it?"

She frowned. "Sang to Yarrow, you mean?"

"We've appeased spirits with music before." He waggled his head. "Well, I wouldn't expect Yarrow to be...*appeased*, exactly. But if it lets us approach it without violence, it could be our way into actually talking to it."

"I..." Cal bit her lip, searching for an argument. "Well, I mean. I suppose we could..."

She looked at Aspen, who turned once more to Shrike.

"Sing to it?" Shrike said, his ears just as flat as his voice. "Sing to the ancient, killing spirit? That's a terrible idea."

"It *is* a terrible idea." Iris grinned wide. "Let's do it."

CHAPTER SIXTEEN

ASPEN

As Aspen feared, no one in the village thought Emry's plan was a particularly good one when Damir pitched it.

"You want to sing. You want to sing to the murderous spirit." Nik set his elbows down on the bar in the gathering hall and hid his face in his hands. "Remind me why I let you into my village again?"

"One"—Damir held up a finger—"I'm not the one singing."

"Thank the gods."

"Shut up. Two, you let me in because I'm your brother. And three..." Damir raised his arms, then let them drop at his sides. "Look, perhaps I've just bought into the Karic lunacy, but I actually think they'll get through to the rotting spirit this way. I've seen it happen before, and the damn kid's lucky enough to make it work one more time."

Nik gave a long, Damir-like sigh. "One more time?"

"I swear it. If Yarrow still refuses to talk after this"—Damir glanced over at Aspen for silent approval—"we'll find another way to sort this all out, won't we?"

Aspen steeled themself and nodded. Any way it took, they would do it. They had already promised it in the letter going back with Joslyn.

"Please," Damir continued, lowering his voice. "I know you don't like to believe me, but—just this once?"

A brief flash of guilt passed over Nik's face, and he straightened wearily.

"Dawn, then. Give ourselves as much daylight as possible, so we can see Yarrow coming when it arrives to kill us." He tossed a cleaning cloth over his shoulder. "And *you're* telling Iris she's not coming."

Damir was the one to balk this time. "Me?"

"It's your bard's plan—"

"But I'm her favorite uncle!"

"You're her *only* uncle!"

Damir eventually lost that battle, but he had won the war. They all agreed to meet back at the gathering hall at dawn for one more venture into the forest. But dawn took its leisurely time, leaving both Shrike and Aspen to pace around the plaza in the moonlight until it arrived. Normally, nighttime brought a sort of quiet peace to spirits, akin to the closing of flowers after sunset.

Tonight, neither spirit could enjoy such a feeling.

"Think it'll actually like the music?" Shrike muttered, nosing at a dandelion growing between the cobblestones.

"It's not a matter of it liking the music." Aspen set their chin on their hand and watched the dandelion grow under Shrike's motions. "So long as it listens long enough to start talking. Then we'll ask it a few questions and see it if can leave Raven's Rest alone."

Shrike gave them a skeptical look. Aspen shrugged.

"What? We might as well ask. We don't even know why it wants the village."

Or any of the villages, really. Human dwellings were nice and all, but Aspen had never wanted to lay claim to one of them, let alone an entire town. There was so much about Yarrow that made little sense to them.

They tentatively reached out across the river, then into the forest, poking about to see if the old spirit hovered nearby. To their surprise, something reached back. Its signature was muddled in the darkness, but it searched rapidly, giving off a sort of urgent curiosity—

Aspen quickly retracted back to the safe side of the river. There was no need to provoke Yarrow before they even set out on their quest.

"I'll try to ask it as many questions as I can"—they turned to Shrike—"but if it tries to attack again, we'll need to work together to get everyone back to the village quickly."

For once, Shrike didn't scoff at that; he merely folded his paws and yawned. "Why not just bring the bard and leave the others where it's safe?"

Aspen snorted. "Please. *You* try taking Emry anywhere without Cal or Damir."

∼

When dawn finally arrived and the humans all gathered, Damir took charge of the debrief.

"There's an old Sada festival ground up on the mountain, past the old hunting lodge," he said, keeping his voice low—as if Yarrow were lurking in the morning mist and would overhear him. "Nik, is the lodge is still there?"

Harvey answered for him, shaking his head as he stuffed Nik's pack with bread wrapped in cloth. "Could be covered in thorns, as far as we know. Can't tell if the forest has claimed it in the past few months."

Iris stood by Damir's side, her jaw set in poorly restrained jealousy. "You have the candles?"

"Yes."

"And the herbs I picked for you?"

Damir patted the top of his pack. "I'll use them to the fullest, I promise."

Iris stepped back, arms folded—just as pouty as her father could be. "You'd better."

Once they parted from Harvey and Iris and stepped into the forest, Aspen kept an easy pace with Damir at the front of the pack, maintaining their human form this time. "I thought Envis didn't do any sort of spirit celebrations. How'd you learn the traditions?"

"Blame Nik."

Behind them, Nik snorted; Damir gave a rare smile.

"Mum thought I was too underfoot while she taught Nik how to manage the village," he explained. "Sent me out into the forest to forage, hunt, and talk the ears off the elders who went with me, like Harvey. A few of 'em still remembered the old ways—even led a few festival celebrations now and then. Not that anyone paid much attention to the *spirit* part of the rituals. We were mostly just there for the food."

Cal stuck close to Emry as she walked, her gaze constantly moving from tree to tree. "I can't claim that Vidanya has been a bastion of spirit tradition until Aspen's appearance, but I hadn't realized that Envis had dropped the traditions as well."

"If anything, we dropped it first," Nik said. "The forest isn't kind here. Maybe we thought that if we ignored the spirits, they'd ignore us. Let us live another day."

Damir gave a pointed hum. Nik rubbed the back of his head.

"Well, I didn't say we were *right* about it."

They passed by the hunting lodge—still intact, if grimy and sagging—then reached the festival grounds by noon. To Aspen's dismay, the festival grounds didn't exactly reflect the joyful times they were once used for. The place was little more than an overgrown stone plaza in the middle of a clearing, riddled with cracks and dead weeds. Cal frowned at the shriveled growth, then the brittle foliage leading into the forest.

"Yarrow's growth seems to be rather smothering here. Can you feel it, Aspen?"

Aspen didn't need to make any effort to confirm it. The natural brush, so dampened by Yarrow's invasive species, was withering away underneath the growth. Given time, the entire forest would look like this. Dead, dry, fragile, even in the middle of summer.

The opposite of what a healthy grove was supposed to look like.

They wanted to rush into the middle of the plaza, revive any plants they could in defiance of Yarrow's siege— but Damir stepped in first.

"Let me set up some of the old Sada decorations first," he said, opening up his bag to reveal Iris' candles and bundles of herbs. "It'll be just a minute, I think."

He arranged the offerings exactly how he prepared stage decorations for a concert: grumpily and with a great deal of muttering.

"See, it's supposed to be rosemary for wards, clover for good luck or something..." He nudged a bundle with his foot, hands on his hips. "Stop *judging* me, Nik."

Nik raised his hands. "I'm not judging you!"

"I can feel you laughing at me. I don't know what I'm doing—"

"Oh, like *I'd* know what to do with them."

After a few more candles, nudges, and bickering retorts, Damir finally stalked back to the edge of the plaza.

"Fine. It's done." He crossed his arms. "At least, I think it's done."

Having never seen an Envisian ritual before, Aspen thought Damir had done a decent job. The candles brought a warm, if feeble, light to each corner of the plaza, while the herbs positioned around each candle gave the air a welcome hint of freshness.

"I like it," Aspen tried to sound encouraging. "It's nice."

They glanced nervously at Nik, expecting some sort of indifference, or at worst, derision—but instead, he awkwardly patted his brother on the shoulder. "S'not too bad."

Damir reddened.

"It's awful, but thank you for lying." He gathered himself together and waved Aspen along. "Go on. You're up, Karics."

Side by side, all three Karics headed toward what constituted a stage—then Cal slipped off to the left and Emry tentatively stepped ahead of Aspen, lute in hand. For a moment, they all stood and waited, watching the ground for any hint of movement, any attack.

Nothing so far. Shrike padded up to join Aspen, and once they were settled in the middle of the plaza, Emry began to play.

Aspen couldn't recall which song Emry had chosen to draw Yarrow's attention—they felt the vibrations through the stone but were far too focused on the surrounding forest to truly hear the words or melody. As they expected, Yarrow moved swiftly down the mountain toward them, away from its current stronghold. It wasn't angry—not yet, at least. More...confused. Curious. A little like the curiosity Aspen had sensed out in the forest the night before.

Then it encircled the plaza, sending a chill skittering across the stone. It took no visible form but remained present just the same.

You, was all it said at first. The one word reverberated deep into the soil, as all-encompassing as the surrounding thorns. *You're still here.*

Its tone was disappointed, edged with anger. Aspen would have to placate it soon or keep this conversation short.

"We don't mean you any harm," they said. Whether the words were uttered silently or aloud, they knew the spirit would hear them. "We come seeking your wisdom."

Wisdom? Yarrow's response was almost a laugh.

"We have a question," Shrike added quickly. "A question meant for a spirit older than us."

Ask.

Shrike took a breath. "How does a spirit sleep?"

Sleep. Yarrow rolled the word around, and it fell heavy in Aspen's head, tumbling like a boulder down a mountainside. *A spirit sleeps until it does not. I slept until I did not.*

"And what woke you?"

THE SPIRIT'S CURSE

Death.

A chill wind buffeted across the plaza, snuffing out the candles. The humans in the clearing shivered, but Aspen didn't dare move, nor utter their conversation aloud. *And how long have you been awake?*

Seasons, was the only answer.

Aspen bit their lip. The anger in its words had dulled, but this conversation would never work if all they got from the old spirit were one-word answers. There had to be something else they could glean...

Their gaze landed on the layers of dead foliage in the clearing. It didn't appear all that different from what they had seen at the spirit fanes. Layers of thorns, energy, memories...

They directed their next words to Shrike alone.

Keep talking to it. I'm going to try something.

The lynx bristled. *Me?*

You can do it. Just don't anger it.

Shrike flexed his paws, then sat straighter and focused once more on Yarrow. *You were...further north once. What was it like?*

While Yarrow responded—something about the cold, the pine trees—Aspen carefully reached further into the foliage around the plaza. Yarrow's memories had gathered here along with its presence, fuzzy and thick. Sifting through them for information was like walking through mist and feeling for a tree trunk to lean on. But whenever they did reach cold, scratchy bark, a flash of memory rewarded them. A glimpse of a bristlecone pine tree at the mountain peak, weathered and twisted against the sky. A blink of a forest, taller and colder than the one surrounding the Rest...

Then a longer memory, seared into the ancient spirit like a burn scar over the land. In this memory, white particles of energy whipped through the pine trees, blackening and withering everything they touched. A surge, Aspen realized, as their own memories of surges roiled in their chest. The event in this memory didn't look like the great wave that had once shattered the other provinces, but it was a surge nonetheless, consuming large swaths of the forest all at once. Throughout the trees, the distant presences of spirits faded, their imprints being torn from the earth—

Except for Yarrow. Still a young spirit then, it hurried to the surface of its grove in fear and confusion, trying with all its might to build a shield and cling to life until the surge passed. And once it was gone and the spirit was left with a weak circle of surviving greenery, it tried to dive back into the soil. To the gentle lull of sleep.

But it didn't work. Of course it didn't work. Aspen watched helplessly as it tried diving again. And again. And again. Panic and confusion rippling and expanding—

Aspen released the memory, the emotions behind it making them feel sick. Was this what the other spirits had felt after the wave? That same sort of fear and panic? They opened their eyes, looking for any sort of distraction—and found Emry and Cal there, kneeling in front of them at a cautious distance.

"Aspen?" Emry said, quiet and distant. But it grounded Aspen all the same, drawing them to recall the dead spirits' memories. The memories of what had happened at the fox fane, the owl fane, the bear fane...

Yes, those other spirits in Vidanya might have been overcome with fear upon not being able to sleep. But what had they done after that? They had spoken to Aspen and Emry and Cal. Sent them letters, helped them research, listened to their music.

They hadn't taken over villages. They hadn't killed other spirits.

Why? Aspen swung their focus back on Yarrow, trying hard to keep their voice steady against their anger. *Why spread from the north? Why kill the spirits, why* do *all this?*

The words could have gone awry so easily. The anger wasn't well-veiled, the tone all but betraying Aspen's promise to not do harm.

But Yarrow simply regarded not Aspen, but Shrike. *Your question was my question, once.*

Shrike stood on all fours, the nub of their tail flicking back and forth. *Sleep, you mean? You figured out how to go back to sleep?*

A flood of new memories suddenly filled Aspen's mind. They didn't have to search or sift this time—the memories came willingly. Of Yarrow coming upon strange, unfamiliar seeds. Of Yarrow taking over a feeble grove with this odd new growth, then digging eagerly, desperately, into the layers of the other spirit's energy. It had burrowed underneath, deep underneath, feeding the grove with the remnants of the last tenant's magic so Yarrow could finally sleep...

And sleep it did. For a time.

Then the grove came clawing down, seeking out Yarrow's magic once the other spirit had faded entirely. Yarrow woke again, and in renewed anger and fear, rushed off. Letting desperation take over its every waking thought, it used its new leaves and flowers to spread, and searched for another grove to hide in. Then another, and another—

It paid little attention to the villages in its way. Humans lived near spirits; sometimes, the quickest way to the next grove was through them. Cobblestones were ripped up, houses taken over by trees. The energy of past groves fueled its momentum, pushing itself down mountains, through valleys—

Until it reached a familiar river and a familiar village, with the distant promise of more groves even farther south.

"No." The word came from Shrike, ripping the memories to pieces in an instant. "No. That can't—that can't be the only way!"

Every human in the plaza jolted; those were the first words they had heard aloud in minutes. Cal gripped Emry's arm tight.

"What's the only way?" she asked, but there was too much going on for Aspen to even try to respond. The humans' fear filled the plaza, a strange energy shifted beyond the trees—and Yarrow pressed in closer, quickly muffling everything else.

Your groves, it said, focusing on Aspen's lute and the vines that encircled Shrike. *They will not help me sleep.*

"Of course they won't!" Shrike spat, his fur on end, his teeth bared. "We're not going to help you with anything—"

Yarrow didn't so much as flicker against the protective display.

But your energy is strong. All around them, the shadows deepened. *I will make use of it.*

The temperature in the clearing dropped. Frosty air slipped out of Emry and Cal's mouths, and their limbs shook with cold. A sharp wind sent white flecks across Aspen's vision. A surge, they thought in fear—but then the flecks melted on their hands, their face. They looked up, and nothing but deep gray clouds looked back at them.

They stood in the middle of Yarrow's territory, deep in a growing midsummer snowstorm.

CHAPTER SEVENTEEN

EMRY

E*MRY ONCE THOUGHT* he enjoyed winter.

He enjoyed normal winter weather, certainly. Soft snowfall, clear skies, crisp air. Hot cocoa waiting at home.

This was not, by any stretch of the imagination, normal winter weather.

The summer breeze vanished in an instant, replacing the air in his lungs with cold knives. He blinked, and snow had already buried the dead grasses in white. By the time Aspen reached him, he could barely feel their fingers against his numb arm.

"We have to run," they said breathlessly, eyes wild as they rushed him and Cal toward the path. "We have to—"

Another blink, and Aspen was gone. A thorny whip tore them away from the others and dragged them back next to Shrike in a sharp, shrinking cage of briar.

"Aspen!" Damir bolted back but waved Nik away. "Keep going!"

Nik didn't listen nor did Emry and Cal; they all descended on the cage, pulling hard on the makeshift prison wherever they could find space. Inside, Shrike yowled and slashed at the growth with his paws, while Aspen tried to push the humans away.

"No, you have to"—they flickered—"you have to keep running!"

Emry ignored him and yanked out his knife with shaky hands. It had done the trick before, hadn't it? All he needed to do was—

He brought it down, and its edge glanced off the thick vines.

"Come on, come on..." He tried again; nothing. Panic buoyed his voice. "Cut *through*!"

He lifted the knife again. Something flashed white, the vines shrank—

He stared at the blade. The knife hadn't touched the thorns at all that time.

"Do it again." Cal tugged on the withered vines, snapping them easily. "Whatever it was, do it again!"

As if recognizing the small victory, the wind whipped harder, and snow gathered faster on their shoulders and in their hair. Beyond them, Emry could barely see the path out. If he didn't get the spirits out soon, none of them would make it back to the Rest.

His grip tightened around the blade, then loosened. It hadn't been the knife. It hadn't helped now, and it hadn't helped before, had it? What else had he been doing? Nothing. Just shouting—

He stepped back. Just shouting. Just using sound.

Without thinking, he swung his lute around and strummed a chord. Any chord, latching onto the sound and rushing one single, magical command out with it—

Break.

The thorns shattered with a scream. Behind them, the spirits gasped for air, and Aspen stumbled into Emry's arms.

"You—!" Their eyes went wide, but Emry just reached for their half-frozen lute and slung it over his shoulder.

"Later!"

Holding tight to both Cal and Aspen's hands, Emry followed the others down the mountain, hoping beyond hope that the path had magically shortened since their ascent. But Yarrow refused to let them escape so easily—with a shrieking howl, the snow descended in hard, icy droves, trying to separate them as they ran. Somewhere to Emry's left, Damir slipped and stumbled away from them. Off to his right, he could no longer see Cal's face. Soon, the only evidence he had that he wasn't alone were fumbling moments of touch—Cal's grip on his hand, Aspen's fingers pulling on his, Shrike's bulk huddling against his shin.

"Damir?" he tried to yell, squinting against the snow to search for the others. "Nik?"

Someone stumbled into his back—Nik, his dark beard barely standing out in the white fog around them.

"Is Damir with you?" he asked in a panic, then threw his voice out to the trees. "*Damir!*"

The wind ripped away Damir's weak reply. "Keep running—!"

Nik lunged forward, but Aspen grabbed his hand, their wide green eyes glowing in the storm.

"Don't! If you leave us now, we won't be able to find you again."

"But he's out there—!"

"And we'll find him together." They held up their hands; a shield flickered to life around them, a white bubble against white snow. For a brief second, it held the ice at bay and quelled the sharp, freezing wind...

But Yarrow had siphoned too much of Aspen's energy. The shield sputtered and fell, sweeping everyone back into a whirlwind of cold. Emry's breaths grew shallow. They had no hope of finding Damir, nor even moving from their spot on the path. Snowdrifts piled around their feet. Both lutes on Emry's back felt like ice cubes pressing into his clothing. Shrike grew smaller and smaller, his lynx shape impossible to maintain against such a deluge.

"Em?" Cal's voice wavered. In jerky, shivering movements, he pulled her close, taking little comfort in her arms wrapped around his torso. He tried to form commands in his head—*warm, melt*—but instead of words, he could only cough. His throat was frozen, his voice raw from breathing in the frigid air—

A new presence entered his mind like a shadow, large and barreling through the storm.

"Aspen?" He quickly wrapped as much of himself around Cal as he could. "What is that?"

"What is *what*?" Cal's voice was muffled against his chest. But Aspen didn't respond—their wild gaze tracked some sort of movement out in the snow, and at Emry's feet, Shrike began to cry out. Emry stiffened and prepared himself to shield Cal any way he could. If it was Yarrow, he'd make sure its thorns struck him first. It was all he could do now.

But no thorns came, no roots or sharp branches. The presence kept lumbering forward, steady and…warm. Warm, earthy. Raging in a way that shot through Yarrow's anger like sunlight—

A massive elk stormed through the brush, its form a stark, deep brown against the snowstorm. With a raging bellow, it stomped on the ground with both front legs, and summer returned to the path. The snow around them melted with a hiss; the fog slithered away. Warmth shot back painfully into Emry's fingers and toes.

Then the great elk, antlers draped in curtains of moss, huffed and swung their round, angry gaze on Aspen.

"What have you *done*, young one?" Cedar demanded—but before Aspen could defend themself, Pigeon flapped between them.

"Never mind that right now!" she shouted. "Follow us!"

Emry was fully prepared to melt like the snow in relief—but there was no time. All through the surrounding forest, the storm still raged, and Nik stumbled forward, hands pleading.

"My little brother's still out there. A man with blonde hair—"

"Damir! I'll find him!" Pigeon darted off into the snow, her feathers trimmed in ice-encrusted flowers. Cedar pawed the ground with a heavy hoof.

"Come with me," they said. "There are others of your kind beyond the bridge."

"The bridge," Cal repeated, then frantically extricated herself from Emry's arms. "Wait. Cedar, you can use the bridge!"

Her legs still numb, she struggled to run alongside Aspen and the elk, but her words flowed faster than the snowmelt downhill.

"The root barrier we made yesterday," she breathed. "You could grow the trees upwards as well. Keep Yarrow from following us into the village!"

Together, they burst out of the tree line, the village in question just ahead. Under any other circumstance, the Rest would have looked beautiful after such a snowstorm. Dark stone under white blankets, a half-frozen river glittering in the sunlight. Today, the sight only sapped life away from the village. The only signs of hope were those waiting for them at the end of the chase—Harvey and Iris, pacing at the bridge beyond the northern ruins. Emry was relieved to see Damir limping ahead of them, Pigeon perched on his shoulder. And two other spirits, a hawk and a badger, hovered in wait at the edge of the ruins.

"Aspen!" The badger hurried toward them first, her voice just as panicked as the humans'. "What can we do? How can we help?"

Aspen wasted no time. In the spirits' presence, their form had returned to its full strength—and on Emry's back, ice fell in shards from their lute.

"We'll make Cal's barrier." They looked at Shrike and Cedar. "All of us."

The ragged group stumbled through the icy ruins and across the bridge, then parted in two exhausted halves—the humans into the arms of Harvey and Iris, and the spirits to the water's edge.

"Uncle Miri!" Iris helped Damir onto a bench while Emry and Cal fumbled with a blanket. "You're hurt!"

Damir rolled his eyes. "I'm fine."

"He's hurt." Nik blew past them in a rush. "I'm getting the bandages—"

"You're getting hypothermia if you don't put this on first." Harvey shoved a coat against the man's chest with a surprising amount of force. "Fire's already going in the hall. All of you, get over there and—"

The earth jolted under their feet.

For a moment, Emry could almost hear what had caused it—the spirits' collective command shouted into the earth. A silent plea for the rue and rowan to defend more than just the soil. To break out from the stones, to defend every inch of the southern village with all the energy they could muster.

And the earth obeyed. Trees burst up at the base of the bridge and ripped up stones around them. Dark green leaves and fierce red berries tangled with the yellow rue flowers, forming a jungle around windows, doors, rooftops. One by one, every branch grew to stand sentinel, until nothing of Yarrow's cold and death could take one step into what remained of Raven's Rest.

THE SPIRIT'S CURSE

As the spirits stepped back from the tangled bridge, the cold slunk away in defeat. Snowmelt dripped from the rooftops, and the summer sun worked quickly to reclaim the air. Emry took a full, deep, warm breath and relaxed against Cal, who half-collapsed onto his shoulder in relief. Looking up at the strong, vibrant trees, he felt the safest he had since arriving in the village.

As he held Cal tight and kissed her hair, Harvey shuffled forward to greet the newcomers.

"My new friends." He spread his arms out wide. "I cannot thank you enough for the gift you've given us today. We have nothing to offer you but our welcome." He smiled at Aspen. "It isn't much, but—how would you feel about another yeda for our new guests?"

CHAPTER
EIGHTEEN

ASPEN

AGAINST THE HARROWING backdrop of the forest and Yarrow's memories, the gathering hall took on the air of a festival.

It was warm. It was safe. It had *friends*, old and new, all huddling and talking in the light of the hearth. Even the hall itself seemed to enjoy having newcomers. It let their chatter linger in the rafters, warming up the vast space as much as the fireplace did.

And Harvey—bless him—wasted no time in having the spirits sit, or approximate sitting, for their yeda.

"Now, you stay put while I fetch the tea." The old man shuffled off to the kitchen, while Otto did his due diligence and sniffed each of the spirits in turn.

Nik, who hadn't once sat still since entering the hall, tried to beat Harvey to the door. "I'll get the—"

Harvey waved him back. "You'll get nothing but an earful if you try to do any more work today."

"But I haven't done any—!"

"What, *surviving* isn't work?"

Surviving certainly felt like work to Aspen. After Yarrow's attack and all the effort they had poured into the barrier, they could hardly keep up their human shape. When they went to the hearth to check on Emry and Cal, they almost walked right through the armchairs.

"So, you think it works with any sound?" Cal was saying in a low voice, her questions further muffled by the blanket wrapped around them both. Emry nodded as he rubbed life back into one of her hands. To Aspen's immense relief, both appeared largely unhurt, if still a little cold.

"It's not just my voice," Emry replied. "It worked when I—" He looked up at Aspen and smiled. "Here to join us?"

He held up the edge of the blanket in welcome. Aspen gladly wiggled their way into the huddle, wanting to join the conversation about Emry's magic—but Cal immediately reached for them with her free hand.

"That barrier you all made was simply incredible." Her eyes sparked. "You *must* tell me the specifics of how you built it. And did Cedar and Pigeon tell you how they found us? And Yarrow, what exactly did they reveal to you about—?"

Emry kissed her knuckles. "Darling, I think Aspen needs a bit of rest before they get interrogated."

"Of course, of course." She drew back and wrapped her arms around Emry's bicep. "Are the other spirits settling in all right?"

She tried to peek up over the armchairs, her curiosity back in full force, while by the tables, Iris, Harvey, and Damir all fussed and flitted. Aspen smiled. Humans were terribly fragile, yes—but they were also wonderfully resilient.

"Are *you* settling in all right?" they asked, noting Emry's wince at Cal's movement. They instinctively reached for the flowers in their lute, hoping to grow a moonflower for the pain—but all the blooms were still half-frozen from the storm. "I'm sorry, I—"

"It's fine." Emry gently touched their wrist. "Just a small flare from all the running."

"Aspen?" Pigeon called from the table.

THE SPIRIT'S CURSE

"Go join them." Emry nodded toward her. "We aren't going anywhere, I promise."

"But your magic—"

Cal pulled her blanket close and rested her cheek against Emry's shoulder. "We can discuss all of it later. Emry's right—keep up your strength and go be with your friends."

Despite their reluctance, Aspen's chest warmed at the word. Friends, their *friends* had arrived. Cedar, Pigeon, Badger, and Hawk all sat—or hunched, or perched, or stood—at the long table in the hall, taking in the human structure and murmuring to themselves.

Aspen had never been so delighted, nor so utterly confused, to see them.

When they approached, Pigeon hopped up onto the wooden planks at the edge of the table. "The nice man is getting us some tea." She lowered her voice. "Does he know we can't drink tea?"

"'Course he does. He's just being nice." They cleared their throat. "Pigeon, not that I'm not happy to see you, but… How? And why?"

"Sage and Riley, and Sage and Riley," Pigeon said proudly. "What, you thought they didn't share your letters with us?"

The warmth in Aspen's chest grew. "You came because of our letters?"

Badger toyed with the necklace of flowers around her neck, just as anxious as she had been when she and Hawk had joined the circle back in Vornik. "Sage was convinced a forest spirit was going to poke your head off with a giant thorn."

"And Riley wanted to send a champion to fight in her stead," Hawk said proudly.

Pigeon tilted her head. "Honestly, neither of them was that far off."

"There are other spirits as well," Cedar said. Even with their limbs folded up on the floor, their antlers branched high above the other spirits. "Not here, but beyond the mountains and in the villages leading back to Vornik. The raven you sent was…quaint…but Pigeon communicating with them will be faster."

"Really?" Aspen tried to seek them out, eager to sense this chain of spirits—but their weakened reach fizzled at the edge of the stone plaza. They'd have to try again tomorrow.

Once Harvey arrived with the tea, they all declared that the liquid smelled very nice and welcoming and began asking a dozen questions about Otto. The only spirit that didn't acknowledge the tea, the chatter, or the dog was Shrike. He curled up at the base of the table, staring into nothing.

"Shrike—?" Aspen started, but the hall doors groaned open, letting in a bedraggled Nik from his inspection of the new tree barrier.

"It's holding just fine, and the snow should be fully melted within the hour," he muttered, tugging gloves off his hands. "Will need to check on the garden next. Make sure it didn't all freeze over."

Damir, his ankle propped up on a barstool, nodded over to the table of spirits. "Wouldn't worry on that front, Nik. I think you've got a few folks willing to help get the garden back on its feet."

Nik stared at the table, his lips pressed into a line. Now that he was back in the safety of the gathering hall, his stoicism had returned. "Suppose I should thank you all for helping us get away from Yarrow."

"You suppose?" Iris said, slurping tea alongside Badger.

Nik opened his mouth, then gave a tired nod. "Thank you," he said, strength returning to his voice. "For helping us and protecting the Rest. Your barrier is..." He twisted his gloves in his hands. "Well, I can't say I've ever seen anything like it. But it'll protect us, that much is certain."

One by one, the humans dragged chairs over to the table to join the spirits in their yeda—but the group's questions far outweighed the welcoming air the tea had briefly provided.

Pigeon went first, her voice almost jarring in the hall's silence. "I don't understand this Yarrow. Why would it attack you? You never meant it any harm."

Shrike flexed his claws but said nothing. Aspen straightened and tried to solidify their form, gathering the half-frozen energy left in their lute.

"We didn't threaten it. Shrike and I were just trying to ask it about going back to sleep."

Hawk perked up. "What did it say, then?"

Some part of Aspen had hoped that the spirits wouldn't ask that question. That they had forgotten, or had decided they didn't want to know the answer after all.

Aspen certainly didn't want to know, now that they had heard it.

"I should...start from the beginning."

THEY DESCRIBED everything they had seen. From their journey in the tunnel, to the dead spirits' fanes, to Yarrow's memories of killing them. The deeper they waded into the memories, the more their human audience stiffened, as if they still stood in Yarrow's frost. Iris looked pale; Cal kept twisting the pendant at her neck. Emry and Damir just stared at their respective cups of tea.

The spirits, on the other hand, couldn't sit still.

"Why would it do such a thing?" Pigeon flapped hurriedly from rafter to rafter, the flowers on her legs shedding petals left and right. "Any spirit I know would *never*. Never in a thousand seasons—"

"Yarrow might well have lived a thousand seasons," Cedar replied, their voice as deep as ever—but even their words faltered. "Even through its memories, it is unclear how long it may have slept up north before being woken."

Iris scooted closer to Nik. "Is there a way to make it go back north?"

"Or go away entirely?" Damir cut in bitterly. "It doesn't belong here. That much we know. But sending it north won't help, either." He glanced at Aspen, and his gaze softened. "Tree kid, I know you won't like this, but Yarrow is a threat to everyone in southern Envis.

Possibly beyond, if it gets through the mountains. If we're going to solve this...the solution should be permanent."

Even with the memories lingering in their head, even with their anger still simmering, Aspen reeled back in horror.

"What, *kill* Yarrow?"

They couldn't do it. Killing spirits was what Yarrow did. It was against everything they knew.

"No, we could..." They scrambled for another idea. "We could convince it—no, *command* it to leave. To not...bother anyone else again..."

The words all rung hollow. Words and pleas would do nothing now. They had tried that already.

Cedar bowed their head toward Aspen, their tone both strong and gentle.

"In your grove. Do you allow everything within it to flourish?"

Aspen frowned. "Of course," they began—then hesitated. "Well... no. Not entirely."

Sometimes the mint tangled up with the honeysuckle and they had to cut it back. And every now and then, they had to dig out the ragweed. And there was seasonal culling, weeding...all trims they did without a second thought. But surely that didn't—

"And the wolves in Tazlo," Cedar pressed. "Do they subsist on air alone?"

Aspen didn't have to answer. Of course they didn't. They killed. They killed so they and their pups would survive. Death allowed them to live. That was simply what nature did.

Cedar gave a slow nod at Aspen's silence.

"If we allow Yarrow to flourish, it will soon be the only creature left in the forest," they said. "Weed it out now, and Raven's Rest—all of Envis—has another chance at life."

Aspen balled their hands into fists, then released them. They hated it. They hated the corner they had been backed into, the violent words spoken over a welcoming yeda.

THE SPIRIT'S CURSE

But Cedar was right—it was simply what nature had to do. "All right," they said quietly. "Yarrow must be defeated."

CHAPTER NINETEEN

ASPEN

By the time they left the gathering hall, every trace of the snowstorm was gone. Puddles of melted snow were evaporating in the sunlight, giving the impression of a village washed clean by rain. Iris couldn't help herself—she stretched her arms out to the fresh summer sun, absorbing the warmth and letting it chase away the last of the chill.

For a moment, Aspen stood there with her, wishing the warmth would chase away the murky feelings that lingered around their decision.

When they had suggested a bit of rest before making any further plans, the other spirits had quickly agreed. All of their groves, from lute to vine to moss, still needed time to shake off the ice and soak up the snowmelt. A forest clearing would be ideal for this, Aspen thought. Surrounded by trees and shrubs, not metal and stone.

But straying too far from the humans, even south where the forest was safe, felt too risky—so Shrike led them back to the side yard by the cottage.

"S'not much, but I think we can all fit," he said—the first words he had uttered in over an hour. The yard wasn't much, but the patch of grass and overgrown garden did indeed fit them all. Cedar settled into the middle of the garden and let flowers form a comfortable bed around their limbs. Pigeon and Hawk fluttered into the apple tree, its leaves still dripping water from the storm. Badger paced nervously around the tree trunk.

"About Yarrow's"—she wrung her dark paws—"*solution* to the sleeping problem."

"Despicable," Cedar muttered. "Disgusting to even consider."

"But what if..." Badger hesitated to even say it. "What if that's the *only* way?"

Pigeon hopped confidently along her tree branch. "It can't be. Just because we don't have the answers yet, doesn't mean they don't exist. That's what Lydia always says."

Hawk flicked his tail. "And Yarrow is just one spirit in one forest. There are others, aren't there? That man Zeke showed me something he called a *map*."

He looked around, expecting the others to be awed by his new word—but Pigeon bowled right over his presentation.

"I bet you Cal has one of those!" she said eagerly. "After we, uh, you know"—she glanced at Aspen—"we could always try the next forest! Meet new spirits. Ask them if they know anything."

Cedar nuzzled the soil by their leg; a legion of bright pumpkin flowers all bloomed in unison. "We would be wise not to limit ourselves to forests alone. Lakes may offer older spirits. Oceans, as well, if we can reach such a thing."

The word *ocean* sent them into a tizzy of excitement.

"I've never seen one, have you?" Pigeon peered down at Badger. "I hear it's very large."

Badger gulped. "Hopefully not too large. I get lost so easily."

Cedar shook their antlers, moss fluttering in the breeze. "You will not be alone. We will all be together, will we not?"

Mutterings of agreement gradually dissolved into silent, expectant looks at Aspen, who could do nothing but fidget.

Of course the answers were out there somewhere. They were out there, and Aspen had promised to find them, no matter what it took. On that topic, Cal and Emry would have strongly agreed with them.

But Cal and Emry hadn't agreed to travel to other forests, or lakes, or the ocean. They had agreed to stay for a week.

"I could...always ask Emry and Cal for a map of the oceans?" they offered weakly. That seemed to satisfy the other spirits for now—they all immediately delved into various rumors they had heard about the great body of water.

"I hear there's very large fish," Hawk said proudly. "Larger-than-this-*tree* sort of fish."

Pigeon snorted. "That's not possible. Have you ever seen a land animal bigger than this tree?"

Badger lifted a paw. "Ooh! Ooh, I have! There was a bear once who—"

While they all chattered, Aspen looked around for the one missing voice: Shrike, who hadn't chimed in a single word on oceans or travel. He crouched near the fence in the back, watching the others silently.

Aspen carefully set down their lute in a patch of sun and sat on the grass next to him.

"A copper for your thoughts?" they asked. Shrike frowned at them.

"What?"

"I don't know. Emry says it sometimes. I don't actually have a copper for you." They tugged at a few pieces of grass, willed them to grow long, then began to braid them together. "Will you tell me your thoughts anyway?"

Shrike slowly relaxed from his crouch, tucking his paws underneath him—but he still couldn't bring himself to look at Aspen.

"I was thinking about home," he said quietly. "When I left it."

Aspen kept braiding. They knew there was more behind the words, but they had to stay quiet in order for Shrike to let them out.

"I woke up after you sent out the warning," Shrike finally started.

"Right before the wave hit the edge of the Cima mountains. I was fine—I mean, obviously I was fine, I'm *here*—but I didn't know what to do after that. I didn't know what was going on."

Aspen stiffened. Yarrow's memory flashed through their head, of trying to go back to sleep, only for the soil to reject it.

"Turned out farmers lived near my grove. Didn't take them long after the wave to learn that spirits were actually real." The nub of Shrike's tail twitched. "They had just gone through something called a drought. A long one. I didn't know what it was until they brought their torches and yelled at me about it."

Aspen's heart dropped, and they looked up from their grass braid. Even now, they could smell the lingering scent of ash on Shrike's words. "No. They didn't."

"They did. They set fire to the whole grove, starting with an old fane at the corner. Didn't leave a single tree standing." Shrike suddenly stood, his claws flexing angrily into the soil. "If they had just asked, I could've grown something for them. If they had just— just *talked* to me, rather than attack my grove, I could've—"

Aspen set a hand on his fur, their fingers sinking deep into the thick layers. "I know."

Shrike huffed and shook out his legs, as if shrugging off the anger —but he couldn't settle down. He paced around Aspen, grass growing in sharp blades wherever his paws stepped.

"I wandered around the mountains after that," he continued. "Played some tricks on the humans. Changed the roads, that sort of thing. Was a good distraction for a bit. Eventually, I found a few spirits who kept mentioning someone named Aspen. The one who warned us all about the wave. The one who saved us."

Aspen flinched instinctively, but there was no bitterness to his last few words. Just sadness and exhaustion.

"I thought going back to sleep would help me forget. Forget about the fire and the stupid farmers. And now, seeing what Yarrow did..." Shrike finally sat, facing north, and his voice almost went too quiet for Aspen to hear. "What if I had come across another fane in the Cima mountains? Would it have taken me a thousand seasons to go mad and kill a spirit in order to sleep?"

Aspen shook their head. "You aren't like them. Not at all—"

Shrike rounded on them. "But I could have been! If I hadn't found you at the festival, if I hadn't come here—what if I had gone down that same path? What if I..." Fear clouded his eyes, and his voice cracked. "I don't want to be like Yarrow."

"You won't." Aspen knelt and placed a hand on the lynx's shoulder; a sad, broken purr thrummed underneath his fur. "You won't be like that spirit. You'll have me, and Cedar, and Pigeon, and everyone else to help you. Even though we don't know what's next, and we don't have any answers..." They swallowed. "We'll figure it out together. All of us."

CHAPTER
TWENTY

EMRY

DESPITE THE EARLY MORNING SQUAWKING, Emry had come around a bit on the old raven tower.

Yes, it had an impressive amount of birds, creaky steps, and... droppings. But once he had won over the birds with Harvey's guidance and a few berries, he found it wasn't a bad place to write letters and think.

"Harvey?" he called from the doorway, paper in hand. "You in here?"

Though no one responded to him, proof of life filtered back to him in the form of footsteps, giggles, and something new—Harvey's singing.

Eager not to miss whatever was happening, Emry hurried up the steps as fast as his achy knees deigned to take him. He had never heard Harvey sing before, and it was just as he would have imagined it: a warm, throaty bass, and a delightful rumble that only came with age.

And when he reached the top platform, he found that Harvey had an audience for his song.

"One, two—no, no, your left foot, my dear," he instructed Iris, then began to clap and sing again. As he sang, Iris hopped through a dancing routine with inordinate focus, her tongue sticking out as she landed each step. "Yes, that's it! Now, spin, and..."

She spun, then curtsied to him with a final laugh. He grinned and bowed as low as he could manage—then upon seeing Emry, raised his hands in faux regret.

"Ah! You could have had a dance partner after all, Iris."

She blushed and giggled; Emry held up a hand.

"Please, you don't want me as a dance partner. Just ask Cal—she's lost at least three toes to my clumsiness." One of the ravens landed on the sill near him, and he stroked its beak. "It's a lovely dance. May I ask what it's for?"

Iris' joy faded. "Nothing," she said quickly. "It's just—it's nothing. I'll see you at supper, Harvey!"

With a wave, she hurried down the steps, a few of the ravens gliding alongside her. Harvey watched her go with a bittersweet smile.

"The midsummer festival," he explained once the door below had closed. "It would have been next week."

Emry's heart sank. Iris may have several years' worth of decent festival memories—but Harvey had decades' worth to remember, and they all clearly played before his eyes now. Emry set aside his half-finished letter and leaned against the sill. "What was it like?"

Harvey busied himself with pouring birdseed into his hand. "Oh, I'm sure you've been to more exciting festivals in your time."

"Vidanyan festivals, sure." Emry scooped up some birdseed as well. "But not any Envisian festivals." Then he smiled—he knew what question would make Harvey talk. "Did Damir dance at any of them?"

It worked; Harvey grinned from ear to ear and leaned in, as if imparting deep secrets. "Don't tell anyone, but when he was a young boy, he was the one who danced the *most*."

After that, there was no stopping Harvey. He described how Damir had made friends with every traveling bard and wailed when his mother tried to get him to stop dancing to the music. Nik, on the other hand, only danced when there was a pretty girl to woo—the rest of his time was spent trying to join his father at the gambling tables. Partly for the shiny coins, and partly for the conversation: leaders from Warwick and Beldam would ride in for the whole week, all serious and authoritative and the very people Nik wanted to be.

"And Yvette—oh, dear Yvette." Harvey chuckled to himself as he wiped birdseed off his palm. "Nearly broke someone's hand for trying to steal her pie before the contest. But when little Iris took a swipe of the whipped cream right before judging?" He held up a hand. "Nothing. Said that sweet angel deserved all the cream in the world and just patted over the spot with a knife like it hadn't happened."

Emry could almost see the festival—the pie tables, the dancers, the lights strung about the plaza. The visitors from Warwick, Beldam, and beyond, turning Raven's Rest into a bastion of joy.

He couldn't blame Iris for not wanting to venture back into those memories, given the current state of the village.

"Well, I'm afraid I've talked your ear off." Harvey gestured to Emry's forgotten letter on the sill. "You take your time with that letter. The birds aren't going anywhere, and neither is Vornik. I'll send it off when you're ready." He paused at the top of the steps. "And thank you, son."

Emry looked up in confusion; he didn't think he had fed the birds all that much. "For what?"

"For all of it. For bringing the spirits here. For fighting back against Yarrow."

Joslyn landed on his shoulder and cawed; Harvey stroked her beak.

"For giving me and my birds a chance at getting our village back.

I truly wish you could've seen it. And maybe we'll get you on that stage one day, eh? Would do the village some good to have some music there again."

Emry tried to add confidence to his voice; it was the least he could give to Harvey. "We'll get Yarrow out of here, then come visit again once everyone's back and settled. I promise."

Once Harvey shuffled down the stairs, Emry finally turned his attention back to the half-finished letter intended for Vornik—the one Aspen hadn't added anything to the other day. He certainly owed Sage and Riley a great deal of thanks of his own. Without Cedar, Pigeon, and the others, he would be a frozen icicle in Yarrow's forest.

But his troupe wouldn't be satisfied with simple thanks, and Zeke wouldn't be satisfied with Cal's summarized reports of her findings. Those in Vornik wanted both of them back. They had lives to resume, after all—and not just the doldrums of responsibilities and research. They had family to visit, friends to tend to, music to play...

"Good morning, Cal!" Aspen's voice echoed below the tower, quickly followed by a chorus of other voices and animal sounds. They had stayed in the yard with the other spirits last night, talking until dawn. That morning, the little garden overflowed with the natural side effects of a spirit's presence: flowers, vegetables, fruit...

Iris had been overjoyed at the sight. Emry had felt queasy, somehow.

He pushed the feeling aside and finished what was assuredly an unsatisfactory letter to Vornik. A quick, downplayed recount of Yarrow's attack; a paragraph of thanks for sending the spirits to help; and a terribly vague estimate for when they might come home.

Aspen, Cal, and I should be on the path home in perhaps a few—

The spirits' chatter grew stronger as they passed by the tower. Aspen laughed loudly at something Pigeon said.

Emry bit his lip and crossed out the sentence.

Will be home as soon as possible.

By the time he wandered downstairs and left the letter with Harvey—combining it with Cal's research notes for Zeke, of course—only Aspen and Cal remained near the tower. The other spirits had moved on, wandering toward the barrier they had grown the day before.

"Off to join them?" Emry asked. Aspen held their hands behind their back, the flowers in their hair furling and unfurling in nervous thought.

"Yes," they said with a blink, as if just discovering that Emry was there. "Yes. Um, soon. They're going to check on the trees. Make sure they're still holding. Then later, we'll, um..."

They let out a breath.

"I don't know how to defeat a spirit. I don't know what to tell them. How to—to command them, or—"

"My dearest." Cal set a hand on their shoulder. "You cannot command anything until you have a plan. All you have to do is start the conversation with them."

Emry prayed that a conversation with the other spirits would be enough—he himself didn't know where to start when it came to taking down a spirit—but he couldn't show any of that doubt to Aspen.

"This isn't all on you." He nodded along with Cal. "You have other spirits with you now. You'll come up with something together."

Aspen pressed their lips into a line. "Together. Right. That's what I told them. Together to find answers, no matter what."

But the words didn't seem to bolster their resolve very much. Emry quickly searched for something comforting, something they both enjoyed.

"You don't have to join the other spirits now, right?" he said. "Why don't we dabble with the song for a bit?"

Aspen paused. "The song?"

"Yeah, our song." He shrugged. "It helped you relax back when we were basking. Maybe it'll help you now."

To be honest, he quite liked the idea himself. He had played for Yarrow yesterday, but playing a relaxing melody in a garden was worlds away from that poor, dry excuse for a Sada festival ground—

"No, that's all right," Aspen said. "I should join the other spirits. Get the conversation started, like you both said."

"Oh." Emry's calming thoughts stopped short. "Yes, of course."

Aspen drew themselves up, then gave them both a hug. "Thank you. You're the best."

Then they dashed off to join the other spirits, their confidence returned.

If only Emry could say the same for himself.

An hour later, he stood in the garden the spirits had left behind, with just himself and his lute.

Aspen was off making themself useful to the cause, so he determined that he should be, too. He did have a bit of magic to sort out, after all.

He played a few test chords to clear his head. The music itself didn't reach for his magic nor was the sound a requirement to use his power. He could grow small, simple things just fine on his own. Leaves, grass, flowers...

But pushing his magic through sound—even just through humming—made it flow so much easier. Like playing on an instrument crafted by a master, rather than an old, broken hand-me-down.

He turned to the garden flourishing around him and reached back into his memory. All those times his magic had felt stronger during concerts; all those times he had noticed tiny flowers growing around him while playing...

He had always assumed it was because Aspen was beside him.

In some way, the realization made him feel worse than before, and the next few chords came out off-key and jangled. He huffed and tried again—

"Em?" Cal leaned against the back door of the cottage, a fresh cup of tea in her hand. "My love, are you researching your magic without me?"

"What?" Emry pretended to hide his lute behind his back. "No! Darling, I'd never so much as form a hypothesis without you."

She smiled and wandered out to join him. "May I ask what you've discovered so far?"

"Well, I..." He pulled his lute back around and stared at it in thought.

This lute wasn't the one that Aspen had first lived in—that one firmly belonged to Aspen's grove now—but in honor of them, the instrument had been carved with aspen leaves along its face. The leaves fanned outward, dappled in the warm sunlight filtering through the apple tree.

A knot formed in Emry's throat.

"I've discovered I don't want to do this without Aspen," he said quietly.

Cal's smile faded, and in that moment, he silently begged her to reassure him. To say that Aspen wasn't going anywhere, that they'd come home to Vornik like they were supposed to, answers or no. That other spirits could lead the charge for answers in their stead, now that Yarrow had given them worse than nothing.

But she just laid her hands over his.

"I know." She softened her voice. "But Aspen is their own being. They can choose their own path."

He didn't want to say it. "And if that path is with the other spirits and not with us?"

She wiped a tear off his cheek, her own eyes shimmering. "Then we'll make them swear to write to us every day, won't we?"

Emry gave a hollow laugh, but inside, his heart was in shards. It had only been a few years, but he could hardly recall a time before Aspen. They couldn't just *leave*. Emry couldn't do any of this without them—

"Karic?" Damir's voice floated in from the road. "Where is he? Karic, any update from the menagerie?"

Emry swiped at his face and squeezed Cal's hands before turning. "Over here, Damir!"

His manager strode into the garden, still favoring his left leg but trying not to show it. In classic Damir fashion, he ignored all of Iris and Nik's attempts to get him to rest and take weight off it. "Ah. There you are. The menagerie, any updates from them?"

Emry frowned. "Menagerie?"

"You know, the other spirits." Damir waved his pipe toward the barrier. "Nik wants to know if they've got a plan of attack yet."

"I don't want to *know*." Nik appeared behind him in a huff. "I want to *plan* the attack. It's still an Envisian problem, and Envis needs to help—"

"Take care of its problems, yes, yes," Harvey called from his cottage, shoving open the window. "Look at the lot of good that's done us so far. Iris, have you got the berries?"

"Yes!" Iris' voice shot out from the road. "The good ones, not Yarrow's. They're nice and ripe and—!" She joined them all in the garden, a basket at her hip. "What's going on? If I didn't know any better, I'd say Yarrow put a storm on all your faces."

Emry winced; he hadn't meant for his own gloomy mood to spread. But the weight of the lute on his back gave him an idea. He had promised himself some relaxing music before—there was no reason the others couldn't all share in it.

"I must apologize—I've been a terrible guest." He bowed to Iris. "You asked for a reprise of a song the other day and I never followed through. Why don't I play it for you now?"

Iris brightened, a deep contrast to the others' sour faces. "Oh, could you, please?" She tugged on her father's arm. "Papa, you'll love this. He's a *good* bard. Not like some of those singers that used to come down from Illev."

"Of course he's a good one." Damir sniffed. "As if I'd hire an Illev singer..."

"All right, all right." Nik nodded to the road. "Hall's nice and cool this time of day. Iris, bring along those berries. Harvey, do you still have some of that wine left from Beldam?"

"It's got your name on it, my boy."

As they filtered away toward the hall, a knot crept back into Emry's throat. He couldn't recall the last time he had performed without Aspen around, either on stage or watching him. But, he supposed, performing was one of the only things he was capable of on his own. It would be fine.

"I should go check on the menagerie." Cal kissed him, then briefly stroked his cheek. "But the music is a good idea. Thank you, Em."

He gave a weak smile. "It's the least I could do."

CHAPTER
TWENTY-ONE

ASPEN

WHEN ASPEN REACHED THE BARRIER, they hoped the spirits had started the planning without them. Perhaps they'd already come up with an idea or two—or three, if they were lucky. But when they arrived, it was difficult to pluck their ideas out of all their bickering.

"What's wrong with attacking it directly?" Shrike demanded of Cedar. "Aspen saw that big tree in its memories. I can feel it up at the peak. *That's* where it lives. We just get ourselves together and head straight there."

Cedar sniffed. "Attacking it directly would be utterly foolish. No doubt it will use its multiple strongholds to sustain its defense—"

"Then we find the strongholds and take 'em all down at once, like I said!" Pigeon pecked impatiently at Cedar's antler. "It'll be easy—"

"Easy?" Badger gasped, already half hiding behind a bush. "*Easy?* There's only six of us!"

Hawk swooped from a window to a tree branch above Shrike. "Please. Doesn't Cedar count as at least three of us by themself?"

The spirits had all nestled themselves in nooks and crannies naturally formed by the tree barrier. Cedar and Pigeon rested right in the middle of the stone path leading up to the bridge, while Shrike crouched on the last bit of balustrade not covered by leaves. Badger, just as before, couldn't sit still, shuffling from bush to bush as if testing out different hiding spots, while Hawk simply watched from above. So surrounded by dense plant growth and spirits, Aspen almost felt like they were back in a friendlier forest.

Almost.

Upon seeing them, Shrike hopped down from the balustrade. "Thank the rotting leaves. Can *you* talk some sense into them?"

Pigeon puffed herself up. "It would help if any of your plans made sense in the first place."

That got them all bickering again until Aspen held up both hands.

"Why don't we go back through your ideas together, so I can hear them?" they tried. "Sort out the good and the bad parts, then, you know, take the good parts and—"

"Well, that rules out all of Shrike's ideas," Hawk muttered. Shrike bristled.

"Come down here and say that again!"

Hawk gave a screech; Shrike yowled right back.

"Will you two *behave*?" Cedar stood, sending Pigeon darting off to a rooftop. Badger ducked behind another bush.

"At this rate, it'll be real winter by the time we sort this out," she moaned.

Aspen passed a hand over their face. "We'll sort it out, we just have to—"

"What, too afraid to come up here, kitty cat?" Hawk shouted down at Shrike. Shrike began to sprout wings.

"Oh, I'll come up there—"

"Is everything all right here?"

Shrike froze, half-formed wings still stuck to his back. Aspen turned. Cal stood behind them in the sunlight, her short smile not reaching her eyes.

Oh, no. Aspen knew that look. They found themselves on the receiving end of that look whenever they decided to use something unusual as a planter at home. Like the teapot that had been gifted from her cousin. Or that one boot Emry thought he had lost.

(Aspen had learned that day that dirt was very hard to get out of boots.)

"It's fine," they lied. "Just—you know, throwing out ideas—"

"And hurling insults, it seems." She moved forward with a slow, confident stride, her gaze landing on each of the spirits in turn. "I understand this situation is highly unusual, but every moment we do not form a plan together is another moment Yarrow has to form a counter against us." Her eyes narrowed. "You all came here of your own accord to help Aspen, and of course we thank you for that. If you'd rather not participate in the next action required to keep this village alive, you are free to head back to Vornik at your earliest convenience."

None of the spirits moved.

"Thank you. Now"—she pulled her pencil out from behind her ear—"I believe several of you had ideas to offer. My research department prefers to hear out all ideas first. Rule none of them out until we have a list to narrow down. Is that acceptable to you?"

It took Aspen a moment to realize she was deferring to them.

"Yes." They straightened. "Yes, of course. Shrike, Pigeon, Cedar, and Hawk had ideas. I'd like to listen to all of them. Please."

Cal's list took shape within minutes. Shrike, naturally, wanted to attack Yarrow where it currently resided (a strategy not at all different from his plan onstage back in Vornik). Pigeon and Cedar both argued in favor of attacking the strongholds—the pockets where Yarrow held more sway, where their presence hovered more strongly.

"I can find all the spots," Pigeon said. "Just give me a day and—"

"One moment, please." Cal held up a hand as she wrote with the other. "But I do appreciate the enthusiasm. Hawk, your thoughts?"

Hawk didn't hesitate. "All these plans are too rotting slow. If we're taking on those areas, why not just create a big storm to hit them all at once? We could take over the whole mountain that way."

Badger's nose popped out of the bush. "Again," she said weakly, "we are only six spirits."

"Perhaps we could...ask for more spirits?" Pigeon cooed in thought. "There's the chain of other spirits waiting for us in Vidanya. If we broke the chain and brought a few of them in—"

Aspen shook their head. "If Yarrow senses more spirits coming into Envis, it might attack straight away. I won't endanger them or us by asking them to come in."

"If Yarrow senses *us* move out of the village, it will attack straight away," Cedar said. "We must find a way to navigate around it."

Hawk scoffed. "We fly, obviously."

"And get caught in another storm?" Badger squeaked. "Or the tree canopy?"

"I'm telling you, if we create our *own* storm and control the wind, we can—"

While Hawk continued to argue his point, Aspen settled near Shrike and watched glimmers of the river peek through the trees. If they squinted, they could see through the barrier to what lay beyond on the bridge. It was no longer a simple, clear path, but a swath of angry briar and yarrow flowers. Yarrow had chased them all the way up to the barrier, no longer content to keep its shadows to the northern half of the village.

Aspen grimaced and turned back to the group. "Cedar and Badger are right. We have to move fast, but this is Yarrow's forest. If it senses one of us near its strongholds—"

"Then we'll just move faster," Hawk insisted. "You see, if we start near that river tunnel, we could—"

Something in the river caught Aspen's eye: the shadow of a fish slipping through the water, pleasantly unaware of the thorny treachery that lay on the bridge above it.

"Then I'll start the storm and—Aspen?" Hawk clicked his beak impatiently. "Are you even listening to me?"

In truth, they weren't. They had moved to watch the fish glide along its path. Slipping into the bridge's shadow, then under the bridge itself. Above it, the yarrow flowers shifted in the breeze...and did nothing more. The fish continued on.

Aspen stared at the shadow even after it had disappeared. The water—Yarrow hated the water. Back in the tunnel, it had never dipped under the surface, and here in the village, it hadn't yet forded the river. At such strength, it could have—it *should* have. It would be no more difficult than taking an actual form and flitting across the water.

But Yarrow had never taken a form, and it only grew through ground cover: flowers and thorns that wouldn't survive a sustained dip in such a wide river.

They quickly stood and began nudging the trees aside, politely requesting that the trunks lean back to let them through. Behind them, Cal set down her pencil.

"Aspen? Where are you going?"

"Not far!" They set their lute on the road, then dipped their foot into the river, delighted at the cool rush of the water. Once that joy settled, they tentatively checked the ruins and the bridge for any change. Any angry presence, any sign of movement.

Nothing so far.

They dipped their other foot in, then waded in deeper, splashing around and keeping a wary gaze on the briar the entire time. If Yarrow could sense their approach, they'd surely feel it—

But it didn't. Yarrow let them navigate the waters unopposed.

They scrambled back onto shore, water trailing behind them.

"We'll use the river," they said breathlessly. Above them, Pigeon was still chattering over the others.

"I could make myself into a worm!" she offered. "Yarrow

wouldn't feel that coming, would it? I'd get to the first stronghold in a matter of—um, weeks—"

"Hey," Shrike called gruffly. "Aspen's got something."

Mildly surprised, Aspen cleared their throat.

"Thank you, Shrike." They turned to the others. "I believe we can reach Yarrow's strongholds without it noticing—but only if we move through the rivers and streams. May I—?"

They gestured to Cal's notebook; she eagerly handed it over.

"The river goes this way." They drew a wobbly line across the open page and described what they had observed in the water. "As far as I can tell, Yarrow's been"—they glanced back at the mountains, tongue poked out—"here and here."

"And here." Figeon swooped down and tapped on the top corner of the page with her beak. "Saw it on the way in."

Badger pawed at the paper in turn. "And there's a stream right there! It looked rather sparkly, and it would lead us right to that stronghold."

"The waterways would allow us to move quickly," Cedar agreed. "We could eliminate its tree at the peak without much struggle."

Shrike came and sat next to Aspen. "Let's do it, then."

All eyes swiveled to Hawk, who didn't move at first—then after a grumble and a quick preen, they soared down to perch on the sill behind Cal.

"Fine. I could do a flyover," he offered reluctantly. "Find other streams coming down the mountain that we could use."

Both Cal and Aspen let out a relieved breath.

"Perfect." Cal closed the notebook and nudged Aspen. "See? I had every confidence in you all."

As she spoke, another sound accompanied her—less through the air and more through the soil. Aspen tilted their head. It was both joyful and wonderfully familiar, like a friend's laugh in another room.

"Is that Emry playing?" they asked.

"Oh—can you hear him?" Cal looked behind her. "Yes, Iris asked him for some music. Would you like to hear it? I believe you've all done good work this morning."

They followed her down the road to join the others in the gathering hall. The humans had succeeded in making the large space a little cozier for themselves, dragging chairs together and passing around a bottle of wine. When the spirits arrived, they nodded in greeting, but otherwise let Emry continue playing from his spot near the hearth.

Aspen took a seat next to Cal, easing comfortably into the music that gently settled all around the room. They found it rather funny—they knew this song because they had performed it on stage with Emry last year. In fact, every time they had heard Emry perform like this, it had been while standing on stage beside him. When was the last time they had just listened to Emry like this? Performing with Emry and Sage and Riley was fun and all, but just hearing the music, letting it wash over them, was nice.

Just like the very first time they had heard him sing.

They set their head on Cal's shoulder, quietly unwinding in everyone's presence, particularly the spirits'. Together, their magic hummed along with the vibrations in the wooden planks below, carrying the music not just into the room, but deep into the soil. Aspen closed their eyes and hummed with them, not wanting the song to end. Here in the chords, they had everything they needed.

CHAPTER
TWENTY-TWO

ASPEN

The spirits charted their plan of attack the next day, soaring high over the forest, mapping any hint of water they saw, and bickering about the right paths to take—at least, on Hawk's part. As Aspen waded through the bickering and cobbled together their routes, they worked under the natural assumption that the spirits would be the only ones risking their necks against Yarrow. They were *spirits*, after all. Magical beings capable of great feats, or...something like that. Humans were too fragile for such a task.

But what humans lacked in hardiness, they made up for in sheer stubbornness.

"We'll follow you out," Nik said at dinner that night, talking as casually as if he were discussing the weather. "We'll take the western stream you're not using and weave in and out of it until we reach the hunting lodge."

Aspen stopped spinning the spoon about in their portion of soup, which in a few minutes would be passed to Iris. "Wait. You already discussed this?"

The humans all nodded; Damir leaned back in his chair, for once aligned with his brother. "With any luck, our movements will help distract Yarrow until you reach the first stronghold."

Aspen could only gape at him. "With any *luck*? If Yarrow finds you—"

"We'll take to the stream again," Emry said with a shrug, his tone far too light for all this. "It won't attack us once we're in the water. I've seen it happen before, in the tunnel."

Aspen glared at him—Emry, always shrugging when it came to his own wellbeing—but even Cal was supportive of the idea.

"Staying at the lodge afterward will ensure Yarrow doesn't retaliate on Raven's Rest," she said, gesturing to Harvey and Iris. "That allows us to leave two people to send ravens to the nearest Vidanyan town if"—she faltered—"well, if the worst should arise. Your chain of spirits can respond from there."

Nik visibly relaxed at that; Iris stiffened.

"Can't I just come with you and—?" she tried.

Damir laid a gentle hand on her shoulder.

"Leaders can't always go out on the front lines," he said. "If anything happens to us, it's up to you and Harvey to call for help. That's far more important than you might think."

Harvey shook his head. "She just doesn't like listening to my stories, is all."

"What? I love your stories!"

"She's only in it for the berries." He gave a dramatic sigh. "Just like the ravens."

While Iris tried to win back Harvey, Emry leaned toward Aspen.

"Are you sure Cal and I can't come with you?" he asked quietly, the question laced with none of Iris' bravado and all of his anxiety. Aspen bit their lip. They had no reassuring words like Damir did. They didn't even want Emry and Cal acting as a distraction in the first place. If they had their say, they'd lock all these humans in the tower with the ravens until Yarrow was gone.

But they knew better than to fight against human determination, particularly Emry's.

"I'm sure." They reached out and held Emry's hand. "Just keep the other humans safe."

∽

AT DAWN, they had no more planning or pacing left to do, and no more bags to pack. They all stood at the barrier, the spirits tense, the humans bleary-eyed and somber. Aspen ran over the plan again and again in their mind, just for something to do. The spirits would head upstream, while the humans took a boat downstream, circumventing to a smaller waterway. Then a few strongholds here, a few strongholds there, and Yarrow would be...gone.

They shook their head to rid themself of their last few thoughts. No use thinking that far ahead right now. They just had to get into the water first.

"Are we all ready?" they said, not wanting to look at the others in case they saw fear or worry. They turned to the barrier instead and raised a hand, preparing to command the trees to part—

"Wait."

They frowned and turned; Nik had stepped up behind them, holding something behind his back.

"There's a..." He glanced back at Damir, who looked just as confused as Aspen. "There's something we used to do when my father led hunts. A small hunting blessing of sorts. Haven't done it in ages, but seeing as I didn't believe before, and I..." His voice lowered into a mumble. "Might owe Damir a little..."

Harvey held a hand to his ear. "What was that?"

Nik scowled and held up a tiny bundle of flowers—marigolds, the brightness of the orange petals almost glowing against his hand.

"Come home safe and come home proud." He handed Aspen the flowers. "And may Hara watch over you."

He stepped back and gave his brother a stoic nod. Damir's eyes shone—but he kept his jaw wound tight and managed the same gesture back in a silent show of thanks.

In thanks of their own, Aspen reverently tucked the flowers into their lute, and behind them, several of the spirits sprouted tiny marigolds in their own groves.

"Thank you." They bowed to Nik. "Please stay safe yourself." Their gaze rested on Emry and Cal. "All of you."

Emry gave a smile that did little to inspire confidence in Aspen—but there was no time to try to convince him to stay at the raven tower, or even just stay in the village. The sun was rising and the river called.

They gently bent the trees so the others could get through. The spirits all dove into the water in various fish forms, some clumsy, some sleek; on the other side, the humans clambered into the boat. Aspen waved one more time to Harvey and Iris, then bid the trees regrow—thicker and taller than last time—and dove into the water themself.

Their lute wouldn't take well to the waves, so they slid just under the surface as an otter, the instrument barely skimming the water. They briefly took comfort in swimming in the middle of the other spirits, knowing they were all near—but they only had a few minutes to fight upstream with the group before they split.

Remember, they said, their words muddled in the water. *Only reach out to the others once you're in the water or have destroyed a stronghold. We don't want Yarrow picking up on anything. And*—they added quickly—*please don't get hurt.*

They all knew such a request was nearly out of the question given their mission, but they echoed it back to each other and split a moment later. Cedar, Shrike, and Hawk diverted up the mountain, leaving Badger, Aspen, and Pigeon to continue their fight upstream into the darkness: the tunnel where they had first encountered Yarrow.

After they plunged into the shadows and deftly navigated the twists and turns of the underground river, they finally found their target: a rock jutting out in the middle of the water. They shifted forms and clung low to the rock with hands, claws, and talons. Above them, Yarrow's roots grew only a hand's span over their heads.

All right, Aspen said, still not daring to voice anything aloud— they didn't want to risk so much as a vibration here. *I'll take this area if you both can take that tangle farther up the tunnel.*

They crouched low on the rock and rolled up their sleeves, watching the exposed roots and vines sway above them. Badger instead watched Aspen in curiosity.

What are you doing?

What? They looked at their sleeves. *Oh. I don't know. Emry does it whenever he goes into a tunnel. I just thought you were supposed to do it.*

She anxiously clicked her claws together. *But I don't have any sleeves to roll up!*

I'm sure it'll be fine! Gods, they didn't have time to deal with sleeves— *You two start over there, and I'll start over here!*

As Pigeon flew off and Badger dove back into the water, guilt started churning again in Aspen's chest. It had been gnawing at them all day yesterday, and as they stared at the ceiling of the tunnel, it reared its head once more. They had never intended to kill a spirit. Only to ask it a question.

But it was either Yarrow or the others. Yarrow or the village. Yarrow or the rest of Envis.

They squeezed their eyes shut, reached up, and commanded all the growth above them to wither.

Yarrow didn't retaliate right away. It couldn't, not at such a sudden onslaught. But when it finally fought back, when thorns shot angrily down from the ceiling and tried to snatch them up, the three spirits did as they had practiced. They dove, using the water as their own stronghold. Yarrow's vines whipped and plunged uselessly, allowing the spirits to gather their strength—then in a blink, they were at it again, sloughing off the dark briar until the tunnel walls were free of the smothering growth.

As Aspen had hoped, Yarrow couldn't fight against three spirits in such a space for long. The remaining thorns quickly turned dull and round, and the roots refused to grow back. Once Yarrow was left with a few weak vines hanging limp in the tunnel air, they made one final dive in victory, letting the current of the river carry them back into the sunlight.

This way! Pigeon quickly leapt back into the air and banked into the forest, careful to take the smallest form she could upon reaching the branching stream. Touching any of the trees here could give away their motion, so the three of them landed and stuck carefully to the center of the water, splashing their way up waterfalls and over rocks. Aspen ached to know how the others were faring—if they had moved on, if they were hurt—but they didn't dare send out a signal until they reached a deeper pond.

Cedar? they called, settling in the water so they just barely touched the mud at the bottom. *Shrike, Hawk—?*

Cedar responded in short, crisp answers. *Finished. Moving on.*

Distracting it as planned, Hawk called back, water bubbling in his response. *Humans are, too.*

A new urge itched at Aspen. The spirits, they could hear—but Emry and Cal had no way of reassuring them that they were all right. *Aspen* could reach out, though. Just a quick check through the soil and the roots...

They shook off the urge and kept going, splashing uphill once more. It was far too dangerous to attempt such a check. Even from within the water, they could tell Yarrow was angry and confused, lashing out in random directions in the hope of finding one of its attackers. Its panic gave Aspen a grim sort of satisfaction—it was precisely what their plan needed to succeed.

But even in its flailing, Yarrow still posed a threat. At the next stronghold—an old boulder coated in moss—there was no deep water to shelter in. Just a thin stream they splashed in and out of, muddying but not obscuring their tracks as they ripped up briar left and right.

"Aspen!" Pigeon shouted aloud—there was no point in hiding

her words, not here. "I need help with this"—she slapped a wing against the ground, but the briar before her barely moved—"this *stupid* patch of—"

In frustration, she ventured closer. Aspen whipped out a hand. "No, don't—!"

It was too late. The thorns shot out to grab her, tangling her wings in their sharp spirals. Badger lumbered over in a panic.

"I'll help!"

"No, stay there!" Aspen commanded. "We can't let it take both of you!"

As Badger backed away, Aspen kept their stance in the shallows and tried to fight the thorns. But Yarrow was here now, both victorious and furious, pouring all its stronghold's energy into keeping Pigeon down. To break its grasp, Aspen would have to break the entire stronghold.

"Onto the boulder!" they called to Badger, scrambling over its mossy surface. "We take the place down together!"

"But Pigeon—"

"We won't lose her, I promise!"

They wound their energy together, anger and panic and magic all in one, and shot it straight down into the boulder. At such a force, Aspen nearly fell down with it, briefly losing control of their form, their sense of place above the ground—but it was enough. The earth shriveled into parched, cracked plates. Dead leaves fell around them like snowfall.

And around Pigeon, the thorns collapsed in a lifeless heap.

"Can you fly?" Aspen shouted—but Pigeon was in the air right away, her flickering trajectory fueled by relief.

"Go, let's *go!*" she shouted, and bolted up the mountain in a blur.

Aspen and Badger followed as fast as they could, but Yarrow had caught onto their path this time. A concentrated windstorm whipped up around them, forcing Pigeon back down into the water to make any headway. As they trudged and struggled, they clung even harder to the center of the stream, cursing every time it narrowed. On either bank, Yarrow waited, desperate to ensnare them again in its thorns.

Shrike? Aspen called, narrowly dodging a tree branch that hung over the stream. They flickered with every gust of wind now, fighting to carry their lute alongside them, but they couldn't stop yet. All that was left for them now was the bristlecone tree at the peak: Yarrow's final stronghold. *Shrike, it's time!*

The others' responses came in just as exhausted and stuttered.

On my way, Shrike grunted. *Hawk, is Yarrow nearby?*

Where isn't it? Hawk huffed, then gathered himself together. *No, it's not by the tree. It's near the cliff and the three little waterfalls.*

Fear shot through Aspen's heart. The waterfalls—if they recalled Cal's map correctly, the humans would have stopped there just before making their final retreat to the hunting lodge.

Aspen, Pigeon warned. *We need to keep going and meet the others. Cedar's just ahead of us.*

They couldn't help but slow down. *But the waterfalls are near the—*

They'll be fine! The humans know what they're doing!

No, they don't! Aspen's words came in quick bursts. *They never do, they're always running into danger like this!* They spied the stream widening ahead. *Just—give me a second, I need to know—*

Aspen!

They ignored her and dove into the deeper water.

Thanks to Yarrow, the forest was in chaos. Aspen almost lost all sense of where they were as they tried to sort through it—the whipping wind, the panic, the widespread patches of dead growth that foretold the spirit's downfall. The bristlecone pine lay defenseless at the peak, but they needed to find one of the humans first. Just one of them, to make sure they weren't hurt or trapped or—

Pigeon slammed into their lute, jangling the lute strings and snapping them back to the present: the frigid water, the heaving canopy overhead...and the panicked calls coming from all around them.

Cedar! Badger shrieked. Before Aspen could ask what had happened, Shrike was barreling ahead, their presence a low, fast-moving storm out in the trees.

Hold on! he shouted. He was close now, all of them were, their frightened signatures quickly coalescing up ahead. Aspen silently uttered every curse they had ever learned and rushed to meet them. How long had they been in the water, looking for the humans? How long had Cedar been waiting for them ahead?

Just long enough for Yarrow to find them.

The trees had finally caught the elk spirit. Aspen could hardly tell where the branches ended and where Cedar's antlers began. But Cedar wasn't giving up—they heaved and tugged, a counter-wind thundering about the clearing in anger. All around them, bark snapped and wood splintered.

But Yarrow wasn't letting go. Before Aspen's eyes, Cedar flickered and fell to their knees. The moss swinging from their antlers went gray, then shrank, like a puddle evaporating in the sun.

Let them go! Shrike leapt into the clearing, claws bared. Aspen pulled them back just in time.

No, we do this together! they shouted over the dueling winds. *On three!*

Aspen dug their translucent hands into the soil, feeling Shrike's energy wind around them—then Pigeon's, then Badger's...

They took the energy, weaved it in tight with their anger, and sent it crashing into the ground.

The trees around them shattered. Yarrow's windstorm shrieked in despair and rolled away, too weak to counter. Unable to hold up their head any longer, Cedar fell to the ground.

I've got you! Badger rushed in, scooping up handfuls of soil and rocks in her long claws to start regrowing the moss—but the ground itself was half-dead, and Cedar began to fade in the growing sunlight.

Aspen. Shrike's voice made the spirit jump. *The tree's just up ahead.*

He was right. Aspen could almost see the bristlecone pine

through the thinning trees. It stood there, ready to shatter, just like the others before them.

But if they went ahead, Cedar wouldn't be here when they returned.

We can't. Aspen swallowed thickly. *We need to get Cedar out.*

Hawk screeched in frustration and fury. *But it's right there—!*

Aspen rounded on him. *Yarrow isn't taking another spirit! Not ever!*

Not due to their stupid mistakes, they wanted to say—but the extra words would do nothing for Cedar.

Come on. They poured the energy they had left into the moss that formed Cedar's grove. Yarrow had leeched away almost all the magic the moss held, leaving behind a bare whisper of the elk spirit. *We're getting you to safety.*

Young one, I've lived long enough— Cedar tried.

No, you haven't, Pigeon said firmly. *We're going. All of us.*

With desperate handfuls of moss, dried marigold petals, and soil, they left the dead earth, took to the sky, and banked toward the thin wisp of chimney smoke beyond the waterfalls.

CHAPTER
TWENTY-THREE

EMRY

EMRY COULDN'T DO anything but pace in front of the hunting lodge.

The forest around him exuded emotion as if it were birdsong. The anger and confusion had come first, swift and overpowering, while he and the others were still hiking along the stream. The others couldn't feel it, but he had almost stumbled out of the water in shock. The spirits were doing their job, he'd told Cal. All they had to do was weave in and out of the stream, distracting Yarrow without putting themselves in danger.

And it had worked, for a time. Every time they ventured onto dry land, the trees would bristle, thorns would rise—and they'd rush back into the water to wait for it all to slither away, distracted by the spirits' work in turn. For hours, they proceeded this way, garnering little more than bruises and torn, sopping clothes as they went. If this was all that it took to rid the forest of Yarrow, Emry through, he'd consider it an easy victory.

But by the time the party had reached the hunting lodge and changed into dry clothing, the trees had changed their tune.

Emry was bombarded with a brief flash of malicious victory and self-satisfaction—then panic from farther away, haphazard fear. He couldn't do anything more than stare out into the forest, heart pounding, feet rooted to the soil. He had never sensed the spirits like this before. He didn't even know how to tune them out or shove out the feelings, so he could *do* something about all this—

"Em." Cal tugged on his arm, her face drawn. "We have to get inside."

"We don't," he whispered, eyes still fixed on the trees. It didn't matter that he stood on dry land where Yarrow could catch him. Yarrow wasn't interested in him. Which meant that it had found something else, *someone* else, to claim in victory.

A hundred thoughts rushed through his head in a frantic circle. Thoughts of Aspen, first, of them hurt or lost or worse. Then thoughts of Cal and the others in the lodge, staring at him in apprehension. If Raven's Rest—Hara forbid—lost the spirits, there would be no true defense against Yarrow. Not for the hunting lodge and, eventually, not for Iris or Harvey back in the village. Emry's abilities alone wouldn't be enough. He didn't just need Aspen back; they all needed Aspen back.

But running back into the mountain to search for the spirit was madness.

"Cal." He set his hand over hers, her fingers still wrapped around his arm. "What do we do?"

Another shadow fell over his other side—Nik, his posture straight, face stolid. Like he had done this many times before.

"Same thing I did every time my father went out to hunt," he said. "You wait and you hope. That's all you can do."

The very thought of doing so was going to drive Emry straight into the trees. He couldn't wait, and he was rapidly losing hope. The forests' silent wailing was going to claim him before Yarrow could ever hope to—

A dark speck appeared against the clouds.

"Which one is that?" Nik asked.

The sky answered the question for him. One dark speck was quickly accompanied by another, then another.

"It's all of them," Cal breathed, then hurried back to the lodge. "Damir, they're here!"

Together, they all rushed into the bare patch of path before the lodge—then immediately had to back away for the cacophonous landing party.

"Are we far enough away from Yarrow?" one of the birds called—Badger, Emry realized, just in an unfamiliar form.

"Put Cedar down here—"

"Yes, Badger," another shouted back. "Don't worry. It can't reach this far, not in the state we've put it in!"

"No, no, the soil's better over here!"

The birds all landed in a flurry of wings, then shifted into claws and fur and leaves. Emry could only search for a waistcoat and curly hair in the fray. "Aspen? Aspen, where are you?"

The spirit he was looking for was the only one not shouting. They knelt before a pile of moss, hands dug into the ground, grass and weeds and flowers growing fiercely all around them.

Emry's breath caught in his throat. He recognized that moss. That moss should have been hanging from a pair of antlers.

"Pigeon!" Cal was already rushing off with the spirit, skirts hiked to clear her boots. "There's an old garden out back. The soil there should be better—"

She ran out behind the lodge, with Damir, Nik, and the other spirits quick to follow. Emry instead knelt on the ground beside Aspen, his heart still racing. "What can I do to help?"

Aspen's hands shook, their fingers barely visible against the dirt. "Any energy you can. Please."

Emry immediately dug his hands into the soil and poured his energy into the ground. At first, all he felt was earth—that dark, muddy feeling, choking his senses—

Then he breathed a sigh of relief. The ailing spirit still clung to the moss, their weak signature smelling faintly of cedar wood and distant thunderstorms.

"You'll be all right, Cedar," he mumbled, then kept pushing his energy further and further, trying desperately to make that presence grow. Just like with weaving roots under the soil, shoveling magic into a spirit quickly confused him—so he bolstered the dirt around them instead, hoping Cedar, or Aspen, or *someone* could pull on it themself. But that hope, already threadbare, unraveled quickly. Nothing was happening. No response from the soil, no movement or—

A voice floated weakly from the moss.

"I will"—their voice started and stopped, muffled by earth—"I will be all right, young one."

Tears dripped from Aspen's face onto the ground. "You won't. You need more—"

"If you give any more, you yourself will be gone," Cedar said, commanding even in their weakened state. "Thank you for what you have given. Now let the others take over."

Emry glanced back at the lute Aspen had let fall to the ground behind them. Despite the warm summer sun, the tiny garden inside looked to be on the brink of winter, its growth brown, thin, and exhausted.

"Come on." He left the lute in the sun and gently pulled Aspen to their feet, his hands almost going through the illusion of the fabric on their arm. "Why don't you come inside and tell me what happened?"

Aspen followed him numbly—then as soon as they stepped through the doorway, they pulled Emry into a fierce hug.

"It's all my fault!" they sobbed into his shoulder. "We were going to the tree, but Hawk said Yarrow was close to you and I just wanted to know if you were—"

"Hold on, hold on." Emry squeezed them tight, then guided them to the table. The furniture boasted a thick coat of dust and scratches, just like the rest of the one-room lodge, but that didn't matter. The faded yellow tablecloth looked about as homey as they could get in this forest. "I'm sure it's not your fault. Why don't you start from the beginning?"

Aspen sniffed and began their story in the tunnel, where they had started to attack Yarrow's roots. As they spoke, the other humans filtered back into the lodge, faces drawn, dirt deep under their fingernails. By the time Aspen reached Cedar's call for help in the story, they all had their own dusty chairs pulled up around the table.

"It's not your fault," Damir said immediately, mud still streaking his temple. "You would never have been able to get to Cedar in time even if you hadn't stopped."

"But I—"

"There's no point in focusing on it," Cal said. "It's already done, and Cedar is safe now."

"Aspen?" Badger called from the yard. Aspen's gaze whipped to the window—but they couldn't bring themself to stand. Nik leaned forward, his voice far gentler than Emry had ever heard it before.

"These things happen," he said quietly. "No matter how good the plan is. But as a leader, you must learn to take it as it comes. Support your other hunters. They're likely feeling the same way."

Aspen's eyes went wide. "But it's not their fault—"

"And it isn't yours, either." Cal took their hand. "Come on. Why don't you come see what we've set up for Cedar out there?"

Emry followed the pair out to the side of the lodge, where dirty shovels leaned against the wall. The tools had been put to work quickly—a fresh pile of turned soil now sat under a bower, the pile covered in Cedar's moss. The other spirits all sat on and around it in a stiff, protective circle.

"No one else is hurt?" Emry asked. Pigeon landed on his shoulder.

"We're fine," she said, her voice shaky. "I think."

"It's all right not to be." He watched the tiny flowers around her feet wither and bloom over and over. "You must have had quite a fright."

The word sent Hawk off.

"Fright?" he repeated. "*Fright*? I'm going to pull out Yarrow's roots myself!"

Sitting on the pile was no longer enough; he soared from the dirt, to a branch, to the handle of a shovel, screeching as he went. "We had almost made it to the tree! Just another minute and we would've had it!" He turned on Aspen in anger. "But *you* didn't make it in time—"

Beside Cal, Aspen welled up again. "I'm sorry," they blurted out, "I know I shouldn't have stopped to check the—"

But before Aspen could finish or Cal could open her mouth in defense of the spirit, Shrike leapt up with a growl, his teeth bared not at Aspen, but at Hawk.

"It's not their fault," he said, a hiss underlining his words. "Aspen wasn't the one to encase Cedar in thorns and try to pull their life away. That was Yarrow."

Hawk's eyes went dark. "But they were—"

"I know where Aspen was." Shrike's hackles rose as he moved protectively in front of Aspen. "Even if they hadn't stopped, they wouldn't have made it in time. Cedar was trapped no matter what they did. No matter what *any* of us did."

Badger stood, her voice less wavering than before. "We couldn't have pulled Cedar out without Aspen. We might all have gotten stuck, and then where would we be?"

Murmurs of agreement flurried into the air, while Shrike staunchly remained in front of Aspen. When it was clear no one else was going to agree with him, Hawk huffed and retreated back to the tree branch in defeat.

"All right," he muttered. "But I'm still ripping Yarrow apart next chance I get."

That statement was met with no resistance. Cal squeezed Aspen's shoulder in reassurance and gestured to the pile of soil.

THE SPIRIT'S CURSE

"Why don't we all sit?" she said, her words hardening as her gaze flitted to Hawk. "I'm sure Cedar would appreciate the company as they recover."

She and Aspen settled to form a circle around Cedar, slowly guiding the conversation away from ruminating on what had happened. But Emry was far too restless for that. The echoes of the forest still reverberated in his head, and resting with the spirits wasn't going to get them out.

He returned to the lodge, only to find that the other men couldn't sit still, either. They puttered around the room, cleaning, checking the lodge for rations, and muttering quietly about the journey back to the Rest. Emry silently joined them in their puttering.

Slowly—too slowly—the sun set on the lodge. Emry opened the window as he cleaned, letting in the last of the day's breeze, the scent of soil, and the spirits' waning discussion.

"And what about you?" Cal was asking Pigeon. "Where would you like to go?"

"After all this stupid Yarrow business, you mean?" the spirit responded. Emry smiled to himself as he dragged a rag over the kitchen table; she had never sounded more like Lydia in that moment.

"Will you go back to Matlock?" Cal continued. Pigeon gave a hum.

"I don't think so," she finally said. "I'd like to help find answers. For the others, I mean. I don't mind being awake all that much right now." Her tone brightened. "I mean, I haven't seen all the forests and cities and valleys yet, have I? Hawk told me there are at least a dozen more places to go."

A laugh tinged Cal's voice. "I believe there are a few more than a dozen places for you to visit."

"Then I want to see them all," Pigeon said confidently. "Lydia taught me to write letters if I take a human form. I can write to her and tell her all about the places she hasn't seen."

Badger hummed thoughtfully along with Pigeon. "Do you think

they all have good napping spots? I do like to sit out and just watch all the humans go by. They choose such interesting things to wear."

Hawk pecked at the ground. "If we sort out how to go to sleep," he wondered, "could we also learn how to eat?"

All the spirits perked up at that.

"I've been wondering if berries taste as good as they look," Badger mused.

"Or deer," Shrike added. "No offense, Cedar."

"None taken," Cedar sighed. Pigeon ruffled her feathers.

"Please. No animal food can possibly taste as good as sunlight." She peered over at Shrike. "Hold on. Does that mean you're coming with us?"

Shrike paused as he licked his paw. "What?"

"After we leave here." Badger lifted her head. "Will you be traveling with us? To all the cities and forests and valleys and such?"

Shrike shifted. "I—it might...not be so bad, I think." He quickly glanced at Aspen. "You?"

Emry held himself very still—as if the wind would take away the answer if he weren't listening hard enough.

"Oh," Aspen said. From his angle by the window, Emry couldn't see them, but he could imagine them there. Chewing their lip, sitting cross-legged by Cedar, the flowers in their hair pulsing gently in thought. "Well, I don't know. Travel...might be nice."

It wasn't a commitment. Their resolve had faltered throughout the words. But Emry couldn't help it—his heart dropped to the floor.

Outside, Cal's voice thinned.

"You have always enjoyed seeing new places," she said—but her enthusiasm was weak, and her next words too fast. "Badger, I don't think I ever learned where you first grew. Was it near Foxhill?"

The conversation moved on, but Emry couldn't. The rag remained still under his hand, his thoughts far away. He didn't want this. He didn't want to go back to Vornik without Aspen, he couldn't—

"Karic."

Emry jumped, thinking at first it was Damir—but Nik appeared next to him instead, setting an old straw broom against the wall.

"Place is about as clean as it'll be for now," he grumbled. "Don't worry about the rest of it."

Emry stared at the dirty rag in his hand; he had already forgotten it was there.

"Right. Not worrying," he said quickly and tossed the rag aside. "Done."

But Nik saw through the lie. "You all right there?"

Emry's instinctual response—*fine, all good, how are you?*—lay on his tongue—but then Damir passed outside the window, his dour expression made more haggard by the weak sunset.

"No sign of Yarrow near here, right?" he called to the spirits. "If you tell me yes, tree kid, I swear to Hara, I'm getting Nik's gun and shooting at the rotting flowers myself. No, I *know* that's not how it works—"

Nik smiled and shook his head. The simple gesture threw Emry into the past—of his sister's antics and his parents' tired, loving looks—and in a brief yet sweeping rush, he missed them. He nearly laughed at himself. He missed his family, and he had just seen them a few days ago.

Unlike Nik, who until that week, hadn't seen Damir in years.

Emry's response to Nik shifted before he could reconsider. "When was the last time Damir visited you?"

Damir hadn't been forthcoming on specifics, but it had to have been at least two years since his last trip to Envis. Two, maybe three—

"Three years, five months, and seventeen days," Nik said quietly.

Emry's heart cracked—but Nik wasn't done. As he moved to check the cabinets, his voice echoed in the dusty wooden spaces, stiff and restrained.

"He used to visit all the time, after the war. He was there days after Iris was born. Same when her mother died. He always tried to make it for Iris' birthday after that." Nik swallowed. "Can't claim that anything more than stupidity kept us from talking the last few years. *My* stupidity, at least."

Emry picked his next words carefully. "He...he did mention the letter."

Nik slowly closed the cabinet doors, his words turning bitter. "Shouldn't have written the rotting thing. Thought he was being smug, and I just had to quash it, didn't I?"

"Whatever you wrote, I'm sure you didn't mean it—"

"I *did* mean it," he began, then sighed. "I did and I didn't. If I had known it would chase him away, that I wouldn't seen him for years, like during the war..." He tried to laugh. "Gods. What is it about little brothers that just...?"

He waved away his own words, but they echoed in Emry's head—reverberating not in Nik's voice, but in Georgie's.

Little brothers, indeed.

As Nik huffed and went to test the chairs, Emry leaned against the counter in thought. The Nedrov brothers had lost their parents when they were fairly young, and as far as he could tell, they had no other siblings. They had cousins like Yvette, sure—but that wasn't quite the same.

During the war, Nik must have been terribly alone.

"How'd you do it?" Emry asked. "How'd you deal with him being gone?"

Nik shrugged—but the movement was a lie in itself. "Some days it's easy. Some days you take it hour by hour and hold on to what you had, what you can remember. Same as missing anything else." He pushed in a chair and wiped his hands. "But in his case...well, I know he'll come back. Might not be for a few years, but he will."

Emry's heart twisted again. He could hear his own family once more, back when he had left home. They had always known he'd come back—they just didn't know when.

And Aspen, if they left, would be the same.

He cleared the knot from his throat. "Sorry to bring him back for something like this," he croaked. "I can't imagine you'll want to remember today."

Nik gave a gruff laugh. "Today, the past year. It's all been a pile of dung, if you ask me. Just means he'll have to visit again once this is over." He glanced out the window. "Speaking of…"

Damir strode back into the room, not at all refreshed by his brief constitutional in the yard. The sun had nearly set, throwing most of him—and the lodge—into shadow.

"No sign of Yarrow." He nodded to Nik, who was already igniting a rushlight against the dark. "Karic, Nik and I want to head back to the Rest in the morning. Check on Iris and Harvey. Let them know what happened." He wiped dirt off his sleeve. "But I imagine Cedar will need to stay here a few more days to rest. Will you and Cal be staying with them?"

Emry stiffened. He wasn't sure how much more of the spirits' travel conversation he could handle—and he was hardly being of any use to them here. He'd be able to think more clearly if he went back to the Rest.

"No." He straightened. "I'm not sure about Cal, but—I can come with you. Help fend off Yarrow if it tries to come for us on the road."

"Appreciate it." Damir clapped him on the shoulder. "Never thought I'd need to call upon a bard for defense. Don't tell Ella when we get back. She'll think I've gone weak in my old age."

"You *have* gone weak in your old age," Nik called. Damir glared at him.

"Might I remind you who the older one of us is? Now help me finish these packs, you ancient bag of bones."

As Damir moved away, Emry glanced once more out at the yard, at the shadows of the spirits under the bower, then closed the window.

CHAPTER
TWENTY-FOUR

ASPEN

To Aspen, the hunting lodge was the last peaceful place in the forest.

The little building was just one room, one fragile room of wood and glass and a bit of furniture, where all the humans slept for the night. Their last rushlight had gone out a while ago, leaving the spirits in the glow of the moon and the stars. None of them moved from the bower in hours, all silently insisting on staying close to Cedar until dawn.

But farther out in the mountain, around the remains of its dead strongholds, Yarrow kept pacing.

Aspen supposed it was yet another downside of spirits' inability to sleep. Yarrow was unable to sleep away its recovery, and Aspen was doomed to stay awake to hear it. Hear the thorns slowly growing back, smothering the grasses and flowers and saplings that had only just gotten a chance to breathe.

And while Yarrow grew, it searched. Its attempts were sporadic and weak, but they were there. Hunting for its attackers. Seeking revenge.

Aspen couldn't even blame it—wouldn't they do the same, if anything ever happened to Emry and Cal?

They squeezed their eyes shut and tried to block Yarrow out. To think of more pleasant things. What had the others talked about that day? They had talked about forest animals. About what types of soil were best, the birdsong they missed most...

And they had talked about travel.

Aspen toyed with a leaf on the ground, their fingers still translucent after the day's efforts. They hadn't lied to Shrike—travel *did* sound nice. Seeing new places, meeting new people, hearing new songs. But their journey wouldn't just take them to other humans for a bit of fun sight-seeing. It would take them to other spirits as well. To other Yarrows, possibly...but also to other Shrikes. To other spirits who knew just as little about what to do with their lives.

They watched Shrike drape himself over a tree branch, his form ghost-like as he recovered from the fight. Aspen certainly didn't have any sage guidance for Shrike and wouldn't have any for the other spirits out there. They had...well, themself and the others. Support and friends. Stories and some songs, if they liked music. That would be something, at least.

But if they traveled—if they left to offer support and stories and songs to other spirits—then they wouldn't have Emry and Cal. Or Sage or Riley, or any of their friends they'd made in Vornik. They couldn't just...*leave* like that. Could they?

Their thoughts wandered back and forth like this, pacing just as Yarrow did until a rut formed in their mind. They couldn't leave, they had to leave... They finally let out a long sigh, drew their legs up, and set their chin on their knees. They'd talk to Emry in the morning. He'd know what to do.

Just as their mind finally drifted out of the cycle, Hawk landed silently on a branch above them, their wispy wings tinged blue in the pre-dawn light.

All of you, he called in a flat tone. *Follow me.*

Careful not to alert the humans, they all slipped out of the yard, save Pigeon, who stayed under the bower with Cedar. Hawk led them down the path, toward the three little waterfalls that had been on the map...

And right at the bend in the road, before it dipped into the trees, a patch of weak, white yarrow flowers grew.

Aspen wished they could dismiss them. They were pathetic, hardly a threat. But they grew mere steps away from Cedar and the humans, a quiet, steady symbol of Yarrow's rage and desperation. The cornered animal had almost sniffed them out.

And in their current state, the spirits couldn't fight it.

Aspen turned back on the path. *We need to wake the humans. Now.*

They hurried back to the lodge, Aspen slipping into the lodge while the others diverted to prepare Cedar for travel. No rushlight had been lit, but one of the humans had already roused: Nik, blearily finding his way around in the dim, blue dawn.

"Already packed," he muttered, wiping sleep from his eyes—but when Aspen relayed what they had seen, he straightened, sleep giving way to the urgency of the matter.

"Damir and I were planning on going to the Rest today," he whispered. "If the kids want to stay here with Cedar—"

He glanced at Emry and Cal, who were still sleeping in a corner, Cal nestled against Emry's chest. Aspen shook their head.

"No. All of you are going. Even Cedar."

Nik frowned. "Not you?"

"I'm staying back." Aspen swallowed. "You're not the one Yarrow is looking for."

As they expected, the other spirits didn't exactly like that plan.

"I'll stay with you," Shrike said immediately. "It knows all of us helped with the attack. It'll come for us two and not the humans—"

"And I want you with the humans just in case I'm wrong," Aspen argued. When Shrike's eyes went pleading, they softened. "Please. You'll all be safer if you travel together, and I'll be quick enough to move on my own if I need to. I'll be fine, I promise."

Over by the door, the other humans rustled, their voices growing quickly as they learned of the plan.

"Wait," Emry said, his tone panicked. "No, they can't stay back alone."

"Let me talk to them," Cal tried.

Aspen's throat tightened. If they spent any more time arguing about the plan, Yarrow would catch them all right where they stood.

Stay safe, they instructed the spirits. *I'll meet you back at the Rest.*

Without another word, they took their lute and headed into the forest.

They headed north, away from both the lodge and the village. If Yarrow chose to follow them, they'd be as far away from the others as possible—and if it chose to attack, the others wouldn't be caught in its fury. Any storm Yarrow could summon, any trapping growth, would be centered on them and them alone.

The thought set them on edge. Yes, they could fly away the first chance they got, as they had promised. But in a truth they didn't dare utter to anyone else, they were just as weak as the other spirits right now. The flight back to the Rest would be about all they could manage.

As a result, they jumped at every sound the quiet forest made. They begged for the sun to rise faster, to illuminate the trees so they didn't have to check every shadow. They even hoped for Yarrow to show itself, as an excuse to soar out of this forest and get back to their friends.

But Yarrow did nothing. Not when the sun rose, and not when the morning mist melted away. It just...watched them walk north, into nothing.

Aspen fought the urge to yell at it, to incite it into action. If it wasn't attacking them and wasn't attacking the others, that was good, wasn't it? Perhaps the spirit was too weak to even try fighting. If that was the case, Aspen would still have to fly back sooner or later. Regroup with the others and sort out their next plan...

An image of Raven's Rest came to their mind, strangely vivid and unbidden. They stopped in their tracks. How odd. They hadn't meant to think that.

Then their thoughts jerked in another direction of their own volition. To people in Raven's Rest. To Nik, standing in the gathering hall, and Iris, serving them all tea.

"No!" Aspen shouted out of instinct. They backed away from nothing, hands in their hair. They knew what this was. Yarrow wasn't using its remaining energy to attack. It was sorting through their memories, digging into them for information, just as Aspen had done to it at the festival grounds—

But it wasn't going to get anything. Not if Aspen had anything to say about it.

They screwed their eyes shut and thought hard on other things —things that were far away and useless to Yarrow. Their old aspen grove back in Tazlo. Stages in Vornik, Senne, and Matlock. But that didn't throw off the spirit. It just snarled and dug deeper, forcing Aspen to change tack. They tossed aside the longer memories and rifled through their own thoughts faster than Yarrow could possibly understand them. They thought of Guild musicians they had met, food they had watched others eat, letters they had written. Then songs, books, jokes, plants, soups—

And with each memory, with each random thought and useless recall, Yarrow dug harder. Somewhere in there, it had seen something it wanted. Something Aspen cared about very much.

Emry and Cal.

No matter what Aspen thought of, they were always there. Emry singing at the grove. Cal backstage while Emry sang beside them. Both of them at every soiree, every dinner, every quiet evening in the parlor, every moment Aspen had seen of their short lives—

One final memory bubbled up unbidden and unwanted: the two of them dancing and singing in the Rest. Not far away in Vornik or Matlock, but here, right by the river's edge. Within Yarrow's reach.

Underneath Aspen's feet, the entire forest shifted.

Over the past few days, they had grown accustomed to Yarrow's energy simmering across the entire mountain. Its consciousness wandered, of course, but its signature was always there, just as spiky as the thorns that marked its territory. But now, it all rushed past them, every last scrap of Yarrow's energy, in a wave nearly as great and overwhelming as a surge. Aspen fell to their knees and clutched their lute tight against their chest. If Yarrow chose to direct all that energy at them, they had no recourse. Nothing in their lute could possibly match up to what the spirit was gathering. And they hadn't said a thing to Emry and Cal. No goodbye, nothing, what had they been *thinking*—

But it didn't center on them. The magic paid them no mind as it rushed past. With a cold, growing sense of dread, Aspen followed its path. It barreled south, down the slope, down the mountain paths...

Directly to Raven's Rest.

CHAPTER
TWENTY-FIVE

EMRY

"I HATE THIS."

"I know."

"I'm going to yell at them when they're back."

Cal gave Emry a side glance. "Darling, I don't think you've ever yelled at Aspen in your life."

Emry sighed miserably. "I know."

The hike back down to the village was worse than any other rotting hike Emry had taken in Envis. The dew had turned much of the road to mud. The morning mist obscured every bend and corner. And the downhill on his knees—Hara take him, if Damir thought *he* was getting old...

It came as no small relief to him, then, that Yarrow had chosen not to make the hike even less bearable with its presence. No yarrow flowers or thorns appeared to block their way. Emry couldn't even feel its anger radiating through the forest anymore.

He told himself that was a good thing, but something in his chest warned him otherwise.

"Do you feel anything?" he quietly asked Shrike. The other spirits had chosen to fly directly to the Rest with Cedar in tow, but Shrike refused to leave the humans, insisting he walk back with them. Shrike growled and shook his head.

"Nothing," he said. "Aspen must be too far away."

Emry huffed. Of course they were. That had been their entire gods-forsaken plan.

After a near-slip on the mud and another few bends in the road, his patience vanished. He wanted to ask Shrike the same question over and over again: Did they sense Aspen now? How about now?

It took all his strength to hold his tongue until they reached the northern ruins of the village.

"Are you sure you can't feel them out there?" he asked, trying to pick up his pace. Up ahead, the other spirits waited anxiously for them at the barrier, while Harvey, Iris, and Otto hovered on the other side of the trees. Shrike flicked his ears in annoyance.

"I'm sure."

"And you're"—Emry helped Cal over a root—"you're *positive* Aspen didn't say when they'd be flying back?"

Shrike scowled. "*Yes,* I'm positive." He padded up to the bridge and parted the trees for all of them. "They just said to stay safe and they'd meet us back here."

Emry scoffed. They were perfectly safe back at the Rest. It was Aspen who needed the instructions.

He held back a branch to clear the way for Cal. On the other side, Iris was already wiggling through the trees, too impatient to let them finish bending apart on their own. "Papa, did you—?" She stopped short when she saw the soil the spirits were carrying. "What is that?"

Cal immediately stepped back into her role as physician of spirits. "Iris, we'll need compost and a planter," she said calmly. "A large one. Do you have any—?"

"Got it!" Iris shot off in a panic, Otto barking and following along blithely. Harvey watched them go with an inscrutable look.

"It didn't work, did it?" he finally asked, his voice carrying the melancholy of far too many years. Nik silently shook his head. Harvey gave one short, stiff nod, his eyes dim with disappointment.

"Use the planters by the gathering hall, then," he said, his voice rough. "Let's all stay close today, shall we—?"

Above them, the sun disappeared.

Emry looked up. Clouds rolled in quickly from the mountain, deep and dark, blotting out the sunlight. A summer storm, he thought at first. Shiro's beard, just what they needed right now.

Then the first snowflake whipped past his face.

"The hall." He set a hand on Cal's back. "Get to the hall now."

They all started to rush down the street—Damir taking Harvey's arm, Nik shooting off in search of Iris—but Emry stayed by the barrier. If he could bolster its growth somehow, buy them all a little more time until Aspen came back...

"Here." Shrike was at his side in an instant, nodding to the other spirits to keep going. "I'll help you."

Together, they tried to reach into the growth. To make the branches grow thicker, the roots grow longer—

Ice bit into Emry's fingers. He cursed and yanked his hands away from the tree. Frost had spread over the bark, coating the tree from root to leaf in a thick, slippery sheet. The winter storm hadn't merely arrived. It was *here*, concentrated directly over the bridge in a whiplash of snow and cold.

And behind the barrier, through the branches already stripped clean of leaves, he could see fresh thorns and yarrow flowers creeping in at a steady, malicious pace.

Under the soil, Yarrow seemed to laugh at him.

Emry staggered back. Every breath brought bitter cold into his lungs, freezing him place. If the barrier fell—

A warm hand took his and yanked him away from the incoming thorns. "Get away from there!"

He stumbled and twisted around. Aspen strode behind him, snowflakes frosting their curls as they dragged both him and Shrike down the street.

"What do you think you're doing?" they demanded. Emry wrested himself from Aspen's grip, spluttering in both relief and indignation.

"What do you think *you're* doing?" he demanded right back. "Running off alone like that?"

Aspen shot a weak grin back at him. "I did learn from the best."

Emry didn't have a good answer for that.

"I thought I could lead Yarrow away from you," they continued over the wind, leading them both to the gathering hall at a run. "But it decided to target you in revenge—"

"Oh, how thoughtful."

Aspen stopped in front of the door. "Which means I have to go finish it off myself."

"*What?*"

Aspen opened the door to a chorus of relieved shouts.

"Thank Hara." Cal pulled them into a hug. "Gods, I was half-convinced it had caught you."

Hawk spread his wings. "Good to see you. Can we go out there and kill it now?"

The other spirits all echoed Hawk—even Cedar, whose elk form hovered like a ghost in the corner of the room, standing over a planter that had been dragged inside.

"This is Yarrow's final push," they boomed. "Either it takes the village and moves on, or we end it here."

Aspen nodded. "And that's what I'm going to do."

Badger stared at them. "What, by yourself?"

"Not entirely." They knelt by Cedar, and everyone else gathered around, ignoring the snowstorm whistling outside. Even Otto sat still at Aspen's feet.

"All of Yarrow's strength is here, attacking the village," Aspen continued. "If I borrow whatever energy the spirits can give, then fly straight to the tree, it won't be able to defend itself in time."

Pigeon flew to their shoulder. "I can fly with you—"

Aspen shook their head. "I'll move faster on my own. One spirit, one attack. It'll be gone before the thorns can reach this hall."

The wind rattled the windowpanes and hissed over the rooftop. Emry tried not to get up and pace, while beside him, Cal twisted her wedding ring around her finger. He hated this plan more than the last one. To venture up to Yarrow's last stronghold, *completely* alone—

Shrike stood up.

"All right," he said. "Do it. Take what you need from me."

To Emry's surprise, the other spirits were quick to follow. And while Cedar couldn't offer anything of their own, they bowed their ethereal antlers to the spirit in approval. "May its death be quick."

"Planters." Cal swallowed hard and jumped to her feet. "All the spirits will need planters."

Nik and Damir leapt to drag in more boxes; Iris gathered up her trowel and sack of soil.

All Emry could do was stand there, mouth agape. "You can't do this. We *can't* be doing this—"

"You have another plan?" Hawk's eyes bore into him.

He didn't. He *wanted* to. He wracked his brain for something, anything—but it remained blank as he helped Damir drag in planters. It gave him nothing as he watched the spirits form a circle around Aspen. And when each spirit slowly flickered out one by one, leaving little more than vines and flowers behind, he realized it was far too late to stop any of this.

While Cal and Iris placed each of the spirits' groves in the new planters, Emry approached Aspen, hand outstretched. "Are you sure I can't help give you anything?"

Aspen gently held his hand but took nothing. "You can't grow back like the others can."

"But I—"

"So, you'll need to defend them for me."

Emry froze. He had expected to be denied; he hadn't expected to be given this task.

"The other humans can't do it," Aspen said in a low voice. "And the spirits can't, either. If Yarrow reaches this place before I'm finished, you have to defend them."

Fear shot through him. "I can't," he breathed. "I can't do this without you—"

"You can." Aspen smiled at him, green eyes glowing. "I trust you."

They wrapped Emry in a hug, the scent of mint and honeysuckle briefly enveloping him—then after doing the same for Cal, they headed for the door.

"Tree kid." Damir stood as one final guard by the entrance, his arms folded and face trained to be still. "Come back in one piece, please."

Aspen gave Damir a tight hug. The man blinked, then cleared his throat.

"All right, all right." He patted Aspen's shoulder. "Don't tell the Quartet I'm giving out hugs, now. I have a reputation to maintain."

"I won't say anything." Aspen gave them all one more smile, then slipped out into the storm. After the door closed, a small voice floated out of the planter closest to Emry.

"They'll be all right, won't they?" Pigeon asked, her planter marked by tiny red flowers. Emry set his hand on the soil, pushing just a hint of his own energy into it. Enough to get her settled into the makeshift garden.

"They'll be fine," he said. He patted the dirt one more time, and Pigeon cooed back in mutual reassurance.

But her voice was barely audible over the whipping wind outside.

CHAPTER
TWENTY-SIX

ASPEN

As soon as the door closed behind them, Aspen dove into the sky.

They didn't care that Yarrow's windstorm had turned into a screaming gale—the ancient spirit hadn't left them with much choice. While the air above pushed and shoved, the ground below writhed with thorns. They either fought the wind or fought the briar. But the sky would give them the fastest path to the bristlecone pine, so they took their chances with the storm and shaped themself into the largest bird they could think of.

The details of the bird didn't matter, nor the species. They took on wide, broad wings and strong eyesight, weathering every raging gust and turn with grim steadiness. They couldn't escape Yarrow's emotions, not even here in the air—the clouds hung low and heavy with them. Anger, desperation, fleeting thoughts of victory. Aspen had no choice but to breathe it all in as they flew, acutely aware of the spirit's presence above and progress below. Down on the ground, its thorns crawled over the bridge, through the barrier, past the southern houses. Yarrow's headway came at a cost—every handspan gained shriveled its stores of energy—but it kept going. It had no other choice.

Which meant that Aspen had no other choice but to hurtle toward the top of the mountain, claws outstretched, and land before Yarrow's final home: the bristlecone pine tree.

The ancient tree stood stark against the storm clouds, pale bark gathering snowfall against the slate-gray sky. Much like the rest of Yarrow's grove, it seemed to be losing the fight for its own survival. Bone-white roots poked from the ground. Branches hung jagged and bare. And its vast trunk twisted, as if the winds fighting against Aspen had also wrung the tree to within an inch of its life. But Aspen could still feel it—the spirit magic the tree desperately clung to, even as it was wreathed in long thorns and bursts of crumbling yarrow flowers.

That magic wouldn't last for much longer.

Aspen didn't need to take on a form for their next task. They cast aside their bird shape, as unwieldy as it was, and dug into the ground with invisible hands while their lute rested behind them. The soil lay frozen and hostile here, guarding the roots below with dry, rocky layers. Aspen tore at it anyway, using all of the other spirits'

borrowed energy to rip up everything they saw. Weeds, roots, pools of magic—everything that sustained Yarrow here.

The spirit shrieked—an ear-splitting sound that should have shattered the very clouds—but it didn't fight back. No thorns or vines wrapped around Aspen or blocked their work. Yarrow was too far away, focusing hard on the village. On everyone Aspen loved.

So, they worked faster, biting and tearing and ripping just to be finished with this bleak work. If they kept going like this, they thought, they could be done soon. Within the hour, within minutes, even. They just had to reach a little further, dig deeper into the dead, cold soil, and—

Their fingers reached a dark shadow at the heart of the tree, and they found Yarrow staring back at them.

Not all of Yarrow. Just a glimmer, a spark of the ancient spirit, left behind while the rest of its focus moved down the mountain.

It had been waiting for Aspen this entire time.

You, it spat, wrapping their lute in thorns. The motion of its vines ripped apart the surrounding soil as much as Aspen's efforts had, but Yarrow didn't seem to care. Its grove meant nothing to it anymore, not when it had fresh territory waiting in the south.

This is not your forest, its voice boomed, rattling the lute strings. *Why do you defend it?*

Aspen scrabbled for the instrument, trying to tug it out of its restraints. The thorns only pierced their invisible hands and wrapped it even tighter.

It isn't your forest, either! they shouted, and in a bout of anger, they forced out memories of their own into the sharp growth. Memories of the dead fanes, of the spirits' dying energy shredded in the forest. *It was* theirs *and you took it from them! I won't let you take anything else!*

In a swift and cruel counter from Yarrow, new visions clouded their mind. They came in warped, like peering through a deep pool, but the essence of what Aspen saw still shook them. They watched vines crawl up the gathering hall in the village. Snow piling against the windowsills, roots blocking the door...

No! Aspen tried to block out the visions—they were false projections, they had to be. Only shoved into their mind to scare them.

But with their lute so firmly trapped in the crushing thorns, there was nowhere for them or their fear to go. They couldn't move, couldn't think. All they could do was lash out against the visions until they rippled and distorted even further.

Let them go!

They are in my way, Yarrow rumbled, shaking the earth under the tree. More visions flooded Aspen's mind, faster and more vivid. Thorns broke through the windows. Humans shrieked from within. Deep in the gathering hall, the firelight guttered and went out. *You are in my way.*

The briar encasing the lute constricted with a hiss. The strings all snapped in discordant tones; the wood, cracked years ago and healed, cracked again in a sharp, sickening cry.

But Aspen didn't stop struggling against Yarrow's hold.

Whatever you're looking for beyond the river, they forced out, *you're not going to get it! You can't go to sleep forever this way! It doesn't work and you know it!* They managed to break a few of the thorns, but more grew in their place, thicker and sharper. *We could—we could find another way! All of us—*

The wind lifted Aspen's lute and sent it flying across the dead grove. It crashed against a rock, wooden shards splintering and tumbling into the briar. Aspen briefly wavered, and when they came to, their vision had gone blurry and sideways. Snow whipped upward now in harsh torrents; the bristlecone's branches pointed at strange, cruel angles. It was all they could do to cling to the frozen surface of the soil, desperate not to be swept away along with their lute.

I do not need you, Yarrow hissed, its presence looming over Aspen. *If it takes a hundred of you to return me to sleep, so be it. If it takes a thousand of you, so be it.*

It pulled on Aspen's energy, yanking them into the ground with all the fierce, overpowering strength of a current. There was no escape from the cold soil, nothing they could grasp to keep Yarrow from absorbing them. Only dead grass, discarded roots, and the broken shards of their own grove.

They clung to it all anyway. *You're not taking another one of us!*

Another one? Yarrow's voice rose in victory, sending proud flashes into Aspen's mind. The entire village was smothered in briar now, the river frozen, the southern rooftops black with thorns. And while Aspen fought to blink away the nightmare, Yarrow kept pulling on what remained of their energy—of all the spirits' energy, entrusted to them for this final task.

I will not take one of you, it crowed. *I will take all of you.*

CHAPTER
TWENTY-SEVEN

EMRY

THE TEMPERATURE in the gathering hall plummeted.

The fire in the hearth tried to fight against it, but its flames were as feeble as the spirits in the planters. Within minutes, everyone scrambled for blankets and coats, their own icy breath trailing them like mist.

"Stay by the fire." Nik guided Iris to the chair beside Harvey while Emry and Cal tried to drag the planters closer to the hearth. "We just have to hold on a little while longer."

Soon, the planters formed a makeshift fortress around the armchairs. Harvey held Iris' hand in a wavering grip while Emry stoked the dimming fire, trying to encourage any sort of warmth from it.

"Sorry," he mumbled to the others when the flames refused to cooperate. "I'd go out and get more firewood, but..."

The storm shook the door in response. Cal clutched her notebook tighter—not to write anything in, but simply for something to hold. Emry managed a tiny smile.

"What, you don't want to take any data on this storm?"

Cal gave a weak laugh. "If I survive, I believe I'll recall the details just fine." She twisted in her chair. "Damir, why don't you come sit by the fire?"

But neither Nedrov brother could bring himself to stay inside the tiny fort. Both Damir and Nik stalked from window to window, braving the rattling wind and the cold that seeped through the cracks. Not even Otto wanted to join them; he hid behind Iris' chair, shivering despite his fur.

"There are drifts already gathering against the door," Nik muttered as he crossed Damir's path. Damir grunted in response and rubbed off a patch of fog on the next window.

"The firewood's not that far away," he said. "I could run out there and—"

He gave a loud curse and leaned closer to the window. Emry immediately joined him at the glass and rubbed off more fog with his sleeve.

Even through the clear patch, he had to squint against the driving snow—but movement across the plaza quickly caught his eye. Low, dark vines crept slowly down the road. Slithering over steps, across porches, cutting a path through the gathering snowdrifts...

And the more they filled the plaza, the more the vines spiraled. Tumbling over each other, forming gnarled patches of thorns, each spike longer than Emry's arm.

He froze in place at the window. He had never fought such an onslaught—he *couldn't* fight such an onslaught.

"I don't understand," Pigeon said beside him. He could barely see her form, but he could hear her wings fluttering anxiously against the glass. "Aspen was flying straight there. They had everything we could give. Yarrow should be *gone*."

"Yarrow still has the full strength of the mountain," Shrike hissed somewhere to Emry's left. "Just give Aspen some time—"

Ghostlike badger claws raked the window before he could finish. "We don't have time! Yarrow's right there!"

The spirits' panicked babbling only drew more humans to the windows—first Iris, then Cal, then Harvey.

"What do we do?" Iris wrapped both arms around Nik's, her voice shaking. "Papa, how do we fight it?"

For a brief moment, Nik's eyes shone. Then he pressed his lips together and straightened.

"We don't," he said. "We leave."

A riot of complaints, both spirit and human, cut him off.

"We can't!" Iris pulled away from him in horror. "You promised, you said we'd never leave!"

"And Aspen's still up there!" Pigeon screeched. "We can't just leave them behind—"

But Damir had already gathered up the blankets Iris and Cal had discarded. "Aspen is at the top of a rotting mountain, and Yarrow's at our door," he said grimly. "Even if they do succeed, you think they want to come back and see us torn apart by thorns because we refused to leave?"

Beside him, Cal steadied her shaky hands and started to pile together anything that seemed useful. The bread rolls on the table, an empty sack sitting by Emry's lute... "The southern villages," she said, her voice strung tight. "Warwick and Dav. How far away are they?"

Harvey's next words made her freeze.

"Days," he said softly. "My dear, they're days away, and we have no horse. If we leave, we won't make it."

Low wooden creaks and snaps filled the plaza. Emry forced himself to look out the window one more time.

The vines had crawled around the stage now, their tendrils reaching the side of the gathering hall. Slowly, cruelly, leaves began to cover the windows in thick patches, and little by little, the hall darkened.

"Try to break its growth!" Hawk shouted to the other spirits, their shape fading away in the growing shadows. "We can hold it back!"

One leaf outside shriveled, then two, then three. But they grew back moments later, wider and darker than before. The door rattled; Nik immediately pressed his shoulder against it.

"Iris, get to the back of the hall!" he shouted. "Through the door!"

"No!" Iris latched on to one of the planters. "No, I'm not leaving any of you—"

But Nik pressed on. "Damir, up here with me! We'll tear apart its damn thorns with our bare hands if we have to!"

Damir joined him without a second thought—but Cal stood just as frozen as Emry, watching the door in fear.

"We can't go." Her voice warbled. "Iris is right. We can't leave them."

Emry's chest tightened until he couldn't breathe. Staying would be madness, and leaving would be death. The spirits couldn't move, the thorns were too thick, the back door opened into nothing but snowdrifts and deadly forests... He whipped around for something, anything he could use to defend them, defend his *wife*—

And his gaze landed on his lute, resting by the ash-filled hearth.

He had left it there after his last performance for the others. Back on a gentle, sunny day that, in the dark cold of the hall, felt like it had been years ago. Songs wouldn't be enough to fight Yarrow; songs wouldn't bring it down.

But it was all he had could do—and he had made Aspen a promise.

"We're not leaving them." He picked up his lute and slung the strap over his shoulder, as he had done thousands of times. "All of you, stay here. I said I would guard the hall and I will."

"What does that mean?" Damir looked up from the door, eyes wide. "Karic, what does that mean—?"

Emry ignored him and kissed Cal. Her lips had frozen in the wintery hall, but they still held a hint of what life had been like just days ago: summer wine, berries, a past laugh. Everything he wanted to taste with her again someday.

"Please," he breathed, "for the love of everything, stay inside."

He strode to the door, refusing to think about what he was about to do. She stumbled to follow him.

"Stay inside?" she repeated. "Stay *inside*? While *you're* going out there?"

His heart pounded harder in his ears. "Aspen wouldn't want both of us in danger—"

"I'm in danger whether I'm on this side of the door or not!"

Outside, the wall creaked, and Pigeon's half-visible form darted away from the window. "Get back!"

A large vine, as thick as the planters, slithered up and cracked the glass. Cold air spilled in, the chill reaching right into his bones. He was out of time.

As Nik staggered back, Emry slipped in front of him and rushed through the door. The storm outside immediately reminded him of his poor decision—a blast of wind froze his face, and snowflakes pelted his skin like tiny daggers.

But he didn't let it slow him. He slammed the door closed and staggered away, just in time for yarrow flowers to cover the handle.

"Em!" Cal's voice was muffled by the wood. Moments later, the door shook against the growing vines. "*Emry*! Damir, help me get this open, godsdammit—"

His heart threatened to break his ribcage, and part of him wanted to turn back, rip the flowers apart, open the door—anything to not be alone out here against Yarrow. But Cal was safer there, if only for a moment.

So, he inhaled a knifelike breath, ran onto the creaking, snow-covered excuse for a stage, swung his lute in front of him—

And he began to sing.

You can feel it in the roots below
  As sure as rain and the river's flow

That spring is gone, it's time for her to leave you

At first, he feared the wind would steal his voice. That the words would die in the snow and his magic would die with it. So, he forced his thoughts into the ground instead, where the air couldn't snatch them away. *Break, shatter, wither, leave—*

All around him, the commands took shape, directing his desperation at the growth around the stage and the hall. Vines shriveled at his feet; the thorns at the door snapped in two. Tangles of briar shrank and pulled away from the windows, as if finally cowing under the winter storm.

But Yarrow's determination outpaced Emry's panicked thoughts. The wind howled louder, trying to drown him out, and one by one, each thorn and leaf grew back. Green and purple and black twisted over white snow, lashing at his boots.

Emry kept singing, his voice against the wind.

She stole away into the night
 No kiss left by the candlelight
 Just one thorn from the blooms she always grew you

He struggled to keep his eyes open against the storm, rooting his magic firmly to the earth. His commands weren't enough—wishing for death alone wouldn't save them. But there was life here, too, wasn't there? Life that was loyal to the Rest, and just as headstrong as its villagers. Even through the snow, he could sense flower boxes that hadn't yet frozen over. Ivy that clung to the empty houses. Weeds that slept stubbornly between the cobblestones.

He sang louder and changed his commands, casting them to the surrounding buildings. *Grow, smother, help, please, for the love of everything, help—*

And they did. Weeds sprouted up through snowbanks, tangling angrily with the briar. Flowers spilled over boxes and pots to defend their porches. And behind him, a sharp *snap* ricocheted off the hall as ivy wrenched away the root blocking the door.

Emry's gaze rose to the mountain, a gray peak behind a gray sky. He had done it; he had bought Aspen precious time. He just needed the spirit to—

A thick vine wrapped around his leg. Yarrow still surrounded him, in every leaf and thorn, and the stage couldn't keep him free from its grasp. Thorns reached for his ankle, then piled higher to aim for his arms. He squeezed his eyes shut and tightened his grasp on his lute, his fingers and thoughts both numb from the cold. There would be no retreat for him now. Not to the hall, not even off the stage—

The door behind him slammed open.

"Emry!" Cal came rushing out. "I've got you!"

She grabbed his arm, the glow from his eyes casting a pale light on her face. Relief and fear swept through him in equal measure, and his knees weakened. All he wanted to do was drop the lute and hold her close, to not be alone in this storm anymore—

"Cal," he tried weakly, "the thorns—"

But she didn't listen. She stood in the briar, hands clutching his waist, and sang with him.

> *She cannot stay, you know that well*
>   *No prayer will pull her gray farewell*
>   *Out from your palm, the hand that she once held to*

A moment later, Damir's voice joined hers, his callused hand gripping Emry's shoulder.

> *But if you grow through the sun and snow*
>   *The burnished leaves and the bones below*
>   *She'll dance back to your arms just like she used to*

Though his lungs froze and ached, Emry forced himself to keep going with them, taking their sound and weaving it into his own efforts. The vine reaching for his hand recoiled and withered; the one at his leg loosened.

"Damir!" Nik shouted behind him. "I'm not letting you get ripped apart by yourself, damn you—"

He pounded onto the stage a moment later. Then more footsteps, more voices: Iris and Harvey struggled out into the wind, slow but sure. The spirits shouted with them from the lodge, catching lines and singing them back before the air could rip away their attempts. And Emry caught all of it, both grateful and terrified, scattering the music like seeds with hoarse words and pained fingers. The stage, he just had to protect the stage—

Yarrow's growth snapped and shattered at every turn. But as fast as it broke, it reformed elsewhere, sharper and more desperate. Emry's voice faltered; his stiff, frozen fingers missed one chord, then another. The remains of the village couldn't hold its defense forever, not like this.

Aspen would need to break Yarrow now if Raven's Rest was to make it to the end of the song.

CHAPTER
TWENTY-EIGHT

ASPEN

A**SPEN'S PROMISE** was quickly waning.

They had promised that Yarrow wouldn't take another being, that they would go and end Yarrow themself before anyone else could get hurt.

But none of that had come to pass. Yarrow flooded their mind with horrible visions of hands and necks wrapped in thorns. Nightmares, Aspen told themself as they wrenched away from the thoughts and into reality—but what surrounded them was hardly better. Their lute lay in shards, scattered before the bristlecone pine like broken offerings. Snow piled up around them in tall, freezing drifts. And they couldn't feel any sunlight anymore—Yarrow's pull on them was too strong, its grip too tight. The frozen soil had nearly encased them now, their awareness hovering just over the earth. Earth they didn't belong in, earth *Yarrow* didn't belong in.

But they couldn't fight the spirit anymore. The last of their strength clung to the surface in a final attempt to stay alive.

They couldn't shed tears without a form, but sobs wracked their body anyway, their fragile, amorphous presence that fought against the dirt. They couldn't fail like this. That was their grove down there. The humans and the spirits they had sworn to protect, and guide, and *outlive*, damn them. They couldn't lose now, they couldn't do this—

Something new shook the earth.

Shook wasn't the right word. The vibration was tiny, a pinprick of a star in the night sky. Yarrow ignored it, too victorious, too single-minded to care about such a useless spark. But it shot through Aspen like an earthquake. It was distant, yes, but bright, and warm, and so very familiar—

Emry was singing.

Suddenly, Aspen stood in their grove back in Tazlo. Surrounded not by snow, but aspen trees gilded for autumn. Someone was visiting their grove—the first human in a long, long while. Aspen sat in their favorite tree and looked down upon the nervous bard, who asked for a bit of luck in exchange for a song. His music wrapped around the tree branches and tangled gently with the night air.

Aspen had never heard anything like it. The bard's voice had been so sweet and so—so *sad*. He had asked for something Aspen didn't know how to give, but they had to do something, had to say *something* before he walked away. There was just something about him; they couldn't let him go.

They couldn't let him go then, and they couldn't let him go now.

Aspen desperately reached for the song. It was like trying to gather music notes in their hands, but they made the attempt anyway. Collecting scraps of the melody they knew by heart, the lyrics they had helped write. None of it could put their lute back together or melt the surrounding towers of snow, but it burned somewhere deep inside them, alighting the very last of their determination. Emry was still out there. Their friend, their very best friend, their brother, they had to see him—

Aspen turned their reach to Yarrow. Not to tear it apart or loosen its hold, but to find its memories one more time. To see what it saw at the base of the mountain.

Yarrow had not prepared for such a counter. They had expected Aspen to turn away and close their eyes. Not dig deeper. Not face the mirror. Its malignant visions, so carefully constructed and painted, shattered. Aspen forged ahead, through darkness, down roots, into the cold—

And saw Raven's Rest once more.

There was no blood or death. Emry wasn't on the floor in the gathering hall, being consumed by thorns. He stood out on the sagging wooden stage, eyes glowing, surrounded by every person left in Raven's Rest, filling both the air and the earth with their music.

> *But if you grow through the sun and snow*
>   *The burnished leaves and the bones below*
>   *She'll dance back to your arms just like she used to*

Aspen couldn't help it. With every last vibration they had, they sang along, the words filling the cracks of the frozen earth around them.

Yarrow reeled back from the sound, its pride faltering. It didn't understand—this music here did nothing. It didn't hurt or break or wither. It was out of place, just like Aspen was out of place.

And with that faltering came fear.

It surrounded Aspen as they sang, swiftly replacing Yarrow's pride and anger until nothing else remained. In a blink, the old spirit no longer loomed before them, ancient and all-powerful. It hunched, young, skittish, and desperate.

Aspen almost stopped singing. Behind all the thorns and illusions, that was all the spirit was—fear, sprouted from its very first memory and preserved deep in its roots. After so many seasons, it had rotted and festered, driving each of Yarrow's waking moments... But at its core, the emotion was no different from what Shrike had felt upon waking. What the other spirits had felt, knowing they couldn't go back. What Aspen felt now, for themself and Raven's Rest.

Shrike was right. He could have gone down Yarrow's path once. Any of them could have.

As if knowing how laid bare it truly was, Yarrow gathered itself back together, pushed aside the music, and pulled on its opponent once more. Aspen held on tight to the music as it dragged down and down, through the soil, to the bone-white roots below to finish what it had started—

The song froze in Aspen's throat. The bones below.

Yarrow's roots, the last tethers of the bristlecone pine and the ancient spirit's remaining store of energy, lay just below them, exactly where Yarrow wanted them to go. If Aspen continued to cling to the surface, they could never reach the roots themself. But if they gave in to Yarrow for just a moment, if they let go at the right time...

They'd only have a second before Yarrow tried to claim them. A mere blink to break the bones and take control of the magic there. But down in the village, the thorns grew thicker and the sky grew darker. The humans couldn't sing forever; this moment would have to be enough.

They listened to the music for one more second, grounding themself to it, winding it into their very presence—then let go. In a rush, they plummeted down into the soil. Past not just Yarrow's energy, but the remaining layers of the other spirits that had come before it. The fox, the bear, the owl...then more spirits before that, farther north in pine forests Aspen had never seen. If they succeeded, those remnants would be free. The forest would be free, Envis would be free—

Just as Yarrow reached for them one last time, Aspen stretched down and touched the tree's final tethers.

CHAPTER
TWENTY-NINE

EMRY

The stage was all Emry had left.

At some point during the song, he had fallen to his knees, too numb to feel the boards underneath him. He was vaguely aware of others holding onto him, and the lyrics that slipped out of his mouth, but the cold chased away everything else, including his magic. There was nothing left to pull from, and his commands had dwindled to just one desperate word: *please, please, please—*

A crack shot through the forest. Emry strained to look upward—and far above the village, the mountain moved.

The shift began at the peak of the mountain. Barren slopes, as gray and dead as the sky, roiled with color. Glimmers of gold, shades of yellow and green... The last lyric fell from his lips, and he held his breath as the colors rippled toward him. Over ridges, into the valley, slowly morphing from strange, vivid brushstrokes to recognizable shapes. Trunks, branches, leaves—

Aspen trees. Thousands of them.

They forced their way out of the canopies, claiming the snow and soil in bright, victorious bursts of yellow. And they weren't just aspen trees—new growth from the surrounding trees staked their claim alongside them. Dead branches sloughed off, fresh moss spread. Leaves as tender and green as springtime emerged to greet the sun—

The *sun*. He squinted up at the sky. Something had shoved aside the clouds, dissolved them into nothing, and was letting the full summer sun beat down upon the square once more. Snow melted at Emry's knees. The cold in his bones began to thaw. Thorns shrank away, their owner no longer present. No longer here.

Aspen had defeated Yarrow.

Emry collapsed not onto the stage, but sideways against Cal, his numb fingers dropping the lute and reaching for her instead. "You," he croaked, his throat bone-dry and rattling, "are you all right? The thorns, they didn't—?"

"I'm all right." The lie was a weak one—everyone onstage bore wounds from Yarrow's attack, and Cal hadn't been spared—but she knelt there before him, alive and smiling, snow melting in her hair like a crown. He took her into his arms and kissed every scratch he saw in worship. On her hand, on her wrist, on her neck—

When he reached her cheek, she pulled him in and pressed an exhausted, relieved kiss against his lips, allowing him to revel in the warmth she now exuded—a sun unto herself.

"I love you," he murmured against her lips, then let her lean fully into him, both of them boneless and tired. "I love you, I love you."

She gave an exhausted laugh, her voice vibrating against his ribcage. "Next time you want to barge out and fight an ancient spirit, my love," she murmured, "please just let me come with you the first time."

On Emry's other side, Damir sank to his knees, pale and weary. "And next time, leave me behind."

Slowly, Emry dragged himself away from Cal's warmth to check the others in the plaza. Nik clutched Iris tight at the other end of the stage, letting her relieved sobs soak into his shirt. Harvey allowed Damir to help him to his feet, looking both more tired and more alive than he ever had before.

"I think that's enough excitement for one old man." As he gave a rattling cough, a blur of gray fur barreled into his shin and furiously licked his hand. "Otto. Oh, my dear boy. Did you defend our spirit friends in the hall?"

Otto barked and raced back to the gathering hall, the door still flung wide open in the chaos. But the dog didn't have to go far to retrieve his friends. The ghostlike spirits met him at the doorway, and behind them, small, pale flowers spilled onto the floor in celebration.

"They did it!" Pigeon shrieked, her delicate form flashing in the sunlight. "I told you, I *told* you they could do it!"

She whizzed straight through Cedar's antlers; the elk spirit huffed.

"I didn't doubt them."

"You did too, you doubt everything—"

"Not the young one." Cedar slowly got to their feet in front of their planter. "I learned that long ago."

Together, the spirits all poured out of the hall—or they tried to. Their weak tethers to the planters kept them firmly near the walls, reaching for Emry like excited dogs at the end of their leashes.

"Can you feel Aspen out there?" Hawk asked, his eyes piercing every tree. "I'm too weak to do it myself."

Badger rolled around in the fresh, warm sunlight. "Ooh, tell them to come back! We've got some celebratory basking to do."

The next request was more pleading. "Please tell me they're still out there," Iris said, peeking out from over her father's arm, tears staining her cheeks. "Please."

Emry wobbled to his feet, bolstered by Cal. "I'll try."

He gingerly reached for the closest vine—not one of Yarrow's, but an overflow of ivy from the closest house, come to defend him during the storm. His magic guttered and smoked inside him, a candle melted to the very bottom of its wick, but he did what he could anyway. Pouring gratitude into the ivy alongside a question, not unlike what he had once thought when looking at Aspen's grove.

Are you out there?

For a moment, nothing responded. Just the vibrant, busy sensation of a growing forest making up for lost time. Just the life given back to it. Emry tried harder, hands shaking. Cal touched his shoulder, but he couldn't bring himself to look at her. *Aspen?*

Still nothing.

Then something glimmered in the distance. Not to his eyes, but to his magic. A signature he had known for years, shifting toward him just like the rolling wave of green and gold. Dappled sunlight, honeysuckle, the echoes of a song...

A flower-filled lute, shattered and trailing soil, clattered at the end of the plaza, and a moment later, Emry was enveloped in a tight, invisible embrace.

I heard you. Aspen was too weak to take a form, but their voice surrounded him in relief. *I heard you singing—*

Emry let out a broken sob, even as he smiled. "You did it," he said. "Aspen, you did it—"

Cal leaned in, tears rolling down her cheeks, and for a moment, it was just the three of them, as it had always been.

Well—not always. But Emry didn't want to recall a time without either of them.

Of course I did it, Aspen said, their presence enveloping them both in warmth stronger and more loving than the sun. *I promised you I would.*

But that wasn't all they had done. When Cal finally broke away, dabbing at her eyes and reaching to gather the broken shards of Aspen's lute, the spirit's form wrapped around both her wrist and Emry's.

Wait. Don't.

In a shape akin to a sunbeam, Aspen knelt by their lute—or rather, the pile of wood and soil that made up their lute—and gently pulled together a little mound of dirt. Within it lived the tiniest seedling Emry had ever seen. Barely more than a seed, and hardly bigger than an eyelash, it struggled to poke through the thin earth, yearning quietly for the light.

"What?" Cal said, searching Aspen's vague form. "What is it?"

Yarrow.

As the other spirits and humans gathered around, Aspen collected enough energy to speak aloud—and when they did, their voice was hardly stronger than the summer breeze.

"It's all that's left of Yarrow. It'll take a long time for it to grow back. A very long time, after all the magic it spent."

"But"—Hawk hopped on the cobblestone—"but you said you were going to *defeat* it."

"And it has been defeated," Aspen said. "Look at it. It can't do anything in this state."

Emry swallowed. Aspen was right—the little thing looked harmless like this, as if one stiff breeze would uproot it. Next to him, Nik crouched, his face shadowed as he inspected the seedling. The source of his village's demise, all contained in one tiny plant.

But when the village leader spoke, his voice was steeped not in anger, but in concern.

"And when it can?" he asked. "When it's grown large enough to fight you again?"

"I don't know." The uncertainty didn't shake Aspen; they merely pushed the soil into a neater pile. "Maybe it'll fight, maybe it won't. Maybe we'll know how to go back to sleep by then, and we can return it to its old grove in the north. Or...maybe we won't."

Their form shifted, as if they were sitting back on their heels and considering the tiny plant.

"It was scared," they said quietly. "That's all it was. If I can take that away for a while—if I can give it a chance to be with other spirits, to not be afraid for once..." Their shape glowed stronger for a moment. "I don't know what it'll do. It can decide that for itself. But whatever it decides, whatever it grows into...I want to see it." Their form straightened to address the humans. "I want to give it that chance."

CHAPTER
THIRTY

EMRY

WHILE ASPEN, Emry, and the other spirits recovered, Raven's Rest was busier than ever—and that included the ravens.

"I've got Dina headed down to Warwick," Harvey rattled off when Emry checked in on him in the tower. "Joslyn's off to Vornik, of course. Then I've got two more birds headed down to Tail's End..."

Emry soon lost track of all the towns now being accosted by Harvey's ravens. He had slept through the first day of the commotion, then spent the second just trying to get out of bed—but watching Harvey conduct his birds like a single cawing orchestra had been worth the effort of shuffling up the tower steps.

When Emry complimented the man accordingly, he simply sat on a stool and rubbed his hands together, his eyes twinkling. "I only wish I could fly with 'em, just to see the looks on the others' faces when they open those letters. I've got friends with bets out against this place, you know. Not that I could ever tell Nik about them." He chuckled. "Old man wouldn't be able to take it."

One of the remaining ravens landed on Harvey's shoulder,

pecking at his shirt pocket in search of snacks. Harvey dug into the pocket and pulled out one of Yarrow's berries.

"You know," he mused as he inspected the fruit, "these birds might be the only ones upset that the old spirit's gone."

Emry leaned against the open window to enjoy the warmth. "Really?"

"Sure." Harvey tossed the fruit up once, then held it out for the raven. "Won't have any more of these berries to give 'em."

Whether the ravens were aware of the pending berry shortage or not, they performed their duties with remarkable efficiency: within days, a donkey-drawn wagon appeared at the mouth of the southern road.

"Nik?" A woman hopped off the wagon, trepidation etched into her tired face as she regarded the empty houses. After patting the donkey's nose, she tucked a graying strand of hair behind her ear and ventured slowly, cautiously down the road.

When she came upon the trees towering at the bridge, she stopped in both shock and reverence.

"All the gods and spirits take me," she said softly, then squared her shoulders and raised her voice. "Nikolai Nedrov, are you out there? I got a letter, but I don't dare believe it until I see that damned reckless face of yours!"

Nik dropped the cart of old briar he was hauling. "Yvette?" He tugged off his gloves and started running. "Yvette, I'm over here!"

Emry quickly followed—but when the two of them approached, Yvette didn't dare move.

"The others sent me as soon as we got Harv's letter," she said stiffly, bracing herself for disappointment. "Tell me. Is it true?"

Nik raised his arms, eyes shining. "It's true. It's gone, it's over—"

She broke and ran into his arms like Iris had, her voice caught between a laugh and a sob. Emry pulled off his own gloves and glanced at Damir, who hung back by the briar cart. As Emry gently nudged him forward, the woman looked around, tears streaking her cheeks.

"Where's my obstinate little one?" she demanded. "My Iris flower? My—"

Her gaze landed on Damir, and she froze.

"Shiro's beard on fire, I don't believe it."

Nik gave Damir a proud smile; Damir wearily raised his arms, then dropped them. "Believe it."

The woman strode forward, all determination—then she grabbed the gloves out of Emry's hands and slapped Damir on the shoulder with them.

"All those years without letters, Miri, and *now* you show your face?" She slapped his arm again. "No note! Not a word!"

Damir flinched. "Like you ever wrote, either—"

"Don't start that with me!" But Yvette had broken out into a smile again, and she wrapped Damir into a hug as tight as the one she had given Nik. "My idiot cousins. My foolish beans for brains."

Emry laughed and turned to look for Iris. If the others were getting berated, it was her turn for a good, tearful reprimand—

Then Yvette handed the stolen gloves back to Emry.

"Who's this, then?" she said, eyes narrowed at him. Emry would have bet half his life savings she already knew he wasn't from Envis.

He took back the gloves and gave a short bow. "Just a bard passing through. Welcome back to Raven's Rest, Yvette. You have a lovely home."

A full grin broke out on her face, as if she never thought she'd hear the words again.

"Well, then." She sniffed and drew herself up. "My family's intact, a bard's in town, and there's no Yarrow in sight." She turned to Nik. "It's time to bring the others back."

At the time, Emry had assumed that *others* simply meant those who had once left the Rest: a modest sum of villagers, ready to fill their houses again. He eagerly set to work alongside Cal, tidying Yvette's cottage—under Yvette's own strict supervision—then moving their sparse luggage into Harvey's spare room. Then he joined Iris at the planters in the town square, trowel in hand.

Together with Damir, they had positioned the spirits' planters all around the stage, so the spirits could take advantage of the full sunlight while Iris tended to them.

And naturally, she took their care as seriously as she would for any of her citizens.

"How's the soil?" she asked Badger, patting the dirt around the ferns that had popped up over the last few days. "Do you need any more compost?"

"Oh, no, my dear." Badger appeared above the ferns and snuffled the fresh earth. "This is luxurious, is what this is."

Near Badger, Aspen's lute sat on the stage itself, basking in the sun just as Iris had instructed. Emry and Damir had worked together to gather the pieces of their lute and patch them up—and for any remnants they couldn't find, Nik had carved little shards to replace them. The poor instrument now sat as a patchwork of mismatched wood grains, glue, vines, and leaves, with a few missing tuning pegs and no strings in sight. It was a nightmarish view for a bard—but the flowers inside bloomed as vibrant and happy as any garden.

And in the lute's shadow, Yarrow's seedling rested in a pot, quiet, small, and sleeping. As much as a spirit could sleep, anyway.

"Are you excited to meet the other villagers, Aspen?" Emry patted Yarrow's soil flat, then leaned back and stretched his legs. It was calming to be on the planks here, amidst the melding signatures of all the spirits. Their forms still flickered and faded in the sun, but with every hour, they grew stronger, exuding an earthy, floral perfume throughout the square. "Iris says I have to play something for the village or else she'll kick me out."

Over by Cedar, Cal snorted. Iris looked up from Hawk's planter. "I didn't say that!"

"She did say that. She said she'll throw me right into the river." Emry grinned and turned back to Aspen. "How about it? Will you join me onstage and keep me from getting in trouble?"

The question wavered with more nerves than he had wanted.

Perhaps Aspen was already done with him. Perhaps they didn't want to go on stage again—

But Aspen appeared in front of him, sitting cross-legged as always, their smile warm. "I'd love to."

Holding on to that relief, Emry prepared a small set list in the time he didn't spend resting or cleaning the village. Harvey suggested a few songs; Iris requested a few more. He even had Damir review and rearrange the list, assuming this sort of work was overkill for a small village reunion.

But the "modest sum" of villagers he had promised to play for—that *they* had promised to play for—turned out to be far from the truth.

In a matter of days, the village overflowed with life. More cousins poured into the city, then grandparents, nieces, nephews, neighbors, friends, acquaintances. Even the ones with bets against Harvey rolled in on carts and wagons, their laughter booming as money changed hands. The money didn't matter—they were just glad to see Harvey again.

But it wasn't just Raven's Rest that had come back to roost. Other Envisians, both southern residents and transplants from Yarrow's northern wreckage, had heard of the victory and used the Rest as a stopping point before they trekked back to their old haunts. The gathering hall was quickly converted to an inn; any home that remained unoccupied was opened to strangers.

To Nik's relief, the final group to arrive didn't need any such shelter.

The first spirit was a tabby cat: a graying shorthair who had been Pigeon's closest link in her communication chain back to Vornik.

"So you really killed that thing?" It sat before Pigeon's planter, tail twitching eagerly. "You took it down?"

"Yes, but"—Pigeon flitted to the end of the planter—"I'm afraid we still don't have any answers to send back to the others. We never found out how we could—"

"Oh, never mind that right now." The cat purred and rubbed its cheeks against the edges of the wood. "I'm just happy to see you alive."

Indeed, they all were—a dozen more spirits stationed between the mountains and Vornik poured in, taking up residence on the stage and ogling Raven's Rest just as much as Raven's Rest ogled them.

"You think..." Nik stood at the edge of the plaza next to Yvette and Emry, stroking his beard as he watched a group of children play in the planters and chase Otto around the stage. "You think we should move the spirits somewhere else?"

"Why?" Yvette shrugged. "They won't leave droppings on my house and they won't eat my pies when I'm not looking. As far as I'm concerned, they're perfect guests."

So, Raven's Rest worked around the spirits to transform the old plaza back into the market it had once been. Merchants and traders and tinkerers of all kinds descended upon the cobblestones and set up stalls, just as eager to see familiar faces as they were to sell their wares once more. And many in Raven's Rest were eager to buy—Nik brought Harvey enough wine to replace his stock for a year. Yvette gifted Iris as much toffee as she could hold in her pockets. Emry even found a few pegs and strings for Aspen's lute and a beautiful quill for Cal.

But the best part of all—Emry's unexpected favorite—were the paints.

Raven's Rest acquired every pigment and brush the merchants had to offer, adding them to others they'd cobbled together in their yards and kitchens. The village mixed each color as reverently as they cleaned and weeded and dusted—then quickly got to work giving the entire village a fresh coat of paint.

They painted over the old designs first, refreshing the leaves and ravens, then added a dizzying number of flourishes until their paint ran out. Emry and Cal took multiple strolls through the village to admire the palettes and spot the new designs. Some of the additions were easy to find: yarrow flowers at the bases of columns, thorns in the corners. A reminder of what had happened here.

But as Emry walked, he spotted cheerier paintings hidden amongst the patterns. Aspen leaves. Quills, feathers, antlers, claws—and lutes. Little ones. Some filled with flowers, others empty. As he regarded one, Cal kissed him on the cheek.

"I believe it's time to get Spiritsong ready for their performance." She glanced at the setting sun. A bittersweet feeling swept over the joy the tiny painted lute had brought; Emry pushed it aside and followed her to the plaza with a strained smile.

He found he didn't mind the little stage so much anymore—not when the village had so thoroughly reclaimed it. The paint was fresh here, too, the dead leaves swept off the boards. The spirits, who had all been eagerly mingling with villagers and visitors, coalesced back on the stage when Emry and Aspen arrived. To Emry's relief, the streetlamps no longer shone through the spirits' forms; they were finally strong enough to look whole again.

"What are you going to play?" Pigeon asked eagerly, sitting on Cedar's antlers. "Any songs we might remember? I know you don't have Sage and Riley. We could sing along, if you think that might help—"

Emry laughed. "This concert is just as much for you as it is for the others. Please just enjoy yourself. Aspen and I have it handled."

As he had hoped, Raven's Rest was a generous crowd to a troupe of two. There was no hint of Envisian prickliness here: they shouted out suggestions, clapped, sang, danced. Iris led her friends in a giddy, twirling mess, brighter and louder than Emry had ever seen her. The same could be said for the whole square—despite its size, it contained the energy of an entire Sada festival, all packed into one rowdy, joyful evening.

And, naturally, the flowers helped.

He hadn't been thinking about magic as he played—he was only thinking about the music and how to properly welcome the crowd back to their own village. But his magic came with it anyway, and the flowers in the planters overflowed onto the stage. With a mere thought from Aspen, they glowed like fireflies in the night, happy to join in on the rhythm. And of course, Aspen themself flourished—the honeysuckle from the lute on their back grew down their arms, all the way to the fingers that strummed their concert lute. They danced and sang like they did at every concert, and for a moment, everything was normal. Everything was perfect.

Then Emry stepped off the stage, and the magic of the set faded. Aspen rushed off to join their fellow spirits, babbling about the music and asking them about their favorite songs. Cal met him off to the side, magnanimously willing to kiss him despite how sweaty he always was after concerts.

"Wonderful, as always," she said, wiping his brow with a handkerchief. Iris had handed her a pink flower crown before the set, and she wore it as regally as she did everything else. "One could never guess you were almost killed by a spirit a few days ago."

"What a compliment." He gave a breathy laugh and straightened her crown. "Though I suppose you're obligated to say such things as my wife."

She wiped his cheek, then kissed his freckles. "I don't believe that particular obligation was in my vows."

He lingered with her in the shadows for a moment, arms wrapped around her waist, drinking in the flower crown's soft scent. But as he drew away, he caught sight of Damir over at a table, throwing a hand of cards down in front of Nik with a smug smile on his face. He swallowed, fighting the urge to stay with Cal, but there was no point in delaying it—he had to talk to Damir about Aspen sooner or later.

"Be right back." He reluctantly gave Cal a parting kiss, then made his way over to the table and nodded to Damir. "May I have a word?"

Nik threw down his own cards. "Berate him while you're at it, will you? The man still cheats after all these years."

"I didn't cheat!"

Nik waved off the words with a grin, clapped Emry on the shoulder, then wandered toward Iris, who huddled excitedly with several other girls her age. Ever since her friends had arrived, the gaggle had been inseparable. Sharing toffees, weaving flower crowns...and gossiping about Iris' adventures.

"And then all the spirits gathered at the bridge"—she pointed toward it as the other girls listened in fascination—"and grew those trees there! You can see the tops of them just over the top of your house, Maria."

Damir watched Nik tousle Iris' hair, then leaned back and lit his pipe. "Karic, if you're asking for a tour of Envis to be added to the concert schedule, I'm afraid I'm going to have to pass. I'm going to need at least three more years before I see any of these faces again."

Emry took one look at the flecks of paint on Damir's hands and the smile that crinkled his eyes and knew that wasn't true—but he couldn't bring himself to call out his manager on his lie. Not yet, at least.

"That's not what I wanted to ask." He took Nik's chair, his insides twisting into knots. Compared to everything else that had happened in the last week, he thought this conversation would be easy. "I wanted to talk to you about the upcoming Vornik tour you had planned. Well...all the tours, really."

Damir's eyes narrowed. "All right."

"I..." Emry drummed his fingers on the table, his breaths shallow. He would be fine, he told himself. It would be fine.

"I know everyone has come to expect a certain sort of concert from Spiritsong," he said. "But if Aspen... If it was just my magic at the concerts, and not theirs. Do you think..." He hedged his words before he could even utter them. "If you don't think it would be enough, there's other things I could do for the Guild. I could be, um—a spirit diplomat of sorts. You know, continuing to keep the peace, talking to Councilmembers. Or I could—"

"Emry."

He looked up in surprise; Damir never used his first name.

"Sage and Riley," Damir continued. "Do you think they're terrible musicians?"

Emry gaped. "No, absolutely not—"

"You'd see them in concert?"

"Of course I would! Every night!"

"All right, then." Damir puffed on his pipe. "Back at the Red Rat, years ago. When I saw you onstage. Who was playing the lute?"

"What?"

"When I first saw you at the Red Rat," he repeated, "who was playing the lute? Was it Aspen or was it you?"

Emry frowned. "It was me, but—"

"And who was singing the song? You or Aspen?"

"Me, but I don't see how—"

Damir lowered his pipe and stared at him. "Aspen didn't teach you how to sing or play the lute, and that wasn't Aspen I heard at the tavern that day. You have talent that doesn't come from magic. I could hear it then and I heard it tonight. And while I might not look forward to the constant trouble you and the other two naturally gravitate toward..." He shifted in his chair, breaking his gaze for a moment. "I look forward to all your concerts, Karic. Every single one."

The knot in Emry's throat hardened; he fought against it. "So...so you're all right. If Aspen leaves."

"I'm saying *you're* all right if Aspen leaves." He stood. "You're still Spiritsong. You always have been. And you can tour wherever you like, so long as it isn't Envis. Now"—he pointed his pipe to the stage—"that's all the niceness you'll get from me. Return to your wife before my reputation becomes tattered beyond all recognition."

Emry couldn't help it; he gave Damir a hug.

"Thank you," he murmured. "For everything."

Damir returned the hug, trying to hide the thickness in his voice. "You're easy to tolerate."

"Even when we almost get killed by mad scientists and evil spirits?"

Damir sighed. "Well. We all need new material for that next song, don't we?"

CHAPTER
THIRTY-ONE

EMRY

The concert didn't mark the end of the celebrations for Raven's Rest—every time new people arrived, the dinners and parties and drinks began anew. Emry was called upon to sing several more times, while the entire group was called upon to tell the story of Yarrow's defeat. And the poor spirits in the plaza had to answer the same fascinated questions over and over: What did it feel like to grow flowers? How exactly did they summon clouds? And could they really not drink ale?

But the more Raven's Rest filled out, the more it settled into itself, the more Emry knew it was time to leave. The village still had plenty of healing to do, but it was best to leave them to it, for now.

And the next letter from Sage and Riley didn't help matters.

I'm not sure what will have happened since my sending of this letter—

"Only everything," Emry muttered to himself, then continued reading.

But please stay safe. We'll be here to welcome you back whenever you're ready. Which I do hope is soon, because if Riley has to keep dealing with these Councilmembers by herself, she'll punch one of them, and I simply cannot have a reputation like the Forsgren Quartet. I have worked far too hard to—

The rest of the rant was scribbled out and replaced with a single line.

We look forward to seeing you in one piece and hearing your song. Chin up, my dears.

Emry peered out the tower window and down at the luggage now stacked in a wagon, waiting to leave. Yes, he thought as he folded up the late letter. Chin up, indeed.

When he descended the stairs, he found the wagon wasn't alone in its wait. Aspen and the other spirits had clustered together on the road, while Nik pored over a map with Damir.

"That route should do it." Nik tapped the paper. "It's not the shortest path, but it's the safest and it'll drop you right at Warwick." He folded up the map and handed it to Damir. "You're, uh—you're sure you have to leave today? Road might be drier if you stay a few more days."

Damir forced out a shrug. "Afraid we all have to get back to work."

"But—but you'll write? Now and then, of course," Nik added quickly. Damir pocketed the map with a small smile.

"Suppose I could spare a few words every month or so."

Nik nodded and rubbed the back of his neck. "Good, good. You know, in a few weeks..." He cleared his throat. "Iris and I think we can wrangle a few others to help clear the northern paths. To the fanes, I mean. Clean them up, keep an eye on them in case a spirit decides to live there again. Mrs. Karic gave Iris some sort of... pamphlet or something on what to look out for..."

THE SPIRIT'S CURSE

Damir blinked at him in thinly veiled shock. "And...you'll tell me? If anything shows up?"

Nik gave a gruff laugh. "You'd better hightail it back here if anything shows up. Gods know I won't have a clue what to say to it."

Emry hid a smile at that and headed toward Cal and Iris, who waited nearby with Harvey and Otto. Otto leaned against Iris' leg, his tail thumping against the road, and stared lovingly up at her and her flower crown. Aspen had woven it for her before the concert, and the daisies within still looked freshly picked.

"Could I come visit Vornik one day?" Iris blurted out to Cal. "Papa said I had to ask you first."

Cal laughed. "Of course, you can. As soon as your villagers can spare you, we'll give you the grand tour. Won't we, Em?"

But Emry was too focused on the gaggle of spirits behind the wagon, all conferring quietly with Aspen.

"I hear there's a giant lake northwest of us," Pigeon was saying. "And taller mountains, too."

"Any spirits left around there, do you think?" Badger asked.

"We'll find them, if there are," Cedar said firmly. Emry swallowed and turned back to Iris with a false smile.

"Sure. Yes, of course. Grand tour and everything."

A half hour later, Raven's Rest led them outside the village, then left them at the fork in the road with a firm handshake and an extracted promise to visit again soon.

"The birds'll get sad if you don't come," Harvey warned. "They always remember a friendly face."

But his eyes shone as he said it. Emry shook his hand with as much reassurance as he could muster. "Mustn't disappoint the birds, then."

Harvey sniffed and waved him along to the eastern road. "Off you get. I'm sure a city will do you all some good after your time in the forest."

He turned and shuffled away alongside Nik and Iris, easily navigating paths once hidden by snow and thorns. The birds had yet to truly return to the forest post-Yarrow, but a few of them chirped in the sunlit branches above. As Cal took his hand, Emry stared hard at the canopy, then the path. According to Nik's map, the eastern road gradually bent downward—south to Warwick, then on to the mountains, to Vidanya, and eventually to the city of Vornik, where he belonged.

But not all of them belonged in Vornik.

The spirits stood at the mouth of the western path, the one that led deeper into the forest. Cedar, Pigeon, Badger, and Hawk formed the front line, but the others from Pigeon's chain had all gathered there as well. Together, they stood over a dozen strong, all of them ready to find answers—and friends—elsewhere.

"Well." Shrike pawed the earth, then tentatively bumped his soft head against Emry's hand. "Stay safe. Don't take any boats. Don't talk to strange spirits."

Emry laughed and patted between Shrike's ears. "Don't attack any more bards at the end of their set, all right? Really hurts our chances for an encore."

Next to Emry, Cal crouched down. "If you do find a way to sleep... would you please come visit us first? Say hello one more time?"

"You want me to go back into a city?" But underneath his words, Shrike purred. "All right, all right. I'll come visit."

After a brief brush against Cal's shoulder, he padded over to Cedar and Pigeon and quietly joined their huddle. Badger, her paws wrapped around Yarrow's flowerpot, nuzzled him in welcome.

But the group didn't move on yet; their eyes followed one more spirit.

Aspen stood directly at the fork in the road, weighed down by two lutes: their grove, slung on their back, and their concert lute, its wood shining in the warm forest light. As they looked at Emry, their words trembled.

"I, um... I have to..." They took a breath, made unsteady by tears already spilling onto their face. "I think I should—"

Cal's hand in Emry's grip started to shake. Emry squeezed it, then let go and reached out to Aspen. "It's all right."

Aspen rushed into his arms without a second thought. The force of their embrace couldn't distract Emry from the taste of tears gathering in the back of his throat, but he pushed out the words anyway.

"You can go with the other spirits," he said, his gentle tone cracked by the waver in his voice. "You belong with them just as much as you do with us."

"I have to look after them." Their tears seeped into Emry's hair. "Even if we don't find their answers. I told them we'd do it together, I promised them—"

"I know, I know." He tried to smile. "You'll love all the traveling, Aspen. All the new friends. All the new food you get to ask about—"

Aspen let out a broken laugh and clung tighter to him. "I won't be gone forever. I'll—I'll fly back and visit every few months, I swear it."

"Gods, you'd better." Cal sniffled loudly and wrapped both of them in a hug, turning them into a trio one more time. Emry held on tight—too tight, even with his hands shaking—but eventually, Cal slipped away, wiped at her face, and rummaged in her satchel.

"Here." She pulled out a journal—an untouched one, its pages fresh and clean—then tugged the pencil from behind her ear and handed both to Aspen. "I want to hear about Yarrow's progress and everything new you find. Every"—she sniffed, her composure breaking again—"tree and bird and fish. And I'll need a report every few months. For statistic consistency, you see."

Aspen tucked the pencil behind their ear, and she broke into a sob. Emry let her squeeze the life out of his hand—the most basic of his duties as a husband—while he shoved back his emotions to get just a few more words out.

"Learn a few new songs and teach them to me when you get back, all right?" he said, wiping his own cheeks. Aspen nodded, then glanced at Damir and pulled their Guild pin out of their pocket.

"Do you want—?" They held out the simple, shiny circle. Damir shook his head, his jaw working hard to keep his own expression steady.

"Keep it. You're still a part of Spiritsong, as far as I'm concerned."

"Aspen," Cedar called from the road, gentle but firm. Now that they had grown stronger, their elk form was almost back to its original size, the moss-covered antlers brushing the higher tree branches. "The humans should start on their path while they have daylight."

Aspen took a long, ragged breath, then stepped back, shoulders squared. "Right. I'll look after them," they tried to say bravely. "I love you."

Emry gave them one more hug, closing his eyes against the scent of mint and honeysuckle. "I love you, too."

CHAPTER
THIRTY-TWO

EMRY

NOTHING COULD COMPARE to the first night of Sada in the forest.

Not that Emry didn't love being in the city during the new year's festival. Cities held a vibrant sort of energy on Sada, one that was generous to a bard lucky enough to perform that night. The audience sang louder, danced harder, drank more. The parties stretched endlessly, the hand pies flowed freely. In the city, it was a celebration of the highest proportions.

But to be in the forest for Sada was an entirely different matter. Celebrating amidst the trees kept things simple: food, wine, family, and friends. In some parts of the province, the whole town would be scattered out in the forest, little pockets of festivity connected by deer trails. Back in Senne, Emry used to wander between such parties all night. Giving and receiving songs, sampling what his cousin or friend or neighbor had made and trading it with something of his own. And when it came to music, trees were just as generous of an audience—no drinking necessary.

It had been years since Emry had enjoyed such a celebration on Sada; so, the following autumn, he decided to bring it back.

"Georgie, do you have the—?" He looked around and sighed. "Hara take me, where'd the ladle go?"

"Watch out, Emry." Marley held up a finger. "If you say such things on Sada, Hara might actually whisk you away."

Georgie grunted into her mug. "If I say it, can Hara whisk me away before Nana starts singing?"

Her mother leaned forward to glare at her over the long table. "I heard that. Emry, darling, here's the ladle. Stew's over that way."

It had taken a bit of convincing to break the family—both sides of the family, Karic and Breslin—from celebrating in their respective cities. But after a few letters, they had agreed to do something a little different for Sada this year. They all descended upon Tazlo, sisters and parents and cousins and in-laws, and hauled their finest food, drink, and instruments out to the forest.

To Aspen's grove, specifically.

"You said they like pears, yes?" Cal's mother stood tentatively before Aspen's fane, pear in hand. Cal looked up from her bowl of stew, which had been by far the most treacherous dish they had dragged out to the grove. Half of it had nearly ended up on the moss at the start of the path.

"They'll love it, Mum," she reassured her. Mrs. Breslin turned back to the box and bit her lip, looking very much like her daughter in that instant.

"And...they'll appreciate it even if it isn't *in* the fane, exactly?"

To Emry's delight, Aspen's fane had no more room for offerings. The little wooden box overflowed with food, flowers, and trinkets. In fact, it had already been half-full when they arrived, honored by travelers passing by on the road. Emry couldn't even see his original coin in there, so hidden it was by all the gifts.

Which was just how he wanted it.

"They'll appreciate it," he called. "I promise."

Mrs. Breslin set the pear on the ground, next to another pile of offerings, and hurried on to the cookie tray in relief.

Even though Emry's family was the only group occupying the forest that night, he still had plenty of mingling to do within the grove. His Tazlin friends—Marko, Stef, Bron, and others from his time at the Dancing Rabbit—stopped in with wine and hand pies, wanting to know how life in Vornik was treating him. Sage begged Tessa Karic for stories of Emry as a child, while Riley made a game of stealing Georgie's drink when she wasn't looking. And when his troupe mates ran off to go watch Karlson down at the Lamb's Ear Inn, Emry sat with his in-laws and, in classic Breslin fashion, was interrogated on what he had been up to recently.

"Oh, please, I've done nothing of interest." He smiled and passed the wine bottle down to Cal's aunt. "You all were at the concert in Etris. You've seen my work."

They had seen the work that was meant to be visible, of course. He didn't want to bore them with his Council meetings that quietly quashed anti-spirit laws. Nor did he want to elaborate on Mr. Chamberlain's reluctant, grumbling approval of spirits after a few of them amiably—and rather smugly—fixed his roads in Cima. *Spirits Save Cima Sales*, the papers had said. Emry had made sure that particular headline spread far and wide.

Not that he felt like bragging about any of that here. Let the others see the glowing flowers and the pretty songs—he, Ella, and Damir would handle the rest. Just as the Guild ought.

"And Aspen's truly been writing to you every week?" Mr. Breslin asked.

Cal laughed. "Every week when they recall. Sometimes twice in one week, if they've really forgotten what day it is."

Marley leaned toward the conversation. "Have they made it to the ocean yet?"

"Not yet." Emry tried to recall the map Cal had put up in her study, full of pins tracking where Aspen had last written from. "They were deep in Aviko about a month ago, but then had bounded back east right after. Something about a music festival Aspen wanted to attend."

"I believe I heard about that," Mr. Breslin mused. "Some rumors about a singing wolf?"

Those were Emry's favorite rumors. Clearly, Aspen wasn't lugging around their concert lute just for show. Every now and then, a story would trickle back to him—about a human, a pigeon, and an elk teaching a tavern a new song. About a traveling bard sharing a few lyrics with a young person, only to watch said young person bound into the forest as a wolf moments later. He wondered if Aspen would remember the new songs well enough to teach them to Emry upon their return. His portfolio of Avikan music in particular was rather sparse—

Someone placed the half-finished cookie tray on the table, then set a hand on Emry's shoulder. He looked up to find his father smiling down at him.

"It's almost time for the music," Edward said. "Any word from Aspen this morning?"

Emry's smile weakened. "No word today." Then, more defensively: "But I know they'll make it back. They said they would in their last letter."

"Where'd they write from, again?"

"Just across the Selj border. Near Matlock."

He passed the cookie tray along without taking one, his appetite not quite matching the still-abundant spread before him. Aspen's last letter had been from a week ago, but the spirit could travel faster than any human. All they had to do was fly, or run through the forest, or swim through some sort of river. So long as they hadn't lost track of time...which they most certainly could have, given that Emry hadn't left them with a pocket watch or anything. Gods, he should have thought about that before they—

Under the table, Cal touched his knee, quelling his thoughts.

"They'll be here," she said. "They promised."

Aspen had indeed promised. So, Emry stayed back while the

grove was prepared to host music. The long table—an absolute bear to drag into the forest—was pulled to the side. Blankets and chairs were splayed out over the grass.

And in turn, each family brought their instruments and their voices to Aspen's tree as an offering for the new year.

The tree was not exactly a hallmark of the joy of the festival—still blackened as it had been from the surge years ago—but it proved to be just as kind of an audience as any of the other trees. Emry's cousins went up first to sing a lively drinking song. Then his sisters took their turn, then Cal's aunt—a beautiful soprano—then his Nana—an untenable alto...

Song after song was offered to the goddess Hara and the spirits—and before long, the moon had risen high, the food had gone cold, and the party had nearly had their fill of music.

"Emry?" His mother finally turned to him, her smile both sweet and sad. Emry clenched his jaw tight against his disappointment.

"Sure," he mumbled and headed for his lute case near the tree line. This wasn't quite how he'd wanted the evening to go. He adored celebrating with his family and friends, of course. He loved the low, gentle signature of the grove pulsing under his feet, and the music that gradually collected there. But he had also wanted Aspen to see the grove again. To see all the people here, and the fane that overflowed with offerings just for them.

He steeled himself as he tuned his lute. He'd spent the last few months without Aspen. He could perform just one song without them. After all, he had done it for years before them. It didn't make him sad at all to think he was singing a song in Aspen's grove and they weren't even there to hear it—

A crash sounded through the underbrush, followed by a panicked, rhythmic thump—much like a lute banging against someone's back as they ran.

"Wait, wait!" Aspen called out. "Are you all still here? What time is it? Tell me you haven't left yet—!"

The spirit skidded to a halt in their own grove, bare feet disappearing in the grass, their golden waistcoat glittering to celebrate the festival. The lute on their back shed flower petals in the rush, and their concert lute hung loose in their hand.

But the smile on their face more than rivaled the light of the full moon.

"I made it!" they crowed. "And you're all still here!"

The entire party converged on them, loud, half-drunk, and ecstatic.

"Hey!" Marley elbowed Georgie on her way to the spirit. "I said I was going to hug them first—"

Georgie hip-checked her into the trees and lifted Aspen off the ground in an embrace. "I'm buying you a pocket watch in the morning."

"But I made it, didn't I?" Aspen happily kicked their feet in the air. "I even took the river boats and everything!"

Behind Georgie, Edward sniffled. "I'm so proud of you."

Not eager to pluck leaves out of his hair like Marley was currently doing, Emry set down his lute and let the others smother Aspen first, basking in the chaos of the crowd alone. He even let Cal interrogate the spirit before they made it over to him—a generous move, but it was unfortunately in his vows not to obstruct her scientific method.

"The journal, did you bring it?" Cal squealed and jumped when they handed it to her. "How much did you write?" She gasped as she flipped through the pages. "You even *drew* in it!"

From his distance, Emry tried to peek over Cal's shoulder. Aspen had indeed added little sketches to their notes. Some of them weren't exactly true to life—a few of the flowers, for example, had tiny smiles in their centers—but several of the drawings matched the new blooms cascading from Aspen's lute, right next to Yarrow's tiny seedling.

Still quiet, still growing. Still slowly moving toward its second chance.

"I tried to track Yarrow's height and draw some of the new things

I saw," Aspen said proudly, then faltered. "Pigeon said my birds could use some work. She said I wasn't getting the wings right."

Cal looked around. "Did Pigeon come with you?"

"She's in Matlock for a few days." Aspen brightened. "To see Lydia for Sada. Cedar's visiting Brinna, too, then we'll go and meet Badger down in Foxhill. I can't wait to tell you all about—"

Emry cleared his throat. "Pardon me, but Nana would like to hear our song before she falls asleep."

He blinked, and Aspen was in front of him, lifting *him* off the ground in an eager embrace.

"I missed you, I missed you!"

"Missed you too, Aspen." Emry laughed and swung his feet. "Dearest, if you could please..."

"Oh." Aspen set him down. "Right."

Once they had finished all their hellos and apologized several times for being late, Aspen took in the grove with fresh eyes. Circling around the fane in excitement, inspecting the remains of the cookie tray...

Then stopping before the blackened tree that helmed the makeshift stage.

"I was sort of hoping it had grown back," Emry admitted as Aspen approached to inspect it. "With magic or something. I even tried to help it along myself, but..."

"No," Aspen said quietly, a small smile on their lips. "No, it's far too gone for that." They crouched and drew their hand across the long grass at the base of the tree. Rhythm blooms—the symbol of Sada and a marker of spirit groves—unfurled in a trail leading from Aspen's fingers, their white petals giving way to a soft blue glow. Every time someone behind them spoke or laughed, the glow flared: a loving, silent symphony just below the tree.

Then Aspen stepped back and held up their lute. "Did you still want to sing?"

Emry set his lute strap over his shoulder, just like he had years ago.

"Why not?" He grinned. "For luck."

Want More?

Did you enjoy *The Spirit's Curse*?

Leave a review and spread the word!

∽

Want more cozy fantasy & fantasy romance?

Sign up for my newsletter to get free stories, art, and future release updates:

https://rkashwick.com/newsletter/

∽

Also by R.K. Ashwick:

The Side Quest Row Series

A Rival Most Vial

A Captured Cauldron

Acknowledgments

I made the mistake of thinking that the last book in a series would be easier to write. I knew how it all should end—it was just a matter of getting there, right?

Wrong. I was extremely wrong, and the following people kept me from pulling a forest spirit and disappearing into the woods forever.

First, to my beta readers: Joe, Emma, Kalynn, Sarah, and Lila. Thank you for peeking into the dumpster fire of early drafts and making constructive comments on the burning wreckage. You are all fire-proof wizards.

To my editor, Kim Halstead: thank you for seeing this series through from beginning to end. I am so, so grateful.

To my cover designer, Patrick Knowles, who came through for both *The Spirit Well* and *The Spirit's Curse*: thank you so much for nailing the look and keeping it consistent through the whole series. If I had to change the style partway through, I would have started eating leaves.

To my husband, family, friends, writing groups, and online writing communities: you have dealt with so many half-coherent vents and complaints over the past year. I promise I'm done...until I start running into problems with the next book.

And finally, to Emry, Cal, and Aspen: I love you. I wouldn't be here without you.

ABOUT THE AUTHOR

By day, R.K. Ashwick herds cats in the animation industry. By night, she writes, bakes, and herds her literal cat around the living room. She lives with her husband (and said cat) in California.

For more information, visit rkashwick.com.

www.ingramcontent.com/pod-product-compliance
Lightning Source LLC
LaVergne TN
LVHW040156190525
811633LV00007B/23